IN THE WEREWOLF'S DEN

Rob Preece

Books ForA Buck.com

ePublishing

In the Werewolf's Den

Rob Preece

ISBN: 1-60215-058-3
ISBN-13: 978-1-60215-058-4

Be sure to visit www.BooksForABuck.com for the best in affordable electronic fiction.

Prologue

The alarm's eerie wail cut through Warder Cadet Danielle Goodman's sleep like a blade, jolting her awake. Around her, fellow warders stirred, snapped on equipment, grabbed a quick jolt of coffee--or something stronger. Time to get to work.

Danielle jerked on her bulletproof vest, the fabric heavy and cold to the touch, then snapped on the baby-blue helmet of the warders. This felt good, right.

"Ready, Danielle? Good work." Sergeant Mansfield, a crusty woman of indeterminate age, had been a cop way back, even before the return. Now she was a favorite mentor for graduating officers of the Warder Academy—and the Academy's toughest martial arts instructor.

"Any word on the alert?" Danielle asked.

The sergeant shrugged. "Two quicks, one slow. Got to be a vampire."

Danielle had known that, of course. You couldn't watch television without being bombarded by public service announcements about the warning signs, or by semi-fictionalized accounts of the great battles between normal humans and those afflicted with the return of magic, the impaired.

She pulled the coordinates off the computer, handed them to the sergeant, then climbed into the shotgun position in the heavy half-track the Los Angeles Warders used as assault transportation.

The diesel rumble and muffled clank of Kevlar treads set Danielle's heart beating faster than the alarm. After years of study, countless hours of simulation, and thousands of bruises in the ring, this was the real thing. Her chance to strike back at the bastards who had killed her mother and threatened the lives of countless thousands every day. She'd show her mentor, Joe Smealy, that she was worth the efforts he'd made to get her into the Academy.

The GPS offered driving suggestions, but Mansfield ignored those, taking shortcuts that only a native of Los Angeles would know: alleys that the maps showed had been blocked decades before but weren't, and burned out shells of buildings that a carefully managed assault vehicle could climb through.

The sergeant spun around the final corner and jammed on the brakes in front of an ancient motel that had been dilapidated when built in the late twentieth century and had only fallen on harder times since. They were barely a mile from the zone and few normals want to live that close to the infestation of magic. Only those too poor to have any other choice and those who would rather risk their lives and souls than come into contact with the authorities would live in a place like this.

According to the report, though, at least two who had made that choice could no longer be counted among the living. Whether they were safely dead was yet to be determined.

"Think you're ready?" Mansfield glared at her as if expecting a negative answer.

"I've been looking forward to this all my life," Danielle admitted.

"Right. I'm putting you in charge then." The sergeant punched a couple of keys in the truck's computer, then spoke over her radio. "Cadet Goodman has the command. Two confirmed casualties already. Let's not make a third, Warders."

* * *

For a fraction of a second, Danielle's brain blanked in panic. She was just a cadet. She had planned on taking part in the raid, not leading it. What if she messed up? What if she got a warder killed? What if, after years of work, she didn't have what it took and washed out of the Academy?

Then she caught her breath and nodded. She had the training. She could do this. "Squad two, go left. Squad three, take the right. I want Sergeant Mansfield and two others to circle around back and make sure he doesn't get away. Jones, Peterson, and Cortez, we're going in. One hundred seconds. Travel."

Mansfield nodded, but patted her sidearm.

Damn, she'd almost forgotten the most basic lesson of all.

"Load with silver, Warders," she concluded. "It may not kill the monster, but solid silver shot will sure slow it down."

* * *

Danielle bailed out of the half-track, rolling away quickly in case of sniper fire. Nothing.

Once Jones, Peterson, and Cortez had joined Danielle, Mansfield zoomed off in a cloud of blue diesel fumes, the assault vehicle's treads biting into already eroded concrete.

Danielle's helmet visor included a heads-up display and it ticked off the seconds until her assault was to begin.

With ten seconds left, she took conscious control over her body, sending a massive surge of adrenaline and endorphins through her system.

Time seemed to slow, something the Academy trainers called the blur. That blur, along with the rest of her training, were what gave a Warder Academy graduate the advantage over the magically impaired. Those and massive firepower, of course.

The last five seconds seemed to take forever. With every sense keyed, Danielle could hear the distinctive breathing of the three men she'd detailed to accompany her into the run-down apartment. Cortez was breathing normally, but both Jones and Peterson were sweating and gasping for breath.

She opened her mouth to reassure them, then remembered that she would sound like a cartoon to them. The blur affected her vocal cords just as it did her larger muscles. Instead, she hand-signed to them to take out their weapons.

She double-checked to ensure that she had a silver clip in the assault rifle she carried. Cortez and Peterson carried huge-caliber shotguns that would send dozens of silver slugs through any magical assailant. Like her, Jones carried the standard issue sub-machine gun.

"Now." She signaled as well as speaking, coding the others to move. She hadn't considered how the blur would affect her ability to send orders to the bulk of the warders. It was the type of practical problem that could get a warder killed. Well, this was why they sent academy students into the field for months of internship. To learn the differences between practice and reality.

She fired a pattern at the motel's reinforced steel door and then slammed a kick into it.

The door flew off its hinges, cartwheeled through the apartment lobby, and slid to a stop.

Beyond the echo of the door's final crash, silence greeted her.

The building stank of stale urine. Ancient gang graffiti covered the walls. Trash lay in heaps throughout the lobby and down the long hallway that led to the individual units.

She took a step forward and then stopped suddenly, Jones and Cortez both piling into her back.

One of those trash heaps moved.

Peterson swung his shotgun around, his finger squeezing on the trigger.

"Hold your fire." She spoke as slowly as she could, fighting the speedup of blur.

She might as well have lectured the ocean. Peterson's face was covered with sweat. In slow motion compared to her blur, his finger tightened on the trigger.

Impatiently, Danielle knocked the barrel of Peterson's shotgun toward the ceiling, then ducked as ricocheting slugs flattened themselves around the room.

"Damn it, Peterson, that's one of the victims. I think she's alive."

Peterson glared at her and she detailed Cortez to get the moaning woman out of the apartment.

"Alive or undead," Peterson grumbled. "We might as well kill her. Once a vampire has bitten her it's only a matter of time before she turns."

That could happen, Danielle knew. But it didn't always happen. Besides, even if the woman turned, that didn't mean she had to be killed. Impaired who followed orders and stayed in their zones weren't targeted. The warders' credo was protection of the normals, not violence against the impaired.

"Stuff it," she ordered, cutting off any debate. "We're here for the vampire. Now follow me."

She relied on her nose, sniffing for the faint ozone flavor that the textbooks insisted was always associated with vampire.

Peterson and Jones followed her down the hallway, stepping over mounds of petrifying newspaper, human feces, and abandoned hypodermic needles. Despite everything that the warders could do, the nearby zone created a sort of negative energy that, like the real vampires that escaped the zone, sucked vitality from the surrounding neighborhoods. Evil clung to the zone like ticks to a dog.

She couldn't solve all the world's problems today, but she could see that one escaped vampire was brought down. If this mission helped reach her goal of becoming a full-time vampire hunter, that was fine too.

Peterson was still grumbling to himself, but once she made him take his complaints off the warder band, she ignored him. It wasn't as if the vampire didn't know they were coming.

Finally she caught the scent she was searching for.

It grew stronger as she approached a closed door.

She threw it open, then rolled through, her rifle ready, safety off.

Jones laughed at her as she realized she'd only found a stairwell. "A little paranoid, are we? Your vest should keep you safe from most of what they throw at you."

The Academy taught an ultra-safe approach to vampire hunting, and frankly, Danielle didn't mind the bruised shoulders she got from her rolls if they kept her from getting killed. Jones might be right most of the time. It only took once to get into serious trouble—or dead.

She took the narrow flight of stairs that led to the second floor of the low walk-up. The scent of vampire lingered inside like an ugly scar.

"Climbing toward the second floor," she reported. "Unit one, any sign of movement through the upstairs windows?"

"Repeat please. Your voice is garbled."

Mansfield sounded like she was talking through molasses. She was one of the top blur coaches but hadn't even bothered to blur herself.

Take your time, Danielle reminded herself. That vampire isn't going anywhere.

She repeated her query, speaking as slowly as she could. Other than the victim, the downstairs had appeared empty. She couldn't be sure the residents of the second floor had all been evacuated. Where vampires were involved, the warders cut some slack on collateral damage, but Danielle wanted her first command mission to be perfect.

She controlled her patience, drawing on the years of training in the martial arts to achieve the inner peace of waiting.

Finally, two warders reported movement in separate second-story windows. Either could be the vampire. Or neither.

"Right. I'm going in. Hold the perimeter. Peterson, Jones, stay close. We don't want this one to get away."

She matched her action to her words, running up the stairwell and throwing open the door.

The second victim was past rescue. Two deep punctures proved that a vampire had been at work. Still, she touched a finger to the man's throat to be certain. Her gloved hand came away bloody.

The stench of death warred with the acidic taste of ozone in the musty air of the apartment. But her training had prepared her for that. She looked around the room for any clue to the vampire's plan or weaponry, ignoring the open door behind her.

She had told her partners to follow, expected them to be behind her. When she heard the noise directly to her rear, she assumed it was Peterson.

But the soft footstep resonated wrong. Peterson wore heavy boots.

Danielle whirled around in time to see a black-clad figure step from a supply closet.

The vampire's face was a pale white, marred only by a trail of blood down his chin.

She flashed back to her youth, when she'd discovered her stepfather drinking her mother's blood, then brutally forced down the memory. Then, she'd been helpless. Now, she was a warder intern, intensively

7

trained, already in full blur mode.

She fired three short bursts, silver bullets cutting through the vampire's body like a chainsaw.

The bloodsucker stumbled back as if slammed by a heavy fist. But he shook it off and started back toward her.

She pulled the trigger again and realized she'd emptied the clip.

Damn. Where was Peterson with his shotgun when she needed him? Her high-powered shells pierced through the impaired and exited, allowing his magic-impaired body to repair itself. Silver shotgun slugs, in contrast, might have stayed inside his body disturbing the electrical elements of his magic.

Even in blur mode, she didn't have time to reload. The vampire closed the distance, moving almost as quickly as she could.

Danielle reversed her weapon, slapping it into his head, and blinked as he yanked it away from her.

He laughed, the sound high and piercing, then licked his lips. "I hear warder blood is doubly sweet."

"Why don't you come and try to find out, slimeball?"

"A generous offer."

He reached for her, an obvious feint, then knife-handed toward her eyes.

Danielle ignored the feint and blocked the strike, following her block with a kick to his head.

He wasn't big. Probably only a couple of inches taller than Danielle's five foot eight. But she felt like she'd kicked a concrete wall rather than a man.

She turned a backflip, barely avoiding the vampire's grasp.

Keep your distance, Danielle, she lectured herself. If she got into a wrestling match with a vampire, she was going to get bit. Getting bit would end her warder career forever.

"I've got him here." She forced herself to speak slowly into the radio despite her excitement. "I need backup. Now. Sergeant Mansfield, can you get in here? And bring another stake."

The vampire grinned, his fangs gleaming in the faint light. "More warders? Oh, goody. Dessert."

Either the vampire knew little about fighting, or it simply relied on its magical capabilities to protect it from Danielle because it waded into her.

She caught it squarely in the groin, then nailed it with an elbow to the ribs.

She felt those vampire ribs give way and heard the vampire exhale hard, but he grabbed her anyway, bringing his bloody face toward her neck.

Danielle could feel her panic, barely held down by years of training. No wonder Peterson and Jones had run.

She dug deep in herself, relaxed, let him get close, then head-butted him directly in his hollow teeth.

It was a risky move. She felt her own blood where she'd caught the sharp edges of his teeth, but one of those lethal weapons broke off and the vampire reeled away.

"Bitch."

This time she laughed. "You don't know half of it, dead man."

The vampire reached for her again, but Danielle had figured him out.

She let him come, then grasped his arm and used his own momentum to accelerate him into the wall.

The reek of ozone was nearly overpowering. She wondered what it was doing to her lungs. Not that it would matter if she didn't end this fight quickly. She'd been in blur for too long and felt herself slowing.

The vampire bounced off the wall and headed back to her.

Beneath them, still too far away, she heard Mansfield and the others coming.

"Too late for you," the vampire told her.

"And for you."

She reached for him as if she intended to smash him into the wall again.

He kicked away her hand.

His kick had to have broken something in her wrist. Despite the blur's endorphins, her pain level shot through the ceiling. Still, rather than fighting for balance Danielle used the momentum of his kick to spin her around.

As she moved, she reached into her vest and pulled out the wooden stake that all vampire hunters carry.

Her own strength wouldn't have been enough to pierce the vampire's armored chest, but the very blow that he had landed accelerated her spin, giving her the power she needed to plunge the weapon deep into his heart.

The vampire stared at her, then looked down at the stake sunk into his body.

He should be dead, she thought. Or rather, since all vampires are dead and inhabited by demons, he should be acting dead. Instead, he reached for the stake and began pulling it out.

Danielle didn't fight her panic this time: she used it. Desperate fear added to her strength as she hammered a straight thrust-kick. Her booted foot slammed into the stake driving it more deeply into the vampire's heart.

The undead monster gave her a pathetic look, then slowly crumpled to the floor.

Danielle sagged against the wall.

"Good work," Mansfield told her, slapping her on the back. "Keep his teeth as a souvenir of your first kill. Believe me, I'll recommend you as a vampire hunter. You've got what it takes."

Danielle smiled weakly. She'd done it. Notched up her required kill, managed a successful raid, and gotten a word of encouragement from the woman every cadet dreaded. She should feel great.

She vomited against the wall.

Chapter 1

He didn't look like a werewolf.

Danielle straightened her uniform tunic, then continued to watch the *Were*, her eyes hidden behind her mirrored sunglasses. The *Were* stepped toward her, his tawny eyes staring as if they could pierce the protection of her shades and see into her soul. Even in his prison coveralls, he looked powerful, in control of the situation.

She knew he was young, in his early thirties, but a hint of silver dusted the jet black of his hair. His footsteps were silent on the hard concrete floor.

Danielle took a deep breath and reminded herself that she was in charge. She was the warder. He was just another impaired. Her prisoner.

"Dr. Carl Harriman?"

He stopped. "I'm Harriman."

"The courts have heard your appeal. Pending the results of your research, you are released from interment and remanded into my custody."

She was prepared for gratitude. For earnest shedding of tears. His curt nod was unexpected, chilling.

"About time they got around to it. And who the hell are you?"

Danielle drew herself to her full five foot eight. "Warder Agent Danielle Goodman. On temporary assignment as a herder." Very temporary assignment, she hoped. When Joe Smealy had called her in to his office, she'd expected to be commissioned as a vampire hunter, not relegated to the low-status position as herder. Joe hadn't had time to give her details, but she planned on getting them soon. She'd graduated first in her class from the Warder Academy. She'd taken special training in martial arts, in hypnotic resistance, in emergency transfusions. She had even bought the black-on-black casual dress uniform of a hunter-agent. That uniform took up half the space in the workout bag that held all of her possessions. Wearing it would have to wait until she proved herself once more.

"Wonderful. Danielle, is it? Well, I guess I'm stuck with you."

Discourage fraternization. She couldn't count the number of times that message had been beaten into their heads in the Academy. "My name is Agent Goodman, not Danielle."

Harriman's laugh was short--almost a bark. "If we're going to be living together, I really think we should be on a first-name basis."

She bristled. "We aren't living together, as you put it. I'm your herder. You are a late-arrival *Were*, released on sufferance, thanks to the generosity of the people of the State of Texas."

"Very generous, indeed." He paused a beat. "Agent Goodman."

His sarcastic tone sent her hand reaching for the silver-tipped nightstick that all herders carried. She had to maintain dominance. *Were*, like the dogs many people had kept as pets before the return of magic, needed to know who was master. She pulled the stick slowly from her belt, slapped it against a gloved hand, and stared.

He looked back, unmoved by the threat that the silver represented. Didn't he know what it could do to him? Maybe he didn't. According to his documentation, he'd turned himself over to the authorities as soon as he'd been visited with his impairment. That quick decision had protected him from the fearful mob that would normally surround an impaired discovered living outside the zone.

He was only a *Were*. Even so, Danielle decided his tone of voice was not enough to warrant using the nightstick.

"Let's get you situated in a lab," Danielle said. The sooner she could get him to work, the sooner he could discover whatever it was that had gotten him out of prison and the sooner she could move on to her next assignment. Preferably one involving hunting vampires rather than herding lowlife *Were*.

"I've been in prison for six months," Harriman observed. "I need a shower, something decent to eat, and real clothes rather than these paper things." He demonstrated the flimsiness of his prison garb by grasping the fabric and yanking. Sure enough, the woven material gave, exposing a muscled biceps beneath it. "Preferably food first."

Danielle swallowed hard. The Academy was full of hard-bodied males, but something about Harriman affected her. If she hadn't been wearing her silver-impregnated sunglasses, she might have suspected he was using some sort of enchantment spell on her.

She cleared her throat, then nodded. "All right. We'll get something to eat and some new clothes. Then we'll get you moved into the zone where the government has established your lab."

Harriman smiled. He had a nice smile, Danielle thought. With large, even, white teeth. It even looked like he had all of them--another positive result of his turning himself in before the mob could find him. Unusually for a *Were*, Harriman's canines didn't even look enlarged. He looked like a normal human—except sexier than any normal human she'd ever seen.

She reminded herself that nobody chose the curse. Harriman, her stepfather, and all those others were victims of the return of magic. Just because society needed to be protected from them didn't make them evil. Just dangerous. And Harriman was definitely dangerous.

"Let's go," Danielle finished.

"What about my things?" Harriman objected.

"Everything you had with you when you were arrested has been destroyed," Danielle told him. "Come on. Unless you want me to send you back to your cell."

He didn't move for a moment and Danielle wondered if he would actually call her bluff. If wouldn't look good on her record if she gave up on her job ten minutes into it. On the other hand, she needed to assert her authority--and remind Harriman that she had the power to return him to prison at any time. For any reason.

"Destroying perfectly good clothing is stupid," Harriman observed as he followed her through the silver-spiked doors that closed off this section of the Lew Sterret Justice Center. "But destroying my computer is a crime. It had records from years of research on it. Research I'll have to duplicate."

Danielle suspected that Harriman's things hadn't really all been destroyed. Some government official had probably nabbed Harriman's computer on the not unreasonable expectation that a prisoner wouldn't need it. Government computers were, by definition, a couple of generations behind the type of system a scientist like Harriman would have. By now that computer was lost in the system, sitting on some anonymous desk somewhere. There was no way she was going to admit that to Harriman, though. The system wasn't perfect. But it provided the small measure of safety that remained for the normal ninety percent of the human race. The alternative was unthinkable.

"Then we'd better get our butts in gear and get started on it, hadn't we?"

Harriman narrowed his eyes. "What's this 'we' stuff? Surely you don't think you're going to help with my research."

She hadn't, actually. She was his herder, not his assistant. On the other hand, Danielle had an insatiable curiosity. If she was going to spend the next couple of months with Carl Harriman, she might as well learn something. And biomedical research into the source of the magic that had so infected a large part of the world's population was something worth understanding.

"I'm stuck with you, impaired," she told him. "I might as well do something useful."

He gave her that look again. "Right. So, we were talking about food. After six months eating nothing but processed algae, I'm ready for a huge steak, a baked potato dripping with butter and sour cream, and a salad with real lettuce and vegetables. And a bottle of wine."

Danielle bit off her laughter. She was thinking of Harriman as a prisoner, as one of the thousands of impaired whose property had been confiscated when they'd been sent into the zone. But Harriman was different. He was a late arrival. His timely surrender to the authorities had protected his property. Even with what he'd spent on lawyers, he still had plenty of money in his bank account.

"All right." She pulled out her palmtop and punched in Carl's specifications. "There's a restaurant on Turtle Creek," she told him. "It looks pretty close. We'll go there first."

"You've got a date."

Danielle shuddered. She might have to work with him but she didn't have to like him. "I'll wait in the lobby, *Were.*"

* * *

"Afternoon, Fred." Carl greeted the maitre d' at the Old Main Grill as if they were old friends. Well, maybe they were. The restaurant was the type that appealed to rich businessmen. Like Carl had been.

"Six months of prison slop would make cold oatmeal taste like a gourmet treat. I can hardly wait to taste your Tex-French cooking.

"I'm sorry, sir. We don't have any free seating."

Carl frowned. "It's me, Fred. Dr. Harriman." He looked around at the nearly deserted restaurant.

Danielle checked her palmtop. "I made reservations for one. Confirmation number seven zero--"

"I'm terribly sorry sir, ma'am," Fred broke in. "Our computer system must have suffered from a glitch. We won't be able to seat you today."

"Dr. Harriman is legally accompanied by a registered warder," Danielle said. "Under city ordinance two-C-seven, you are not allowed to discriminate against impaired if so accompanied."

"I'm sorry, ma'am. I simply don't have the seating."

It was a lie, of course. But no policeman would enforce that ordinance.

She shoved herself in the Maitre d's face and grasped his starch-impregnated shirt. "You'll damn-well find a seat for my ward or I'll toss some of your customers and make room."

"I'd better get the manager." Fred fled from her, leaving shirt buttons popping behind him.

"Let's get out of here," Carl said.

A couple, the man in his fifties, his date in her early twenties, walked into the restaurant and stopped suddenly when they saw Carl.

"Guess they aren't being as exclusive as they used to be. Imagine trying to bring one of them to a place like this."

Carl turned on his heels and strode out.

Danielle walked after him. She couldn't really blame the restaurant management or the customers. If her work didn't require her to spend time with the impaired, she'd feel a little queasy about sharing a restaurant with one, too. Especially a restaurant whose entrees started at more than a warder's weekly salary. The funny thing was Carl's surprise. He'd have to have been sleeping over the past decade not to be aware that the impaired were unwelcome anywhere outside of their zone.

"Perhaps we would be more comfortable if we went to the zone first, where they're used to dealing with the impaired."

Carl looked at his hands. "It's strange, but I don't feel impaired. I feel like I always did, except I have a capability now. I'm quicker, more aware of scents and sounds. And tastes, which was why I was looking forward to a well-cooked meal."

"The onset of magic is a legal impairment," Danielle reminded him. "Impaired individuals have limited self-control and need to be properly restrained. It's serious, all right."

"Let's stop by a super-store," Carl suggested. "I'll pick up some steaks and grill them myself. And I've got to get some clothes that don't make it obvious that I'm, uh, different."

Danielle shook her head. "Under Public Law 1627, it is unlawful to attempt to disguise your condition. Tell you what. Let's decide what you need and I'll order it on my computer. It'll be at your new lab by the time you get there."

If she'd needed the reminder of Carl's condition, his snarl gave it to her. "I've devoted the past ten years of my life looking for a cure, a way to bring life back to nature and away from the bizarrely supernatural. And for that, I've got to walk around with the sign of the beast on me. It isn't right."

"Let's go, Harriman," Danielle ordered.

Carl climbed into her warder-provided vehicle and stared straight ahead as Danielle pulled away from the curb and headed into traffic.

Her vehicle's tiny hydrogen motor provided enough power to climb Dallas's small hills and not much more. She made a quick U-turn and headed south.

The Trinity River had swelled with the warmer climate and melting icecaps. Where it had once been a trickle a child could jump over, it was now an impressive barrier between the north side of the city and the south. A barrier made more formidable by electric fencing, dynamited bridges, guard towers, and signs indicating that land mines had been laid.

Danielle stopped at a guard post and presented her credentials.

The guard looked at them closely, then glanced into the car. "Werewolf?" His voice held nothing but contempt.

Danielle glared at him. "Yeah."

The guard spat, the thick glob landing on the windshield in front of Carl's face. "Who'd you piss off to get stuck with it?"

"My first assignment out of the Academy."

The guard raised the barrier, then laughed. "You're an Academy grad and you're doing that? It usually takes years even for us unblessed to screw up bad enough to get stuck on herder duty. I got busted for drunk driving and this is as bad as they got to me. Another couple of weeks and I'm back to chasing."

Danielle sighed. Elf chasing. The guard was fat, probably slow, and if he was smart, he sure didn't look it. So why was he an elf chaser when Danielle was stuck herding? Admittedly, a chaser was not in the same class as a vampire hunter. Even so, Danielle would have given six months of salary to trade jobs with the guard.

She flipped on the windshield wiper to clean off the guard's goober and headed into the Dallas zone.

"Are they all like this?" For the first time, Carl's voice sounded tentative.

"Are what?"

"The zones. I've never been in one before."

Late onset impairment was rare. For the most part, those who would receive the magical curse got it within months of the return of magic. Some in the government even held that late onset was a myth--that a few of the impaired were able to hide themselves for long periods of time, working surreptitiously to destroy normal humanity. Carl's ignorance would have cured Danielle of that theory, if she'd ever believed in it.

For the first time, Danielle really looked at the Dallas zone.

It felt quiet. A few beat-up hydrogen-fueled cars roamed the streets, but mostly the residents traveled by foot or bicycle. The hum of air conditioning, ever-present in the north side of Dallas where normal humans lived, was missing here. Beyond that, the general air of dilapidation was impossible to ignore. Buildings leaned to the side, curtains blew in and out of broken windows, and huge potholes turned the streets into an obstacle course that challenged the limited horsepower in her official vehicle.

Hunters, she teased herself, got to drive gasoline-powered vehicles. They, unlike herders, spent most of their time outside the zones because vampires often used their magical talents to escape the ever-expanding defensive rings guarding the normals from the evils of the zone.

An elf woman with a missing arm pressed against the thin plastic of Danielle's car, her remaining hand held out in supplication.

Danielle fought down her reflexive sympathy. They have no pride, she reminded herself, mentally reciting one of the thousands of creeds that had been drilled into her head in the Academy.

Although the zone lacked normal sounds of machinery, the quiet was not complete. Screams of happy children sounded from a lot where an aging strip mall had deteriorated into a dangerous-but-fun-looking playground. A vendor pedaled by on a three-wheeled bicycle selling frozen fruit bars from an insulated box. Two old men whispered to each other as they played a slow game of chess and drank aromatic black coffee in front of what Danielle would have guessed to be an abandoned diner. If she hadn't seen the hint of a tail hanging below one's coat, they could have passed as normal.

"This one looks a bit nicer than the Los Angeles zone," she said. "In the return-of-magic riots there, the impaired burned about a third of the entire zone. Doesn't look like you had that kind of problem."

"Riots?"

Damn. Danielle had forgotten that the censors had decided the L.A. riots had never taken place. She backpedaled quickly. "A few rowdy kids got carried away. Did some damage to the zone before the warders could intervene."

Carl eyed her suspiciously. "I'd always heard that city services are fully available in zones. Doesn't look like the street crews have been out here lately."

Danielle maneuvered her car around another huge pothole.

"It's hard to offer services to the impaired," she gave the explanation she'd always heard. "They attack city workers, refuse to pay their taxes. You know things have been tough since the return, and since the ice caps started melting."

Carl nodded grimly. "That's what I've been telling the courts for the past six months. If we could just get a grip on the virus, we could dedicate all of our efforts to getting the country back on its feet. Magic is just another disease. We whipped smallpox when the bioterrorists re-introduced it. We finally controlled AIDS and SARS. We were even making progress against cancer before all this started.

"Do you have any idea how much of our resources are wasted in controlling the magical outbreak?" he continued, warming to his topic. "Not even including the ten percent of our population directly affected, how many thousands of warders do we have? Not to mention the concrete and steel we pour into the walls we built around the zones. It's worse than the war on drugs back in the twentieth century. The war on magic is ruining our economy. But unless my research results were anomalous, we can whip this."

When he spoke, Danielle felt herself carried away in the excitement of his vision. Carl truly believed he could eliminate the curse of magic's return, and his personal magnetism made him persuasive. His was the kind of message that could transform the world. Best, he sounded like he knew what he was talking about rather than simply spouting a pipe dream. Except the number of warders wasn't measured in the thousands. It was millions. The nation, the world, was bankrupting itself to control the return of magic. If Carl could pull off a complete cure, returning the impaired to productive life, he could write his own ticket--including getting back into that fancy restaurant.

She pulled onto a residential street and pushed the remote to open the radio-controlled gate.

"I didn't think they had electricity here."

"Your place has its own fuel cell," she explained. "Many of your tools are electronic so, when they equipped your lab, they made sure they would run."

Carl nodded. "Got it. Well, why don't you drop me off and you can get back to whatever warders do when they're not playing chauffeur to local scientists?"

The thought had crossed Danielle's mind--repeatedly. Once Carl was in the zone with all of the other impaired, why would he need a full-time herder? What happened inside was normally a matter for whatever local mob ran a particular section of the zone. If the impaired wanted to kill each other, not many normal humans would complain and, while it might be technically illegal, the warders had more important things to do than look into an impaired getting killed.

After hearing Carl speak, however, she knew her answer. Carl's work was important enough to make protecting him a priority. Important enough that she was stuck in the zone, stuck with a dangerous *Were*, for the duration.

She forced herself to look at the bright side. Joe hadn't assigned her to a trivial case. Its importance meant he trusted her abilities. If she didn't screw this job up, she just might get the promotion she craved.

"You don't understand, Dr. Harriman, I'm part of the package. The government wants what you're working on and I'm here to make sure you keep your nose to the grindstone." And to make sure he really was doing what he'd promised. How many impaired had promised wonderful things, only to disappear once they'd gotten what they wanted from normal human society?

"You're going to be with me for months?"

Months? Living in the zone? Danielle took a deep breath and forced herself to relax. Maybe it would be faster than months. For sure, she would hold Harriman's feet to the fire and make him work his tail off.

"However long it takes."

* * *

Danielle wished she knew more about the technical equipment Carl used in his work. If she could believe Carl, the government had provided him with outdated and inefficient equipment. She suspected that he was telling the truth. The return of magic plague had made everyone tighten their belts and nobody was about to give the best equipment to an impaired, even if he did promise to work miracles.

"But they're not giving me anything," Carl argued when she explained that to him. "They've charged my account for the most current equipment and given me this dreck."

"At least you're out of prison."

He didn't seem grateful. "It'll take me twice as long to get the job done if I have to work with this stuff. And I'll need twice the staff."

She hadn't thought about staff. Somehow she'd had the idea of Carl working alone in his lab with her, weapons in hand, making sure that he didn't try anything. Reality was getting in the way again.

One thing for sure, she wanted him to get the job done quickly. "Get me a list of what you need; I'll see what I can do."

That seemed to cheer him up some. "Right."

While Carl calibrated his equipment, checked out his supplies, and did whatever scientific things people like him did, Danielle checked out the rest of the facility.

She suspected that Joe must have helped specify the requirements, because there were two rooms for bedrooms, one for a gym, and another for a kitchen. She'd be able to maintain her training and not fall too much behind her peers when she finally had a chance to make Vampire Hunter.

Since Carl looked like he would be messing with refrigeration units, DNA sequencers, and fermenting vats for hours, Danielle switched from the stiff and ugly brown uniform of a warder-herder to a pair of running shorts and sports bra to get some exercise in.

"I'll be in the gym," she told him. "Don't leave here without letting me know."

"Fine," he told her. "Want to go for a run afterwards?"

"In the zone?" Any time she'd been in the zone before, she'd been in a vehicle with her weapons ready.

"Can we run in the normal side of the city?"

She shook her head. "Only if I put you on a leash."

He gave her a half-smile as if he thought she was joking. But she wasn't. Before his transformation, Carl had obviously kept his eyes firmly closed. Which meant she was stuck explaining reality to him.

His smile faded slowly as the truth sunk in.

"The zone it is, then."

She hit the weight machines in the gym, pushing herself to failure on every set. Some of her fellow-students had been lackadaisical about their strength and unarmed combat training exercises, but every time she thought about slacking, memories of the vampire stooped over her mother surged.

Carl puttered around outside and she used his presence to motivate herself further. She couldn't stay awake all the time. Yet Carl needed to be certain she could handle anything he could throw at her.

She'd finished her three sets for each muscle group and was running through a Kata, one of her martial arts routines, when Carl appeared, dressed in a pair of shorts, an M.I.T. T-shirt, and running shoes.

He grinned, cocky and full of confidence. "Ready for that run?"

"Think you can keep up?"

He laughed. "Trust me, I can keep up with anything you throw my way. Anything."

Chapter 2

Danielle eased into a lope as they strode away from Carl's new home and onto the street. During the past few weeks of final exams, detailed briefings on the situation in Dallas, and endless bureaucratic paperwork as the courts transferred Carl into her herding, she hadn't had a decent workout. Her body ached from the lack.

She snuck a glance at Carl to see how he was holding up.

Looking was a mistake. He seemed to be holding up fine. Lean muscled legs that had been discreetly hidden beneath prison coveralls were now on full display. His running shorts showed off tight-muscled buns. If he hadn't been impaired, he would have been sexy as anything. Fortunately, her stepfather had cured her of that kind of attraction forever.

She upped the pace and tried to keep her attention on the dangers of the Dallas Zone. Here there be monsters, she reminded herself. More quotes from the Academy.

The zone was deceptively quiet. Male and female impaired wandered the streets, apparently going about their business. Few gave Danielle and Carl a second glance, as if a jogging *Were* and his keeper were part of their daily life.

The impaired might be dealing in illicit drugs, hiring out murders, plotting the overthrow of the human government, and exchange of forbidden books, but to Danielle, things looked deceptively normal. As if these were ordinary humans. A child almost ran into her, then flitted up on wings that beat as fast as a hummingbird's, and it hit Danielle with a flash that she was alone in a zone, unmonitored, beyond the range of backup. She became hyper-aware of the relative silence, the occasional wings, tails, and pointy ears she caught glimpses of, the small shops dealing in who knew what contraband. Suddenly the run took on a more ominous air.

"Are you warmed up yet?" Carl asked, breaking into her thoughts. "We can pick up the pace if you're ready."

His tone was smug, superior. So he was in decent shape. Well, he hadn't just spent four years in one of the most grueling training regimes humankind had invented. Time to let him see that he couldn't compete with her, that she would be the dominant one in their, hopefully brief, relationship. Time to rub his canine nose in it.

"Fine," she told him. "Let me know if I'm going too fast."

Her instructors at the Academy had drilled it into her head that the impaired would always test her, always press her limits. She needed to keep a reserve hidden for his inevitable challenge. In a moment of frank honesty, though, Danielle realized that her sudden surge of competitiveness had nothing to do with *Were* and herder. It had everything to do with wiping the smirk off Carl's smug face.

She lengthened her stride, settling into a brisk five-and-a-half-minute mile.

Carl adjusted, looking at her with what appeared to be renewed respect.

Danielle savored the slap of the concrete under her feet, the moist Dallas air in her short hair, and the flow of blood through her muscles. She let a mile slip past, then another, finally turning toward Carl with a smile on her lips. "Ready to really crank it up?"

She expected to see him blowing at least a little. After all, he had been locked in prison for six months. While he could have managed isometrics, she didn't think he'd been running any marathons inside the Lew Sterrett Justice Center.

To her surprise, Carl nodded. "Let's do it."

She upped the pace to an all-out, sub-five-minute mile. Until now, she had been drawing on her body's natural abilities. To run at the faster pace and to sustain it over any distance, she needed to tune into her warder training, consciously flushing out the buildup of lactic acids from her muscles and filtering oxygen directly from the air to increase her lungs' capability.

Carl settled beside her, lengthening his stride and taking advantage of his longer legs. After a mile, though, he was gasping. After two miles, he started to lag.

"What's the matter?" she demanded. "I thought you were going to keep up with no trouble."

He nodded grimly. Whatever else she might say about him, Carl Harriman was no quitter. He leaned forward, lowering his center of gravity, until it seemed that his arms were almost on the ground helping him move.

His breathing steadied and the pink tip of a tongue protruded from his mouth.

She wanted to laugh. In college, she'd run marathons, taking joy in challenging her body to the ultimate. When she'd been inducted into the Academy, though, the training was too serious to allow simple enjoyment to enter into it. For the first time in years, Danielle simply savored the moment.

Carl's breathing shortened suddenly and she glanced over to see whether he was finally ready to concede the game.

Her blood froze.

Carl was in mid-transformation. As she watched, his arms lengthened into forelegs, his face narrowed into that of a wolf. A black wolf with shots of silver running through his fur.

Those same tawny eyes stared at her, filled with an intelligence that was more than animal, but also a cool calculation she recognized as wholly Carl.

Academy conditioned reflexes took over. She threw herself over the panting animal while simultaneously withdrawing the silver mesh leash she stored coiled within her wristwatch.

Too slow, she realized as the werewolf reacted; his sharp teeth closed around her throat. She'd let herself get distracted and now she would pay the price.

She blurred into high speed, twisting away from the werewolf at the same time as she wrapped the silver coils around his neck. She yanked firmly, choking off his windpipe, then rolled over on top of him to make sure that he couldn't use his superior weight against her.

He shifted, catching the leash with his shoulders rather than his throat and carotid artery.

She'd let her competitiveness and that trace of forbidden sexual attraction gain control and make her forget that Carl was impaired, the enemy.

She yanked the leash harder, even though she knew it was futile as the wolf's sharp teeth tightened around her throat.

Her heart sounded loud enough to shake the street as she jerked the leash even tighter. She should be dead, she realized. Although she moved faster than any unmodified human could even think, she hadn't moved fast enough to escape a magically infected *Were's* razor-sharp teeth. So why wasn't she?

The *Were* struggled briefly beneath her, its tawny eyes glaring at her, then it subsided. Not, she realized, because it was defeated. Simply because it knew that further resistance was futile.

So why, she wondered, had Carl shifted at all? If he wanted to attack her, nighttime, while she was sleeping, would offer the best chance. And if he was going to shift in broad daylight, why hadn't he killed her when he had the chance?

"Damned impaired animals," she muttered as she yanked even harder on the silver cord around the *Were*'s neck. It wasn't attacking her, but it also wasn't exhibiting the signs of wolf submission.

She felt the *Were* shift beneath her and brought her hand up to crush its throat. Carl caught her hand, then grinned. And he was in human form again.

She sat astride him, suddenly and acutely aware that Carl was all male beneath the scientist exterior that he so poorly wore. His arousal pressing against her groin generated an all-too human, if inexplicable, reaction from her hormones.

"That's a little tight," Carl remarked, his voice only slightly hoarse despite the thin silver cord that bit into his windpipe.

"Of all the--" she cut off her reaction. He wasn't talking about her own groin, slick now with her instinctive reaction to a male's excitement. He was talking about the leash she'd wrapped around his neck.

"You shifted on me."

"An accident. I couldn't keep up," Carl admitted. "I was really straining. Then it just happened."

A part of her wanted to finish the job. Nobody would ask any questions when she'd told them that he'd shifted. She would get at least an acceptable rating on this job and be that much closer to her real career.

But Carl's job was important. Besides, she couldn't prove that he was lying. She had joined the Warders to protect people, not to become an indiscriminate killer—even of the impaired.

She loosened the leash slightly. "No impaired can keep up with a warder." Warder school was hard. Only ten percent of the entering class graduated. Another ten percent died in process. The physical exercises and guided biofeedback were bad enough. Building the instinctual reactions to magic that could allow a warder to react more quickly than the magic-infected could think were worse. Yet, without those instincts, a warder could easily fall victim to her charge.

"You were going to attack me," she told him. "Don't try to explain this away."

"Attack you?" Carl's lips turned up into a sardonic smile. "I was minding my own business when you jumped me. I pulled back. Surely you felt the wolf's teeth on your neck. You know I could have ripped your throat out."

"Ha."

He looked as puzzled as Danielle felt. "Didn't realize I could control myself in wolf mode. I've always heard that human thoughts and motivations are subverted when the magical infection takes over." He scratched his head. "I wonder why I didn't kill you."

She'd caught him in mid-transition. Academy doctrine holds that the beast-form takes over the moment transformation begins, but Danielle was experienced enough to know that doctrine can be wrong. The return of magic was only a decade old and it had affected scientists and artists more than the rest of the population, so there were still a lot people didn't know about the impaired. Especially about relatively low-risk impaired like *Were*.

"What did it feel like?" she asked.

"I hardly noticed. I was running as hard as I could, digging deep to keep up with you. You're one fast lady."

"Academy training."

"Well, anyway, it felt like I got a second wind. A new sense of power flowing through my muscles: a heightened awareness of the scents of the zone. But I was still myself. I knew what was going on."

"A human wouldn't go after me with his teeth."

Carl looked puzzled. "I guess that's so. I must have had some wolf instincts inside of me. But I was in control. I caught myself and made myself stop when those wolf-instincts were telling me to finish you."

"Human control is not possible in *Were* form." That wasn't just doctrine. It was a fundamental principle that underlay the need to create the zones, to separate the impaired from the normal whom they threatened.

Carl shook his head. "Maybe I wasn't completely shifted then. But I was still me. And I was still in control."

She realized she still held the silver cord tight around his neck, still held him in the mount position. And that he was still aroused.

She wasn't going to kill him, then, so she sprang to her feet, the silver bond tight in her hand.

"Want to loosen that around my neck?" he asked, choking.

She gave it a twitch and the pressure eased. Then she stared into his eyes for a moment, looking for any sign of the wolf, before finally removing it entirely.

Scorch marks burned deep into the tender flesh of his neck.

"Wasn't that painful?"

He worked his shoulders. "Oh, yeah."

"So why you aren't you rolling on the ground howling?"

He considered. "Wouldn't have done any good, I guess."

But it was strange. Everyone knew that impaired individuals lost their ability to defer gratification. Just like everyone knew that the human side lost control. Why was Carl different? She pushed the matter from her mind. Maybe it was because he was late onset. Maybe he was just an anomaly. But if he could complete his cure, none of this would matter.

"Want to continue our run, or head back?" Carl asked.

"After that? We're heading back." Danielle turned and began retracing the steps toward her new home.

* * *

After a few days, they settled into a routine. They would run together in the morning--at a cautious pace. Then Carl would retreat to his lab while Danielle arranged for any supplies he required, ran through her martial arts drills, and studied for the post-graduate course in advanced vampire slaying.

To her surprise, Carl volunteered to cook dinner every night, although it was catch-as-catch-can for breakfast and lunch. She'd expected his meals to taste like a laboratory accident, but he managed to deliver a treat every time. Of course, after half a lifetime of institutional food, anything would taste good to Danielle.

A week into their routine, he suggested that they go out for dinner.

Danielle remembered the way Carl had been rejected when they'd last entered a restaurant and tried to dissuade him.

"In the zone," he explained. "We live here, remember. We might as well explore it."

"It's a zone. What's to see?"

Carl shrugged. "Every culture has certain needs and develops methods of meeting them. At least that's the way it works for ordinary humans. I'm betting it works the same way for the magically infected."

"I thought you were a biologist, not an anthropologist."

"A scientist is a scientist. We can't help our curiosity."

"All right. So where do you want to go?"

He named a restaurant she'd never heard of on a street that didn't show on the map her photographic memory supplied.

"Sounds like fun," she said. "Uh, how did you happen to know about it?"

She intended it to sound conversational. From the hard look Carl shot her way, she knew she'd failed.

"As in, I thought you were a late onset who's never lived here before, and now you know things about the zone?"

"I didn't say that. I was just--" well, she couldn't tell him he was spot-on right. "--curious," she concluded.

"I've kept my eyes open on our runs," he told her. "And I did research on the Internet. Despite the restrictions, there seems to be plenty of zone-related information out there. It even looks like there's a crossover crowd at this place. You might not be the only normal there."

She wasn't surprised to hear about normals slumming. Zone drugs, exotic sex with impaired persons, and a sort of no-rules attitude guaranteed that the dregs of normal society would seek pleasure in the zone. It wasn't legal, but it wasn't anything the Warders cared too much about. As long as no normals got hurt, anyway. On the other hand, impaired information on the Internet was a problem. Cyber-warders were supposed to keep magic-related information off the web, protecting normal children from zone exposure.

"I hope you reported those Internet sites to the cybers," she said stiffly.

"We've got reservations in an hour," he told her, ignoring her comment. "It's casual."

Casual? Danielle closed the door to her room and looked in her closet.

Four herder uniforms and the Hunter informal dress uniform hung neatly from hangers, each still in its dry-cleaning bag.

In her chest of drawers, she had an assortment of T-shirts, workout clothes, a couple of Karate Gi, along with a three pair of jeans and underwear.

So what did one wear to a casual restaurant in the middle of the Dallas zone?

Not a uniform. Residents of the zone hated warders almost as much as they feared them. Which was fine with most warders, as long as the fear came first.

Somehow, though, jeans and a T-shirt seemed too informal.

There was no help for it. It was time go shopping.

She clicked onto the net and found the store where they ordered their food. It wasn't Neiman Marcus or Foley's, but they did have a small selection of clothing--and they'd deliver anywhere in the zone, something that the prestige stores in North Dallas would never even consider.

Highly aware of the minutes ticking away, Danielle input her size and color choice, then ordered the only halfway cute dress that showed up, along with a totally impractical-looking pair of shoes and, in a brief moment of complete unreality, a pair of stockings.

A pretty brownie dropped off the package twenty minutes later. Danielle almost plowed into Carl as she ran to the door and was glad she'd decided to get something new.

The werewolf wore a charcoal gray blazer with an open-necked shirt and a pair of navy slacks. The required *Were* marker was discretely embroidered into the shirt's collar. He looked more like the millionaire he was than the nerd scientist she'd imagined him to be.

"I'll be ready in a flash," she told him, then headed back to her room.

Three minutes later, she decided to let him go out to dinner on his own.

The dress had looked charming and innocent in the computer display. On her, it was just short. The thin knit of the fabric molded to her slender figure and made it look like she'd added two cup sizes. And the stockings had seams up the back. She didn't have to worry about looking like a warder. Instead, she looked like a slut.

She wrapped her bathrobe around her and went out to deliver the bad news to Carl.

"It's the zone," he reminded her when she told him about her disappointing shopping experience. "Nobody will care what you wear."

"I care," she told him. "I mean, look at this." She yanked off the robe and stood there in front of him. "You'll look like a guy who ordered up his date from an escort service."

"I'll look like a guy any other male will envy," Carl told her. "Come on. We don't want to be late."

She was making a mistake by allowing him to talk her into leaving the house. Still, the look of pleasure in his eyes was gratifying to her. She wasn't interested in him that way, of course, but what woman doesn't enjoy being admired by a drop-dead gorgeous hunk of a man? Even if he wasn't really a human man any more.

After a short drive, Danielle handed her car-keys to a young zombie serving as valet and slipped her hand to Carl's elbow. "Don't drip any body bits into my car," she told the zombie.

"Yeth," he lisped.

"Zombies are very careful," Carl reminded her. "I'm sure that's why they picked them for valets."

She looked at him closely. Again he was showing knowledge that he shouldn't have had. When had he learned about zombie habits? She'd have to bug his computer and his office to make sure he wasn't communicating electronically with other impaired.

The restaurant was casual, but in a very high-class way. Its atmosphere reminded Danielle of a movie she'd once seen about Germany between the first two world wars, a strange combination of decadent sophistication and fear. A jazz band played, the wait staff occasionally dropped everything and broke into song, and a brief cabaret demonstrated the remarkable talents of a myriad of individuals who were simultaneously magic-infested and gender-challenged.

Her attire, she found, was tame by the standards of the restaurant and she became a little more content with her choice.

Better yet, the food was spectacular.

Danielle rarely touched alcohol. For once, she let her emotions overrule her logic and smiled when Carl offered to pour her a glass of wine.

The rich red from the magic-overrun Bordeaux region of France made her tingle from her toes up.

Although Carl had told her that the club attracted some normals, she was still surprised to see a table of normal men, obviously enjoying a night on the town, ogling the cabaret entertainers, pawing at scantily clad waitresses, and generally making themselves obnoxious.

She was at the point of walking over and asking them to desist when the club manager appeared at her elbow. "Leave them alone," he urged. "We don't want any trouble."

She nodded and tried to rejoin her conversation with Carl.

After a few minutes, she lost track of the normals. Carl entertained her with tales from graduate school, where he'd supported himself playing jazz saxophone in clubs something like this. That was before, of course. Clubs like this were no longer allowed in normal neighborhoods.

Since the return, normal society had gotten much more conservative, and anything this risqué was banned. Although he was only a few years older than her own twenty-six, Carl had grown up in a different world. No wonder he was inspired to find a cure and return to what he saw as real life.

* * *

She thought she had things under control until the band slowed it down.

She and Carl had finished eating some time earlier and she wasn't surprised when many of the diners stood and moved to the dance floor. She was surprised when Carl got up and offered her his arm.

"Is it time to go?" A part of her had wanted to continue the evening, wallow in the pretense that she was just an ordinary woman living in a time before the zone.

He shook his head. "I haven't heard music like this since college. I'd love a dance."

She swung into his arms hesitantly, almost awkwardly. "You'll have to show me how," she admitted.

"You don't dance? How can anyone go through life without dancing?"

Maybe if her mother had lived a little longer, Danielle would have been able to have an ordinary childhood and learned ordinary girly things like dancing and makeup. Instead she'd been sent to one of the countless orphanages that had sprung up after the return of magic had torn apart so many families. She'd learned how to fight, but she hadn't learned how to dance.

"Not all of us were born with silver spoons in our mouths."

Carl shook his head. "I hope you're not talking about me. I already told you I needed a scholarship to go to college. My parents were dirt-poor."

At least he'd had living parents. Danielle wasn't especially sympathetic.

"A jock like you should have no problems picking it up," he told her when it became obvious she didn't intend to answer. "Come on, you'll have fun."

Fun with an impaired? She didn't think so. But everyone else was up and dancing and she didn't figure it could hurt.

"All right."

Three minutes later, she wondered why she hadn't learned this stuff years earlier. The band had switched to something Carl called Big Band, and she got to kick up her heels.

"You're leading," he complained.

"Your point?"

"The guy is supposed to lead."

"New times make for new rules." Admittedly the government was big into pushing traditional values, but there was no way Danielle was going to let anyone, let alone a werewolf, control where she went.

On the other hand, being in charge was more fun that she would have guessed. And Carl's muscles felt pretty good when she used his strength to launch herself into the air.

* * *

Danielle handed the parking receipt to the parking attendant, who jogged off, leaving them alone in front of the restaurant.

Or were they alone?

She didn't see anything, but a warder learns to trust her instincts.

"What?"

"Something doesn't seem right." She had her leash, but she'd left her heavier weapons locked in the car. At the time, that had seemed safer. Now, she wondered.

Carl sniffed at the air, his nose raised like a wolf's. "Something's about to--"

"Ever had any impaired ass?" The door to a parked white van swung open and four young men--normal humans from what he could tell--clambered out. The speaker, a bald man with a beer belly, was probably a normal, but he could have passed for a troll with his size and aggressive attitude.

"Can't get enough," a second tough answered. His laughter was cruel and crude.

The group of normals she'd barely noticed when they'd been in the club stepped out behind Carl and her. On cue, she realized. This whole thing was staged. And now eight men surrounded them.

"It seems a shame to waste a piece like that on a dog like this." One of the men from the club pulled a heavy automatic from his belt and pointed it casually in Carl's direction.

"You, scat. And leave the female."

"I don't think--"

"That's right, you don't think. You're an animal and I've got a gun loaded with silver bullets. Time to run away. Or die." He laughed shortly. "I guess I'd just as soon you stay. I can buy more bullets."

Chapter 3

Danielle had seen the punks talking on their cell phones while she and Carl had danced, so she wasn't completely surprised by the situation.

"Warder business," she stated. "Move along, citizens."

"You may be a warder," the bald man told her. "But I don't think that dancing with an impaired is warder business."

"Warder Agent Danielle Goodman, Serial 2738433-763," she told him. "Second warning, citizens."

"Let's not mess with another warder, Billy," one of the punks from the club warned. "Maybe we should--"

"Maybe we should shut up and just do it. Is that what you were going to say? Because that sounds real smart to me."

When she'd first sensed something wrong, Danielle had started storing oxygen and flushing the residual effects of alcohol from her system. This whole thing was ludicrous. She was a warder, charged with protecting normals from the danger that the impaired present. Yet it looked like she would have to fight the very people it was her job to help.

If she simply stepped back, let them take out their frustrations on Carl, no one in headquarters would think worse of her. But she knew she wasn't going to do that. Carl believed in his research, and his faith was as contagious as some of the viruses that had swept across Earth during the bio-wars. If she left him, they'd kill him and she would have failed.

"We're going to walk away now," she told the one called Billy. "When we do, you can go back home or go into the club and have a drink. If you try to make trouble for me and my charge, I'll give you more than you want to deal with."

Carl growled softly at her side. He hadn't shifted, but her warder perceptions let her sense the essence of wolf pressing against his human form. Overhead, the moon, nearly full, shone with silver reflection, heightening the magical powers of the night. Billy took a step forward. Danielle's magic-spotting senses showed her that while Billy might be courtesy normal, he had a touch of the magical within him. A bit more and he would be the troll he resembled. Too often, Danielle knew, those most closely related to magic hated it most. If he lived long enough, Billy might find himself locked into this side of the zone. She didn't think he would live long after that.

"Final warning, citizen," she said, but she moved at the same time, stepping toward Billy, then turning with a jumping crescent kick to knock the automatic from the gunman's hand.

Billy caught her as she came down, using his strength to neutralize her quickness.

She headbutted him, splitting his piglike nose and assayed a palm-thrust to the groin. Billy had come prepared for a fight. Her strike met hardened plastic rather than soft flesh.

A howl split the night and the *Were* lunged at Billy's throat. A gunshot echoed in the narrow street. The lupine form jerked, then spun away.

She felt a vague surprise that the wolf would help her rather than run away. Still, she could worry about Carl later. Right now, she had her own problems. Billy was bleeding from her headbutt and she didn't think his gun hand would work after the kick it had taken, but he wasn't out of the fight. Other attackers closed in quickly.

She slammed a sidekick into Billy's knee and an elbow into his ribs, finally breaking the courtesy-normal's troll-like grip. Then she snap-kicked the man who'd shot Carl, sending his gun into the gutter.

She was in full blur now, pumping stored oxygen into her muscles and flooding her body with adrenaline until her thoughts and instincts became action.

All but one of her opponents slowed down to the relative crawl of the normal when facing a warder martial artist. One, though, blurred with her.

He was the man from the bar--the one who had urged Billy to back off. Now, though, he seemed intent on ending the fight his own way. He lurched forward, apparently uncoordinated and random in direction. Unfortunately for him, she'd trained to become a hunter. She knew the drunken-fighting style.

She blocked his attack, moving seamlessly from defense to counter, but he was ready too, parrying her strike before she could bring the full power of her body to bear. Whoever he was, he'd had Academy training.

Another attack and counter. Danielle knew she was better than he. Given time, she could take him. But she didn't have time. Sooner or later, one of the other normals would find the gun she'd kicked away. She glanced around using her peripheral vision to keep the other normals in sight.

Carl was down on the ground, transformed back to human form. Red blood oozed from a hole in his thigh. Apparently they hadn't been bluffing when they'd said they had silver bullets. Billy rolled on the ground groaning and clutching his knee. And the other six men had only started reacting to the battle.

Her warder opponent tossing something at her eyes, hoping to blind her, then followed it in.

She ducked, caught the scent of pepper, and stepped back.

As if this was a signal to bring the other men back into the fight, she sensed Billy behind her using his arms to pull himself to his feet. Another man clawed beneath his jacket going for his gun. They were certain they had her now. The warder would keep her busy, protect himself, and let one of the others pick her off.

It wasn't a bad plan, but Danielle didn't intend to stick around and watch it play out.

She dropped, rolled to Carl's side, then completed the roll to her feet lifting Carl's heavy bulk.

Another elbow, this one to the throat, took Billy out of the fight for the night.

She dumped Carl's still body into the passenger seat of the normal's van, vaulted over him, and took off.

Behind her, three shots crashed into the stolen van, then she turned a corner and left them behind.

That hadn't gone well.

* * *

"We need more help."

Carl looked like he'd aged twenty years. The silver bullet had ripped through his thigh, broken his leg, and lodged barely above his knee. Danielle had cut into his leg to remove the poisoned bullet, but he was still hurting.

A *Were* heals quickly, though, and Carl already looked a lot better than he had the previous evening, so Danielle wasn't sure what he was getting at.

"You're going to be fine. Besides, no doctor will come into the zone." She could take him to a normal-side hospital, but his treatment there would be no better than it had been at the restaurant that first day. He'd be lucky if he was ignored. It was possible that some doctor would decide to finish what the thugs had started.

"I'm not talking about that."

"What, then?"

He ticked off his slender fingers. "Last night proves that things are getting worse. Those gangsters would have killed both of us for no reason beyond simple prejudice. If we wait too long for the cure, it'll be too late. There'll be too much distrust between normals and the impaired."

"I'm in as big a hurry as anyone."

"I need a research team." He held up a hand to forestall any suggestion that she play that role herself. "People with training. I mean, let's be honest. I'm trying to save the world and I'm working by myself."

"I can see that."

"And second, I need some field workers. The return of magic is the most important event of our generation and you know what? No one has even bothered to undertake a systematic analysis of the DNA sequence of the different magical talents. We've assumed that something in the makeup of the victim defines the type of magical being that they become, but we don't really know this. We've assumed that the normals have some sort of resistance, but we don't know that either."

Danielle put up a hand. "Everyone knows normals are different. That the magic infected the already defective, people with holes in their souls."

Carl laughed. "Show me somebody with a perfect soul and maybe I'll believe that. Come on Danielle, I'm no different than I was a year ago."

"Then why is late onset so rare?"

"That's another good question. I proved that magic is a virus, but what is its vector? Does it spread from person to person, or are there some intermediate hosts? We don't even know that. Why did it hit once, then mostly stop? If it was a one-time event, why are there any late-onset victims at all? I need to know that before I can be sure I have a cure. It's up to me to do the basic field work the NIH should have done ten years ago when this whole thing started."

Danielle stood, paced across the living room a couple of times and then stopped in front of him. "Bringing in additional people will increase the risk of your project. There's still rioting going on in the zone, you know. After we left, those lowlifes called in some friends and went on a rampage. Seven normals were killed. If we hire someone and they're killed, the authorities will shut down your project so fast you'll be back in jail before you know what happened."

"Seven normals and how many of the magical?"

Danielle shrugged. Nobody counted magical deaths. In this case, Danielle knew that the normals were at fault, but surely that was exceptional. And if a few impaired got hurt as a result of their own terrorist activities, nobody was going to cry.

"Once we finish our cure, they'll be normal again," Carl reminded her. "So their deaths do matter. Your normals are killing people who can be saved."

Danielle didn't like to think about it that way. If her stepfather had been cured after killing her mother, would he simply have used the impairment as an excuse? Still, many of the impaired hadn't killed anyone. And they did deserve to be saved.

"Can we afford to take the chance, Carl? Bringing normals into the zone is asking for trouble."

"I'm not looking for normals," he explained. "I need people who can work the zone without warder escort. People who don't mind going door-to-door asking for blood samples. People who will make the magically enabled open their doors rather than hide under their beds."

Danielle froze. "It's unlawful to hire an impaired for any job for which there is a qualified normal applicant."

Carl's knuckles whitened. But he managed to hold himself in check. "That is one of the stupid laws that causes all of the problems."

"I think you're blaming the victim here," Danielle reminded him. "Normals need to protect themselves. And don't give me crap about impaired people not being responsible for their actions. They kill without caring."

He shook his head, and she wasn't sure whether he was angry or just frustrated. "Forget what I said because it doesn't matter. We're not talking about jobs that any normal would want, anyway. Or jobs any normal could do. First, they'll have to work with the magical, get their trust, and gain their sympathies. Second, no normal could be qualified for this job. Third, I'm an impaired. No normal would work for me and I'm not even sure it's legal for me to hire one."

Danielle nodded even as she looked for some trick in his logic. "Okay. We'll post a job listing. You know you'll have to pay for the team yourself?"

"As if I hadn't paid for everything since you sprung me from prison."

"Going back is still an option."

He smiled. "Then again, my money wasn't doing me much good when I was rotting at Lew Sterrett. Of course I'll pay."

* * *

Danielle's warder senses almost overloaded at the long line of magically impaired waiting outside the building that she and Carl shared. She'd posted a small notice on the web and had wondered if they'd have any job applicants at all. Instead, it seemed that half of the zone turned out.

The scent of magic, normally a low-level irritant, welled up in her like an agoraphobic panic. Except it wasn't a smell, exactly. It was a special sense that warder training had developed in her. A sense that made her skin want to crawl back, away from all of this disease. Worse, there were vampires in the group. She could understand keeping some of the impaired alive, but vampires had lost their souls anyway. She didn't understand why the government didn't outlaw them completely. According to Joe, they were working on it. And it couldn't happen soon enough.

Danielle's distress over the crowd was made worse by Carl's attitude. He seemed totally unsurprised by the turnout. She'd always thought scientists were nerds with unrealistic views of any reality they couldn't see through a microscope. Carl had confounded that belief, just as he'd turned around so many of the other understandings that had been pounded into her head by years of government television, ignorant teachers, and even warder instructors who taught to kill first and think second.

Her fingers itched to do something. It was illegal for impaired to gather in large groups like this. It could be dangerous. Hell, it was dangerous. If they decided to attack, they could swarm her under. All of her warder skills wouldn't keep her alive for more than a few seconds.

Carl limped out to the landing in front of their building and began organizing the throngs into groups by job function, potential lab assistants on the right and potential field workers on the left.

"How about you interview the field workers," he suggested to Danielle. "I'll have my hands full with the technical folks for the lab."

Just what she needed. Up-close contact with the impaired. She suppressed the shudder. "You haven't told me what sort of skills you're looking for."

Carl shrugged his shoulders. "You know. The usual. Initiative, intelligence, a way with people, and enough physical strength and stamina to pull some long hours. Some medical training would be good, too. It doesn't take a genius to get a blood sample but I'd like to know that they won't faint at the sight of it."

She nodded. She could do that. Those were the same abilities, or at least some of the same abilities, required for potential warders. Certainly no warder could let a little blood make them queasy.

"Let's get to work, then," Carl concluded. "See if you can hire me about five for a start. But get a list of any more that we might want to add later."

Five was more than she'd thought, but she trusted Carl at least as long as his invention was involved. She turned to go, then stopped. "How much should I offer?"

He didn't even pause. "Let's start them around eighty thousand."

She felt her jaw drop, but couldn't help staring. "That's twice what I make. You can get one of them for about five thousand, tops."

Carl glared at her. "Please don't forget that I am one of them. I'm going to put a lot of demands on these people and I want them to know that I appreciate their work."

"But--"

"And it isn't my responsibility that the government chooses to pay warders so little. Maybe it's because all of the warders' expenses are picked up by their prisoners."

Danielle's body shifted into blur mode without her conscious volition. Carl's last slam had been too close to an attack.

He must have sensed the changes within her because he shifted his weight into a cat stance. Now that was interesting, a wolf imitating a cat. She hadn't known he'd studied the martial arts.

She forced herself to back down. She could take Carl, whether in human or werewolf form. She'd done that before. But getting into a fight wouldn't prove anything. It certainly wasn't going to get her promoted into the hunters. Not that she'd have much of a chance for that if word ever got out that she was the reason for the latest Dallas riot.

"Hey, it's your money," she told him.

"Yeah. For now."

"What's that supposed to mean?"

He closed the distance between them. "Read the tea-leaves, Danielle. The magical community is being systematically deprived of basic rights. Do you really think the government won't see whatever fortunes we've amassed as fair game? If I can't get to the bottom of this magic virus or mutation or whatever it is, I won't have anything anyway. I might as well spend it while I have it."

She thought she should argue, but she couldn't really disagree. Even four years in the Academy hadn't prepared her for the reality of the two worlds, normal and magical. She hadn't suspected the misunderstandings, the ways that the two groups could see exactly the same evidence and come to such radically different conclusions. She knew the rules were put in place to protect society, but they could be rough on those society decided were on the outside.

"I'll hire you some good ones, Carl." It was as close as she could come to backing down.

He nodded his thanks and called for the first of the lab assistant applicants.

* * *

A terribly long day later, Danielle stepped into Carl's office.

"Don't you ever knock?"

She shook her head. She didn't have to knock. She was Carl's herder. If he had any secrets from her, it was her job to know them. Not that he was likely to have any. She'd bugged his computer and office so completely that she knew it every time he blew his nose.

"I'm finished."

"Yeah? Have any luck?

"Sort of." She was going against everything she believed in, but the vampire had convinced her. After all, who could be better at collecting blood samples?

When Carl heard what she had waiting, he was surprised. Not as surprised as she had been.

"You said you wanted people with a good attitude," Danielle reminded him.

"Yeah, but--"

"So, who would be more interested in picking up blood samples than a vampire? Who would be less likely to be fooled by someone trying to substitute someone else's, or coming back to give for a second time?"

"Nobody, but--"

"Look, Carl. I don't try to tell you how to run the lab, now don't you try and tell me how to run a street gang."

"That's just it, honey. This isn't--"

She held out a hand. "Don't call me that. Ever."

He stopped abruptly. "It's been a long day."

Finally she put him out of his misery, slamming her hand into the table so hard all of the resumes jumped. "Just shut up, Carl."

"Good thinking. Now back to the vampire. What's the idea there? Besides the fact that he likes blood and wouldn't mind taking a few samples?"

"The idea is that he's got ambition, drive, and energy. Plus the fact that he was involved in medicine before the return and knows how to do the basics. Like you asked for, remember?"

Carl pressed his palms into his forehead. "Vampires are demon-possessed, Danielle. That's a lot different from a *Were* or an elf. We're only DNA challenged."

As if she didn't know that. "Hey, don't think this was an easy decision for me."

"It isn't like the demon is going away if you don't hire him," she continued. "Besides, demon or not, Mike the Vampire seems qualified, anxious for the work, and fearless. I don't know of you noticed, but a lot of the applicants seem afraid of their own shadows. It's pathetic."

"It's the environment. They're denied basic rights, terrorized by the normals, and forced to live without basic services like running water."

Danielle shrugged. "Everyone has problems."

"But a vampire?"

"Talk to him, Carl. If you don't like him, tell him to get lost. But he's the lynchpin. I don't think the rest of your mob will amount to much without him."

"It's not a mob. It's the key crew for my research."

Danielle's smile didn't even reach her lips. "Sure."

"All right. Let's have a look at them. Mike first."

He sat there waiting. As if he expected her to get up and show the candidates in. Clearly power had gone to his head. Fortunately, Danielle was real good at fixing that problem.

She just stared at him.

Finally, he got it, went and opened the door himself.

The magically infected tended to be a disorderly group--part of the reason the zones had been established in the first place--so Danielle was surprised to see the two lines of finalists neatly queued, each holding their resumes in neat, matching, folders. "Which one of you is Mike?"

Carl must have asked the question before thinking, because the answer was obvious. The pale face, lean body, and distinctive black outfit would have identified Mike as a Goth in an earlier decade. Today, it marked him as a vampire.

He wasn't especially tall--about three inches shorter than Carl, but his presence made him seem larger than he was. The accent wasn't Bella Lagosa Transylvania, but it was distinct. Possibly caused by enlarged canines.

"At your service," the vampire told him. He bowed deeply to Danielle.

"Ms. Goodman and I will be interviewing each of you finalists together," Carl told the remaining creatures. "There's coffee on the machine in the kitchen. Help yourself."

A couple of young dwarves got into a scuffle as they tried to head to the kitchen, their short bodies too broad to allow both of them through the door at once.

"Billy. Willie. Behave."

The vampire's voice was soft--hardly more than a whisper--but it cut through the sudden chatter and froze the two dwarves in place.

41

"Sorry, Dr. Harriman," the vampire told him. "It's been a long day and coffee prices are through the roof here. I suppose you know that many dwarves have a serious coffee dependency."

Maybe Carl had known that but Danielle hadn't. There were so many different impairments that the warders had to specialize. She supposed dwarves had been covered in one of the overview classes but they weren't seen as a serious threat and she hadn't known anyone who had looked more deeply. And she'd already seen enough to know that the overview classes had left a lot out.

"If you'll follow me, Mike," Carl said, "I think we can make this quick."

Mike moved with the easy grace of Fred Astaire from the ancient movies. When he smiled--which he did as Carl offered him his hand--his lengthened canines gleamed an ivory white.

"I'm going to be honest," Carl told Mike. "I haven't heard much good about vampires. Ms. Goodman tells me that you're qualified and talented and I believe her. But I want you to tell me why I should hire you."

Mike's shrug was barely discernable. He was impossibly thin, but his clothes fit so well that it looked like a choice rather than the result of starvation.

"How long do you think your crew will last if they don't have someone like me to help?" Mike pulled up a chair and sat, his body almost gliding into the seat.

"I don't--"

"You're right. You don't know what it's like out in the zone. You've lived here for what, a couple of weeks? Secure behind your gates and fences. Almost a zone within the zone. But for the others, it won't be like that. They have to go home at night. They'll be sitting ducks for every gang out there."

Danielle had heard Mike's pitch earlier, but Carl seemed stunned. "Why should a gang bother with my workers?"

"Because they'll have money," Danielle answered for Mike.

Carl held up a hand to forestall Danielle, but Mike went on ahead. "Warder Goodman is right, of course. In the zone, if you've got money, then you're a target. In our case, though, there is even more. Word is out about you, Dr. Harriman. Word that you've got a lab full of treasure-- drugs, chemicals, food. Uh, blood. They'll pressure your poor workers, blackmail them to steal your materials, steal your research, even sabotage your work."

"And you can stop this."

Mike looked satisfied. "Oh, yes."

In the end, Carl hired the whole lot of them. Six outside workers, five lab assistants, and Mike.

"I'll shape them into the best mob in the Dallas zone," Mike promised.

"We're not a mob. We're a laboratory team."

Mike nodded gravely but Danielle didn't need any special warder skills to know he was lying. Intentionally or not, Carl was assembling a mob and Danielle had helped.

She felt uncomfortable, torn between the very real dangers posed by the impaired and the importance of Carl's vision and of her mission. Carl had persuaded her that they needed a staff, and Mike the Vampire was dead-on that they needed to be able to defend what would be seen as an increasingly attractive asset. But that didn't mean she had to like it.

Chapter Four

Danielle sent the two dwarves into far south Dallas looking for blood samples from the earliest of the affected. During the night, Carl had come up with the idea that those who were infected first might somehow be different--might, in fact, have been the elusive vectors of whatever virus or mutation had set off the return of magic. It didn't make a lot of sense to her, but then again, nobody had ever accused Danielle of being a scientist.

Rather than worry about that, or what he'd meant by the slip of his tongue when he'd called her 'honey,' she decided to ask Carl whether he was up for a run. Her cell vibrated just as she reached his lab door.

She suppressed the frisson of fear when she saw the calling number--the Dallas district Warder headquarters. Had they finally found out about her role in the riot?

"Goodman," she said as she pressed the on button.

"Warder Goodman. You are directed to appear at the Dallas District Office, Warder Central at two o'clock today. If you have any questions, please press one. If you accept, please press two."

Warders who want to get ahead didn't have questions. That was lesson one in Warder school. Don't ask questions: follow orders. She pressed two and listened for the confirmation of her choice. Then she continued into the lab. The run was out but she needed to tell Carl he was on his own.

He was buried in his research. Five assistants scurried around, bringing him their work, looking for the next assignment, or trying to anticipate his next request.

She'd thought of Carl as an impaired, like millions of others. Occasionally, especially when she was sleeping, she would think of him as a male, superbly fit, good looking in a rough and masculine way. Naturally she tried to suppress those thoughts. As the rioters had pointed out, dating between normals and infected was simply not allowed. Forbidden by both law and the law of the mob. And her stepfather had cured her of any interest along those lines anyway.

The lab workers, and there were a couple of females along with the three males, thought of Carl as the next best thing to an Old Testament prophet. The reputation he'd made when he'd run his own company had grown in the telling, or maybe his warder dossier simply understated his importance in the field of biopharmaceutical research. For just a moment, she allowed herself to think about what might have been, if Carl hadn't become infected.

She shook her head. She never would have met him if he hadn't become *Were* and the responsibility of the warders. As a normal with a hundred million or so in the bank, he would have his choice of women.

Carl's smile raced her heart.

He dropped everything, making her realize that she hadn't been into the lab since they'd hired the assistants a couple of days before. Well, it wasn't as if she was going to do serious science.

"What's up, Danielle?"

With the call to Warder Regional fresh in her mind, she wondered how she'd let things get to a first-name basis. He might be a science genius, but he was still one of them. She almost reminded him to call her Agent Goodman but stopped short. Twenty seconds before, she'd been wondering if he'd call her honey again.

"I've got to head into town," she told him. "Need anything from the north side of the pale?"

His forehead creased for a moment, then cleared. "I don't think so. The guys have an incredible talent for turning up just about anything."

This was a talent that she should technically report to her fellow warders. Danielle wouldn't bother, though. No warder would follow up on crimes against impaired. And she'd look like a rookie, not halfway ready for hunter work, if she reported every petty theft she ran across.

"Right. Don't know how long I'll be then. Don't mess up." She could feel his eyes on her back as she walked out. That awareness wasn't a surprise. Warder training made you aware of anyone looking at you--it could save your life. Still, Carl's gaze was hardly the stuff of threat--at least not threat in a violent sense. She knew his frankly male appraisal was disrespectful, an implicit statement that a normal might be interested in a *Were*. She couldn't decide whether she really minded.

* * *

Dallas's Warder District Office was the top half of the old Dallas Federal Building. Surrounded by acres of parking lots recalling the days when Dallas had been a commuter town filled with gas-guzzling cars, the building made up a non-distinctive part of the Dallas skyline.

How long had it been, she wondered, since Dallas, or any big city, had added another skyscraper? The return of magic had brought construction to a stop across America—maybe everywhere in the world. Not that anyone had much contact with the rest of the world any more. The return had destroyed whatever tourism industry was left after the bio-wars, so Danielle, like everyone else in the country below the senior diplomatic level, had only a vague idea what went on beyond the nation's borders.

She turned in her knives, her automatic (silver bullets and all), and her electronic pulser at the gate, keeping only the choke leash, which was truly part of her uniform.

A couple of security guards seemed interested in striking up a conversation, but abruptly went silent when they found she lived in the zone. Although there was no evidence to support the contagion theory, there wasn't much evidence to support any other theory of magic infection, either. So plenty of people, including most warders, figured that the less time spent with the impaired, the better. Another reason why herders, of all the warders, got the least respect.

With the delay at the gates, she'd had to hurry down the corridors to get to Joe Smealy's office on time but it turned out it wouldn't have mattered. She had to wait an hour outside his office, contemplating all of the trouble she was in if Warder Headquarters had found out about her role in the riots or in bending regulations to let Carl hire his assistants.

Joe Smealy finally opened his door and ushered her in. Joe hadn't aged at all since the day she'd met him--the day she'd discovered her mother's dead body. The then cop had taken a parental interest in the young orphan girl, encouraged her dreams of becoming a warder, and persuaded her to adopt the rigorous academy route rather than simply join as a patrol officer. More than anyone else, he was her mentor, the man she looked up to. When she was tempted to stray—tempted, for example, by a sexy werewolf--she relied on Joe's example to keep her straight.

Joe was living proof that medical science continued to progress. Danielle had done her research. She knew that he was a good fifty years old. But he could have passed for his late thirties.

He gripped her hand firmly and slapped her on the back, then led her to a small table.

Relief. He probably wouldn't greet her like this if he was going to ream her out.

"Sorry I didn't have more time when you arrived in Dallas," he said. "Visitors from D.C., if you can believe it."

She nodded. "Yes, sir."

"But I wanted to welcome you to the region. I put in a special request for you, you know."

She made herself thank him although she almost wanted to spit. So Joe's request was why she had ended up a herder. Some friend.

"Hey, I know you had your heart set on being a hunter," he said, his warder talents letting him picture her thoughts. "And that's going to happen as soon as I can work the angles. But Washington insisted on letting that werewolf go and," he laughed shortly, "well, you know herders."

She shrugged. "It isn't exactly a prestige job." Had he really said she was going to be a hunter?

He nodded seriously. "Damned right. Because nobody with balls, nobody with ambition, will volunteer to be tied down to a group of impaired. We all want to go where the action is, to fight crime and protect the people."

"Right."

"There are a couple of things, though." Joe's voice sharpened.

"Sir?"

"The unscheduled riots last week are unfortunate. They aren't to be repeated."

She didn't ask what she was supposed to do about normals who crossed over the line looking for trouble. Yes, sir was the only possible answer--and she gave it.

"All right." He nodded crisply. "We won't discuss that any further."

Thank goodness. She had a sneaking suspicion that he did know she was involved somehow and was giving her the only warning she was likely to get.

"Back to your current job. Dr. Harriman is important." He lowered his voice. "Washington thinks that he might be able to come up with a cure to the return of magic. Not just an inoculation, but a full-fledged turn-the-disease-around cure."

Bad news. If Washington thought Carl was important, that meant that she'd be herding for a long time.

"That's what he claims," she admitted.

"But what do you think?"

"Harriman is smart," she said. "And he's committed."

Joe nodded. "Don't let him fool you, though, Danielle. Whatever else he is, he's impaired. They don't think the same as people, don't have the same loyalties."

He stood, closed his office door, and sat closer to Danielle, lowering his voice as if afraid of being overheard. "Don't get me wrong, I've got

48

plenty of capable herders here in Dallas. But I've been watching Harriman. He's smarter than any of them. A few weeks and he would co-opt them. I need someone in place who can see through the story he spins and," his breath was hot in her face, "I need someone who won't hesitate to terminate him if that's needed for the people's safety."

Her face flushed at the compliment, but she knew she hadn't earned it. She knew Carl was smart, but she'd thought about it in terms of being a scientist. She hadn't really thought about how his intelligence meant he could manipulate people around him. Even trained people like Warders. Even suspicious people--like her. She'd tried to be careful, but Danielle was honest enough to face reality. At some level, Carl had gotten through to her. He had manipulated her. She'd been way too careless and if it hadn't been for Joe's warning, she wouldn't even know it.

She promised herself that she wouldn't let up her vigilance: that she'd live up to Joe's confidence in her.

"I understand, sir," she told him.

"I'm still Joe," he urged her. He rang his admin and called for coffee, then got down to business.

"Headquarters is always willing to try some scheme that's guaranteed to end the return forever. Of course, they make darned sure some remote district office is stuck holding the bag with any failure. And guess what? It's been ten years and we still have the impaired. Every single plan has failed. They just don't seem to get it that we're stretched thin out here. We need you hunting, not babysitting a tame werewolf.

"I'd like to do what I'm trained for," she admitted.

"The Academy trained you for anything. What I figure is, if they're going to let an impaired do research, at least we'd give him a herder that he couldn't shake off. Can you imagine what would happen if he was untended? Hell, he might just decide that the magic plague hadn't gone far enough. I'm no scientist, but I'm willing to bet that it would be easier to infect the rest of us than it would be to cure those already impaired."

Joe was right. Danielle nodded grimly. She'd needed this warning.

* * *

"I won't let you down, Joe."

"I know." He paused, then rushed ahead. "I'd like to get you out of herding and into something worthwhile right away, but Washington insists on this project and you're my best hope to keep it from blowing up." He took a sip of his coffee and leaned forward across the table. "Once the job is over, then we'll get to work on your career." He chuckled. "Hell, with your grades from the Academy, I won't be surprised to wake up one morning and find out I'm working for you."

Danielle shook her head. She didn't see that happening.

His smile faded. "But first, we've got to get through this mess. If you see any danger, it would be your job to blow the whistle and bring it to a premature end. Any danger at all."

"Yes, sir. I'll keep that in mind."

The weight that had settled on her chest when Joe had told her that Carl was a Washington directive lifted. She had her ticket out. At any time, she could simply call Joe, tell him there was a danger, and she'd be wearing her informal dress Hunter uniform to the next Warder cocktail party. Cool.

"Yes, sir."

He grasped her biceps and squeezed. "I hope you've kept your training up, Agent Goodman. Because if you decide to cancel the project, I'm ordering that you also terminate Harriman immediately. And be careful. Harriman may only be a *Were*, but he was a third-degree black belt before his impairment. And now he's got wolf reflexes to go with his skill. Don't underestimate your opponent, Goodman."

Her momentary elation evaporated like a mirage. She could have her dream job, but only by killing the man she'd learned to like and admire. Still, Danielle was a warder. She'd do her duty.

"I've been continuing with my training, sir," she answered honestly. "And I have no concerns about my ability to take Harriman and any mob he assembles."

Joe pulled a red bandana from his pocked, wiped his sweating forehead, and peered at her. "Assembling a mob. Is that what Harriman is doing?"

"He's hired some lab assistants and gofers," she said. "He wouldn't call it a mob, but you know the law."

The law made it illegal for more than four impaired to gather together in one place. It was a law that made absolutely no sense in the zone, but that provided warders legal justification for any activity they deemed necessary. Not that the courts had bothered to question the warders legal abilities since the Supreme Court handed down the People vs. Delaware Impaired decision.

Joe nodded. "It's a mob when we need it to be. Good work, Danielle. I knew I could count on you."

She nodded, torn between her pride at Joe's confidence in her and the empty certainty that killing Carl would be the most difficult thing she would do in her life.

* * *

Danielle returned to Carl's compound filled with a grim

determination to keep Carl in line--and to make sure she wasn't forced into terminating him. She expanded her bugging to the entire lab complex, spent late nights reviewing every questionable computer file, and battled down any temptation to see Carl as a man rather than as an impaired.

Then she worked on integrating herself more closely into his activities. Like helping with security.

A few days after her meeting with Joe, an outlaw gang's attempt to extort one of Carl's lab assistants created an opportunity to do just that.

She and Mike tried to keep Carl out of it, but he insisted on going along when they told him they were going to spike a shakedown on Dean, a lab tech.

It ended up with Mike, Danielle, Carl, the two dwarves, and a troll all trying to look inconspicuous on a narrow zone street.

"Perfect. We can see his apartment from here." Mike the Vampire plopped down on at a little cafe-style table outside a small bar.

Danielle joined Mike, Carl, and the dwarves at the table, but kept her eyes busy looking for Dean. Snori, the troll whom Carl had hired that morning, stood across the street, blocking the intersection like a statue.

The waitress, a little fairy-like creature with non-functional wings that flapped at hummingbird speeds and merely stirred the moist Dallas air around them, made sure she stayed a good six feet away when she took their orders.

She squealed when Mike ordered a Bloody Mary.

The two dwarves wanted coffee, but settled for beer when Mike shot them a glare.

"You don't want to see dwarves hyper on coffee," he explained to Danielle.

Danielle nodded and asked for bottled water from across the zone line.

That got more attention than everything else put together, including the vampire.

The waitress fled, not even waiting to take Carl's order, and returned with the beer, the Bloody Mary, and a gnome. She dumped off the drinks and left.

The gnome tapped a small club against his palm. "No magics in normal shops, no normals in mine."

"She's with me," Mike said.

"Yeah? Well, then maybe you're not welcome here either. I had a nice place in Lewisville before they passed the zone laws. Know what they did? Had the health inspectors out every day for a month. I ended up with no customers. Had to shut down. Wasn't doing anything illegal. Just pure nastiness."

Carl sighed. "We're trying to change that, sir. I understand your anger. But retaliating just makes things worse. Besides, Danielle is different. She's one of the few who can see how silly these distinctions are. She's one of the normal who will treat you like a human rather than some sort of inferior."

Danielle kept her mouth shut. Carl was right. She had been heading down that road before Joe had given her the warning and brought her back to the warder path. A warder protects the humans from the magical. That is the whole of the job.

"I don't serve normals," the gnome repeated as if Carl had said nothing. "And I don't serve normal drinks. You think I'm going to go to the barriers and haggle for bottled water when we get perfectly good water here?"

Carl reached into his wallet, probably looking for a cash means of resolving this argument but Mike held up a hand. "The dwarves and I will sit and enjoy our drinks. The human and the *Were* will simply keep us company. Is that a problem?"

Mike never raised his voice, never changed his tone, but that last question carried a load of menace that would have sent most normals into convulsions of fear.

The gnome was no coward, but neither was he a fool. "The zone is still a free country," he observed. "Not like the outside. Sit where you like. Finish your drinks. Then go somewhere else." He stomped back into his bar.

"He won't be back," Mike told Carl. "And we definitely won't see that waitress again. Just leave three dollars on the table."

"But--"

"Three dollars is plenty. In the zone, your money goes a long way."

They sat silently for a while, watching the alleyway entrances to the courtyard where they sat, and where Dean would soon be returning from his day in Carl's lab.

Danielle wouldn't have thought it possible, but both Mike and Carl blended into the background looking completely at home, completely nondescript, and completely harmless. The two dwarves didn't look harmless, but everyone knew that dwarves will leave you alone if you leave them alone—and if you didn't mess with anything they lay a property claim to.

Which left her standing out like a giant in a normal kindergarten.

Tough. Running interference with impaired gangs was exactly what she needed to be doing.

She slouched in her chair, but Carl laughed at her.

"You look about as natural as a catfish trying to dance."

"So, what should I do?"

"Look bored and disdainful. Like you're a rich normal looking for kinky pleasures. You can't help standing out in the crowd so let them see what you want them to see, not someone who's obviously faking it."

"But I'm not some pervert looking for kinky pleasure. I wouldn't know how to begin acting like one."

"You've got the bored and disdainful down. That should do it."

As compliments went, she could have done without that one. Still, she pulled out her compact, powdered her nose, adjusted her lipstick, and thought she did a decent job at the disdain. Boredom was easy. She'd barely passed her stakeout exams at the Academy.

Carl's research assistant, Dean, squirreled through the near alley a good hour later. The little imp wore a short-sleeved white shirt with a clip-on tie that had lost one of its clips. His face dripped with sweat and he clutched his plastic briefcase like a lifesaver. To Danielle's surprise, the imp's glasses-covered eyes glanced over her and moved on without a hint of recognition. Either he was so afraid he wasn't seeing straight, or her disguise was better than she'd thought.

Dean was halfway across the courtyard when the doors of three nearby shops opened and an assortment of elves, *Were*, and trolls surrounded the imp.

"I guess you missed your rendezvous point, Mr. Dean," one of the elves observed. "Perhaps you forgot that we had a meeting scheduled. But you didn't forget to bring us the research report, did you?" The tall elf wore black jeans and a western-styled shirt covered, despite the heat, by a long coat. Her warder training practically shouted out the warning. Strangely, the elf's face was serene, calm, and beautiful.

She could barely see Dean but she couldn't miss the stark fear that filled his eyes. Even more fear than when she'd caught him rifling Carl's files that morning.

"I, uh, thought I saw someone at the rendezvous," the imp explained. "Naturally I knew you would track me down."

"But?"

"But I did get the papers, Mr. Arenesol," Dean said. The imp could have won an Oscar if the impaired were eligible. They weren't, of course. "It wasn't easy," the imp explained, possibly gilding the lily. "But I was able to make a copy when the others were at lunch. They'll never notice it was touched. Exactly as you ordered."

The elf reached for the briefcase the imp clutched under his arm. "Good. So you never told anyone about our meeting?"

"Of course not." Dean let go with a sign of reluctance.

"Excellent." The elf laughed, an almost silent exhalation, then tossed the case to one of the *Were*.

"I guess we'll just have to give him his reward, then Rocky."

Danielle blurred.

She pressed the detonator as she jumped from her chair, suppressing the urge to duck at the sharp slap of explosion.

She was prepared for the noise and the bits of *Were* that landed around her. The mob that had attacked Dean wasn't so lucky. Several ducked. One ran, cutting down on the number that she was left to deal with. The troll, Rocky, barely flinched.

But that flinch was enough to let her close the distance from the cafe. She blocked the troll's knife inches from Dean's throat, slapped a finger strike at Rocky's eyes, and then brought a hundred and twenty pounds of angry woman straight down onto the troll's instep.

Rocky howled, but earned his name, keeping to his feet as he swung the knife at Danielle. Dean had the sense to drop to the ground and start crawling away from the fight, which had expanded with the arrival of Mike the Vampire, Carl, Snori, and the two dwarves.

Rocky was strong enough to be dangerous. If one of his grasping hands caught her, he could pick her up and snap her spine before she had a chance to do much. On the other hand, he was so slow that Danielle could have evaded his grasps even without warder training. So she had the chance to watch the others in her impromptu mob as they waded into the battle.

After only a little training from her, the dwarves, Billy and Willie, had perfected street fighting as an art form. The two worked together, one distracting while the other pounded rock-hard punches into any body part they could reach.

Snori seemed clumsy even for a troll, but somehow managed to knock down two of the trolls in the mob and then picked up a gnome by the ears.

The troll and dwarves concentrated, Danielle noticed, on the lower-ranking members of the mob that had surrounded Carl's research assistant, leaving the core of the organization to herself, Mike the Vampire, and Carl.

Mike was a martial arts machine. With an economy of movement that would have made any of Danielle's instructors green with envy, he reached through ineffectual blocks to touch pressure points, sending his opponents reeling in pain or temporary paralysis. Carl had half-shifted. He'd kept enough of his human form to deliver powerful kicks and punches, but fought low to the ground, threatening his enemies with powerful wolf jaws. While Mike and the dwarves kept the elf's bodyguards from coming into play, Carl attacked Arenesol.

Thanks to Joe's warning, Danielle could see the art in Carl's attack. Perhaps in those six months of solitary confinement, he'd developed a scheme to integrate martial arts designed for humans into his new form. Or perhaps his style of Kung Fu was one of those already based on animal movement.

Still, the elf was good. All elves had a grace and economy of motion that would make a human ballet dancer look clumsy, and this elf clearly practiced. He blocked Carl's attack and landed a raking straight-fingered thrust that nearly took Carl's eyes out.

Conscious that his allies were falling around him, Arenesol stepped back, reached into his coat, and pulled out a stick of dynamite. "Not yet," he muttered.

He stuck the dynamite back in his shirt and produced a pair of sai, the three-pronged fishing daggers that show up in tacky kung fu movies but that Danielle had never seen used in a real fight. Weapons in hand, he faced Carl calmly.

Almost absentmindedly, Danielle popped a hook kick to her troll's ribs then smashed a ridge hand to his temple. Rocky crashed to the ground in a satisfying avalanche and she turned her attention to an elf that had circled behind the two dwarves.

With Rocky gone, the elf decided he'd had enough of fighting, picked his teeth up from the ground, and ran. Danielle was free to watch Carl, to learn his moves and, if necessary, to step in and give him a hand. Third-degree black belt or not, he didn't have the warder training.

Arenesol blocked Carl's next strike, then launched an attack of his own.

The sai, Danielle noticed, gleamed the distinctive white of alloyed silver. Carl could be in trouble. She moved in to protect her herd.

Danielle watched for her opportunity knowing that Carl would need her help. She'd spent plenty of time at the Academy learning about elves—most dangerous of the impaired species after vampires—and she knew that no *Were* could stand against one. Especially not one with Arenesol's talents.

The elf didn't need the silver in his sai. It would simply make his job easier.

Carl arched a sloppy kick at one of the sai, overextending his balance.

The elf reacted to the opportunity Carl had given him, avoiding his kick and thrusting for the kill.

Against a human, Arenesol's move would have been fatal. But Carl wasn't exactly a human. He'd shifted to full wolf form just as the elf reacted. What would have been an insane, head-leading collapse in a human became a poised leap by a wolf.

Not that it mattered. Danielle's kick knocked the sai from the elf's hand leaving him unprotected to the attack.

Under two hundred pounds of wolf, the elf went down.

When Carl's teeth closed at the elf's throat, Arenesol smiled and went limp. "I take it there's something you'd like to discuss with me."

Carl loosened his jaws.

"Tie him up." In his wolf form, Carl's words sounded like a cross between barking and coughing but Danielle knew what he wanted. She whipped her leash out and wrapped it around the elf's hands and neck.

"Why don't we step back to the bar and discuss our next steps with Mr. Arenesol?" Mike suggested. "Billy and Willie, there's some refuse lying on the street and blocking traffic. Just shove those critters into the gutters they came from."

While Carl managed the transition back to human appearance, Danielle and Mike dragged the bound elf back to the bar.

"Can we have coffee now?" asked Billy, or Willie--Danielle had a hard time telling the dwarves apart since they always wore identical jeans, t-shirts, and the hooded cloaks that the law required dwarfs to wear at all times.

"I don't think they want our business," Danielle reminded the dwarf.

"They'll take our business," the other dwarf grunted. "Or else we'll--"

"Beer when we get back to the lab," Carl promised.

"Beer is good too," Willie, or maybe Billy, offered.

Arenesol, to no one's surprise, was perfectly willing to talk. A normal had offered his gang, the Tigers, ten thousand dollars for the results of Carl's work. In the zone, ten thousand will buy a lot of secrets. What it won't buy is loyalty. Danielle quickly picked up the fact that Arenesol's loyalty was to his mob and to his family, which it turned out, were pretty much the same thing.

Danielle watched Carl as he handled the interrogation. From his reaction, he wasn't thinking simply about preventing another attack. She wasn't sure what the elf had said, but something had sent Carl's mind off in a new direction.

Which meant danger.

Danielle rubbed the hand that she'd almost broken when she'd slammed a fist into the troll and wondered if she'd done the right thing protecting Carl. Because Carl was too smart, always planning steps ahead.

Chapter 5

Danielle wasn't sure she liked Carl's expanded plans, but she couldn't bring herself to cancel the project and terminate him. Carl's work was important. She tried not to admit, even to herself, that she didn't want to terminate Carl. Even thinking about the possibility sent her into involuntary blur mode. Too often she woke up during the night, shaking with the realization that she might have to kill him.

After frustrating the attempted assault on Dean the Imp, it only made sense for Carl to buy the houses surrounding his lab and turn the entire block into a sort of campus where his workers could live and work: where the rules of the zone were suspended and the rules of Carl imposed.

Naturally, with the generous salaries Carl was paying his staff, that made the campus a highly attractive region for new restaurants, clubs, and even light manufacturing operations to spring up. With no zoning or regulation to worry about, they did, virtually overnight.

Bars willing to cater to all, even normals, offered beer and watered-down coffee for the dwarves. Carl funded creation of a bakery that soon made bread for the entire zone, a computer center, and a combined brewery and ethanol plant.

Danielle had objected, of course. Carl was supposed to be researching the causes of the return of magic, not undertaking the economic transformation of the zone.

Carl had simply laughed off her concerns. When he'd started his own company rather than take a prestige university research job, he had proved he was more than a science wonk. He liked business, liked money, and liked getting things done. As he told her, curing the magic infestation wouldn't take care of the country's problems all by itself. They needed economic renovation as well. And that might as well start here.

Still, plans for major new construction, the first she'd seen in since she'd been a child, profoundly disturbed Danielle. What would an economic miracle in the zone mean? Could it be good for normals? And what if Carl was ultimately unsuccessful with his research? In her nightmares, Danielle worried that economic growth might allow the zones to grow more important, to the point where they could make demands of the nation rather than the pathetic requests that had been common up until then.

Carl had met her objections with a dogged determination to move forward.

"Dogged is a good word for him," Danielle muttered to herself. Despite her doubts, he'd even managed to talk her into participating in his economic miracle. She'd opened a dojo, training mostly young impaired in the martial arts.

She knew that the money behind all of the building and growth had to be coming from Carl's fortune, but she wondered how long it could last. Even with the low prices common in the zone, he'd been down to only fifteen million dollars after the legal expenses had drained most of the proceeds from the sale of his original company. Property was cheap in the zone, and impaired lives were even cheaper, but Danielle had seen the invoices for lab equipment, the salaries Carl insisted on paying his staff, and the basic supplies they all needed to keep the compound running. At this rate, his money wouldn't last a year--yet, instead of scrimping, Carl kept spending more.

Again, Carl shrugged his muscular shoulders and told her that money in circulation had a way of coming back. He was a businessman, he reminded her, not a philanthropist.

She reported her concerns to Joe, but he simply gave her blanket authority to support Carl or terminate him. There were times when she could have done with a little less trust and a little more authority.

She dismissed her last section of martial arts students, a fairly hopeless group of gnomes, imps, brownies, and fairies, together with a pair of trolls who could easily pick up an old-style gasoline powered car but who seemed barely manage to walk without tripping over their own huge feet.

Snori, the troll who had helped her and Carl rescue Dean, had joined along with one of his friends. Despite, or maybe because of their extreme clumsiness, these trolls were her favorite students. They were always eager for new assignments, spent countless hours committing even the easiest Kata to memory, and showed endless patience with the younger students. Even better, Danielle thought she'd seen a hint of gracefulness in their movement lately. The idea of a quick, talented, graceful troll was a little disconcerting to Danielle when she chose to think about it--so she tried not to.

Carl walked into her dojo just as the two trolls, glorying in their new green belts and sweating from the intricacies of basic Kata four, finally wandered out the door, squabbling like trolls, but also discussing the new Kata and, to Danielle's complete shock, analogizing the movements of the Kata to the current status of the relationship between humans and impaired. That was a direction Danielle wouldn't have taken her martial arts, and a direction she would have bet money no troll would consider. Could there be more to the impaired than the warders knew?

She forgot everything when she turned her attention to Carl. She hadn't been neglecting him, but he had been busy and so had she. The surge of pleasure at seeing him surprised her. <u>He's your herd,</u> she reminded herself. <u>Never develop a personal relationship with a herd.</u> Lesson twenty-three from the warder handbook.

"We've isolated the original virus," Carl announced. "And we have at least some ideas about the initial vector. I think it's time for you and me to celebrate."

The last time she'd celebrated with Carl, it had led to a riot. She reminded him of that, together with the fact that he had a whole tribe of lab assistants and fellow scientists working on the project. They, not she, should be involved in the celebration.

"You're the one whose faith let us get started and keep moving," he assured her. He winked, "Besides, you're a lot more fun than most of the scientists. I hate to stereotype, but what a bunch of nerds."

And there were more and more scientists. Carl kept hiring, adding anyone who had the experience and scientific background he was looking for. All of which meant more late-night work for Danielle as she bugged their computers, phones, and offices, then analyzed the results.

She kept waiting for warder scientists to request particular results or data points for replication, but so far, her reports to regional headquarters had dropped into a black hole. That, however, didn't keep her from doing her job. Aside from Carl himself, she doubted if anyone had a better idea how the project was coming than she did.

Still, getting an English language summary directly from Carl could help her get a handle on some of the more confusing bits of his research. She almost persuaded herself that she was accepting his invitation for that reason. Unfortunately, she'd received advanced training in detecting lies. Her pulse, steady even while running through the Kata with the trolls, had accelerated considerably when Carl had walked into the room and jumped again when he asked her for what she could reasonably consider a date.

She told herself that, as long as she was stuck here, she might as well enjoy it.

Not that she was really stuck here. She had to keep reminding herself of that. She could terminate the project any time she wanted. All she had to do was turn herself into an uncaring psychopath and murder

61

Carl.

"Celebrating sounds fine," she told him. "But first, you'll have to explain to me why isolating the virus is a good thing? I would have thought that would be dangerous. An opportunity for further spread of the infection." It was, after all, one of the dangers that Joe Smealy had particularly warned her about.

If Carl laughed at her, got all smug and superior, it would make it a little easier to kill him. If he refused to tell, she could persuade herself it was her patriotic duty. Maybe.

Instead, he nodded. "I've wrestled with that question myself. Some of the researchers believe that there was a special set of circumstances that led to the infection and that, unless it is repeated, we are safe. The existence of late onset impaired seems to disprove that theory. That and my preliminary findings on the vector itself."

"So isolating the virus is dangerous, then." She slipped out of her gi jacket only to see Carl's eyes tracking her every move. Well, it wasn't as if he hadn't seen her in a sports bra before.

"You're looking good, Danielle. I think you've got a real knack for teaching, especially for working with the children."

Oh, yeah. She'd be a great mom, too. If she didn't assassinate her children the way she suspected she'd eventually have to terminate Carl.

"Thanks. And they're not all children. But don't change the subject. I'm concerned about the virus." The bio-wars two decades earlier had made everyone critically aware of what damage a virus outbreak could do. If a new return of magic infestation broke out among the normals, civilization itself might fail. That, more than anything, was the nightmare the warders had been set up to prevent. This was the kind of risk that Joe had warned her about. Exactly what she'd feared from the moment she'd left Joe's office and returned to the zone.

Carl shrugged. "It became pretty obvious that there was some sort of DNA shift in us magics. There are some interesting DNA segments in the human genome that have always been considered to be junk but, when zapped by the virus, translate themselves in a way that brings about the magical talents."

"Magical impairments," she corrected. This was a critical distinction. If magic became seen as anything other than an infestation, there was no telling where the world would end up.

He paused and looked at her. "Magical impairments, if you insist."

"So the virus goes in and changes DNA and all of a sudden you're a werewolf or a zombie or a dwarf? How likely is that?"

Carl shrugged. "It's not impossible. There's pretty good evidence that it was a virus which led to the speech gene mutation a few hundred thousand years ago. In some ways, this is similar. And there aren't that many other ways to alter DNA once it's been formed. Using genetically altered viruses for gene therapy was one of the key discoveries of the twentieth century. So, I'd have to say it's pretty likely that it happened. I won't try to guess the likelihood that a naturally evolving virus just happened to release multiple latent magical, uh, impairments, though."

Danielle nodded, wiped her body down with a towel, and threw on a silk robe. Years in the Warder Academy had made her less than self-conscious about her body. And one of the fundamental lessons of that training had been that the impaired are not fully human. She shouldn't have minded stripping down in Carl's presence any more than she would in front of a dog. But she did, and she didn't want to think about what that might mean.

"Okay, but a speech gene is just one change," she continued, trying to keep her mind on business. "So, if a virus attack made us turn into vampires, or *Were*, or goblins, or whatever, I might be able to buy it. But how could it result in all of the different changes we've seen?"

Carl smiled at her as if she was a talented student. "That's what we're working on next. After all, we need to discover a cure that will work for all of the infected, not just for vampires, or *Were*, or goblins. I mean, how would it help if we turned a bunch of *Were* into vampires?"

She nodded, although she wasn't so sure about anything any more. Things were changing too fast, seemed too chaotic, too out of control.

"But tonight," Carl concluded, "we celebrate."

* * *

Carl knocked on her door at seven that evening.

Sweltering Texas heat enervated her, made her wish she'd never agreed to this crazy idea.

Carl looked as cool as if he'd just stepped from a freezer.

His eyes widened when she opened the door. "You look great."

He looked like a complete hunk in a suit that had obviously been tailored to show off his broad shoulders and narrow hips. It kept getting harder and harder to remind herself that he was one of them—impaired and not a man at all. To Danielle, Carl looked all man. And a part of her wanted to tell him to forget dinner and drag him into her bed.

"You look pretty good yourself. Let me get my bag and I'll be ready."

He brushed his hand against the mark of the beast, the wolf's head sewn into the lapel of his linen jacket. "Yeah? Thanks."

"I mean it. But what's that?" She pointed at the gas-burning car sitting outside.

"I figured I'd drive. Somehow, it doesn't seem like much of a date if I make you do the driving."

She let the date word pass without comment.

"That's a gas burner."

It had taken way too long, but America had finally caught on to global warming and greenhouse gasses. Petroleum burners were limited to high status warders and government officials. Even normals drove hydrogen carts like the one Danielle had been assigned, or one-person electric scooters. The zone was littered with cars like his Chevy, abandoned by magical or normal alike when gasoline became government controlled and warders began making midnight raids on those who found a way around the regulations.

"Alcohol conversion," he explained. "A lot of car buffs ended up on this side of the zone."

She still looked suspicious. "Where do you get the alcohol?"

Carl laughed. "That is the least of our problems. Comes from the algae plant."

The algae recycling plant had been a stroke of genius on Carl's part. One Arenesol and his gang, the Tigers, had been, indirectly at least, responsible for. Without city services, the Trinity River was their only source for water. Since the river was a slimy mess of sewage, poorly disposed-of chemicals, and whatever flotsam the normals of Dallas cast off, it made poor drinking water.

Elves were particularly susceptible to water impurities, so Arenesol's Tigers had come to Carl with a proposal to filter the river water. He had financed the plan, then added an algae growth facility to handle the filtered algae and chemicals, mixed the organic mass with yeast, and fermented it. The stuff couldn't be drunk raw--not that a few dwarves hadn't been fired for trying--but it could be distilled to pure alcohol.

Danielle hadn't realized that Carl's plant had progressed that far. It seemed like he made more progress each week than the normal side of the zone line had made in the decade since the return of magic virus had struck. Although he hadn't given up on his cure, more and more he seemed embedded in the zone—becoming one with the enemy.

She wondered how many laws Carl had broken, then decided not to think about it. Joe had given her the grim answer. When she decided Carl had crossed the line, she would have to terminate him. Best to ignore what she could. She also ignored his hand when he tried to help her into the car and slid into the passenger seat.

A blast of cool air met her. Wow.

"It's cold."

"Yeah. Air conditioning. Isn't it great?"

"But--"

He let her sputter out. "I'm not that much older than you, Danielle, but I can remember the way things were before the return of magic, when air conditioning was normal, when Dallas was thriving, and when malaria was something that happened in Africa rather than here. And I want those days back. Now come on. We're going to have some fun tonight if it kills us."

* * *

She might have to kill him this evening.

Danielle had always known it would come down to this. Certainly since her meeting with Joe, she'd been continually aware of the knife-edge Carl lived on. But she'd hoped that things would work out. Now, though, she was at a decision point. The knowledge drained the joy from what should have been a wonderful evening. Carl ordered Champagne, poured two glasses, then raised his glass in a toast. "You were the first person to believe in me, Danielle. I couldn't have made it without you. Thanks."

She barely nodded, took a small sip of the drink, and set it down.

The club's owner recognized Carl and hurried over to take their orders and to ensure that everything was to their satisfaction. It hadn't escaped Danielle's notice that just about everyone in the zone knew Carl now.

Danielle had reported to Joe that the zone seemed more organized, less chaotic, than her academy training had led her to expect. As usual, she'd gotten nothing in response, leaving her to make her own decisions and worry whether an organized zone would be better for the human world because it controlled its impaired, or could constitute a threat.

"Any normals around?" Carl asked. "I'd just as soon not get ambushed again."

The owner wrung his hands, told Carl that, as far as he knew, Danielle was the only normal who had ever set foot in his establishment, and hurried off to supervise their dinner.

"What is he?" Danielle asked softly once the owner had left.

"Pete? Oh, he's the owner, of course. I'll introduce you."

"I mean, what's his impairment? He looks normal. He had a generic magical marker which, I thought, was used only for children before they develop their specific handicap."

"He organized a protest against forming the zones. Everyone who protested got sent here. Some had talents. The warders decided that those without talent were latent. They don't believe that a normal could protest their benevolent rule."

Danielle's hand instinctively touched the hidden hilt of the small fighting knife she carried in a sheath on her thigh. Carl's words were close to treason. The penalty for challenging a government classification was death. And any warder was authorized to carry it out.

She told herself that she was letting Carl slide because of the potential he offered, but wasn't sure. She had let herself get emotionally involved with Carl.

"You've gotten a lot more cynical since we met," she told Carl. "You're putting yourself in danger, you know."

Carl's laugh was relaxed, easy. "Hell, Danielle, I'm not a cynic. I'm a blooming optimist. I'm the one who thinks that we can undo the mess we're in and get back to normal. I don't know if you've been paying any attention, but hardly anyone else thinks that's even possible. On either side of the line."

"And you think your anti-virus will do the job?" she asked. She wanted him to give her an excuse not to kill him. That's why she tossed him softballs like this one. But would he bother to swing at it?

Carl frowned. "The virus we isolated shows how the original infection occurred. With the proper vector, we could even recreate something like the return of magic. If we decided that the normal were the sick ones and wanted to cure them by giving them magical abilities, we'd be as good as done. Since we want to do the reverse, we've barely started."

He lapsed into pure gene technology jargon and Danielle's comprehension of the next three minutes of his lecture were complicated by the difficulties of keeping her eyes open. Finally, Carl realized he was talking to an empty skull and nodded. "Sorry. Science is a language. Some things you can't explain to someone who doesn't have the vocabulary. Let's just say we have our work cut out for us and celebrate getting as far as we have."

Carl turned on his charm for the rest of the evening. He entertained Danielle with amusing stories about the problems they'd had in their research--about a mob of vampires who had tunneled under the lab and raided the blood samples, a white mouse who had been given the virus-- and had turned into a zombie stalking and murdering the other mice, and about the dwarves who, hearing of a coffee shipment, had turned one of their own number into a battering ram, using the dwarf's own head to break into the storeroom and secure the forbidden stimulant.

Danielle found herself laughing, relaxing, and even telling Carl stories about her own experiences--about teaching martial arts to trolls, and about life as the only normal in the zone.

Only when Carl's gentle probing touched truly sensitive areas did she realize she'd opened up to him more than she'd ever opened to any male, normal or impaired.

"What about your family," he inquired gently. "How did they feel about your career choice?"

"I'm not going to talk about my mother," she told him, her voice rising despite herself.

"Ooookay. Note to self. Don't talk about family." When she didn't even smile at his attempt at humor, Carl turned serious. "I'm interested in you, that's all. Well, fascinated might be a better description."

Danielle wasn't sure she wanted to fascinate a man—or an impaired.

After dinner, they walked along the swollen Trinity River.

Strands of barbed wire, new in the three months since they'd first entered the zone, and continual probing of searchlights added a sense of danger and adventure to the evening. Hooting alarms and a flurry of tracer shells briefly disturbed the peace of their walk.

"I don't know how we can go on like this," she admitted to Carl. "Keeping the impaired under control is absorbing so many of society's resources."

He nodded grimly. "That's why my work is important. Sooner or later, some politician is going to get the brilliant idea that normals would be better off without the magical."

It was a curious statement. "They already have. That's why we have the zones."

He shook his head. "The zones just contain the problem. They're not a solution."

She shuddered as she caught his meaning. Before this assignment, she hadn't really seen the impaired as human. But living with Carl, seeing the magical struggle for life, made her wish for a solution other than death.

"It's getting late," Carl said. "I'd better get you home."

An alarm almost drowned out Carl's words and Danielle's memory flashed on the vampire she'd killed in L.A. Dallas didn't need an escape.

"Get your head down," Carl hissed.

A searchlight blinked past them, then returned, joined by others.

"Warder Business," she shouted, raising her badge.

Carl tackled her just before a ricochet threw shards of concrete in her face. The crack of a high-powered sniper rifle sounded a fraction of a second later.

"They're after us," Carl hissed.

Walking near the barrier had been a bad idea, Danielle realized. An idea that just might get them killed.

She let herself blur, sending her senses out to be sure that no warders were on this side of the river before leading Carl on a long crawl back to safety.

By the time they made it back to his car, Danielle was a mess, but she was also filled with adrenaline and wound up like a spring.

After the short drive, home Carl walked her to her door.

She decided she'd shake his hand, thank him for a wonderful evening, and go inside.

His lips descended on hers before she could get the first word out.

The combination of Carl's potent male sensuality, the adrenaline rush from being shot at, and the romantic evening swamped any vestiges of common sense. For weeks she'd kept her libido under control by continual workouts, by sparing with vampires and fast-moving elves, and by resolutely refusing to think of Carl's lips, or Carl's body.

None of those tricks worked now.

The problem, she eventually realized, was that her lips and tongue were already busy--busy kissing Carl back as hard as he was kissing her.

Chapter 6

Danielle brushed her hand down Carl's naked chest.

Now how had that happened? Her mind whirled with the past minute's activities: a simple good night kiss at the door. Then a frantic search for the key.

Oh, yes. Memory returned with a hot flush of embarrassment. She'd grabbed Carl and physically dragged him into her bedroom, torn his shirt from his broad chest, and buried her face in the pure maleness of it.

If she was clueless, Carl seemed to know exactly what he was doing.

He nibbled down the side of her neck sending delicious shivers rocketing through her body. His large strong hands held her firmly, let her believe that she was protected despite a lifetime's experience that she could never truly be safe.

She sighed and leaned against him. All of her training, all of her reasoning told her not to let down her defenses, not to let Carl do more. He was her herd, off limits. He was male and therefore risky. He was impaired and therefore a killer.

Yet she could do nothing. Rational thought yammered away inside her, ignored and muted as if locked in a nearly soundproof room. Danielle's reaction to Carl was driven by something more primal than logic.

His hands left trails of liquid fire behind them, left her panting with burning desire and need. He stroked her back and she purred like a cat.

"If you want me to stop, tell me now," he warned.

His tone should have frightened her beyond thought, but she was way beyond thought already. Way beyond fear. Instead, the knowledge that she excited him this much, that she drove him past his ironclad control, made her feel powerful, desirable.

"I've waited too long already," she answered. Her hands fumbled at his belt.

He groaned with need, then grasped both sides of her silk blouse and pulled.

Silk may be thin, but it's incredibly strong. Against the power of Carl's grasp, her blouse disintegrated as if it were made of rotten cotton.

She brought up her hands to cover her breasts, but he caught both her arms in one of hand, holding her immobilized while he lowered his lips to the exposed tip of one breast.

The touch of his hands had been fire. The hardness of his teeth as they grasped her nipple, the warm touch of his tongue against its very tip, raised her heat to levels of pleasure that she had never imagined.

She took advantage of his distraction to free her hands from his grasp and reach, again, for that hard bulge.

Carl laughed, pulled away, then peeled her from her pants as if they weren't even there, left her standing naked and exposed in front of him.

His eyes gleamed with passion as he admired her, his hands everywhere, stroking, touching. His lips following with gentle kisses and firm nibbles.

"You too," she urged. "I want you naked."

"Soon."

He picked her up and put her on the bed, then slid beside her.

One of his hands brushed against her sensual folds and she responded with a liquid surge.

"Don't torture me," she urged. "Hurry."

"You've been torturing me for weeks," Carl answered. "It's turn-around time."

She hadn't been a deliberate tease, even when she'd worn skimpy workout attire in Carl's presence. But she had noticed the way he looked at her. Had savored the knowledge that he desired her.

Slowly, deliciously, he slid a finger into her, then brushed his thumb against her sensitive nub.

She moaned, again pressing herself against him. She didn't need artful lovemaking. She needed to be taken, to be ridden hard, to find release. But Carl's touch sapped her protest, tore her between the urge to sink back and savor the pleasure and the need to feel Carl inside of her, driving toward their fulfillment.

His belt buckle finally gave way against her probing hands and she seized the evidence of his hunger.

"Two can play at this game," she breathed as she squeezed down hard on his erection.

Carl gasped. "Easy, honey."

She hadn't been able to admit it before, but she realized she liked his pet names.

"Oh, no," she answered. "I don't want easy. I want you hard and inside of me. Now."

Carl looked rebellious. She was disturbing his fantasies. Well, tough.

Danielle was a big girl. She knew what she wanted and wasn't about to accept the next-best thing.

"I mean it," she added. She released his erection and wrapped her arms around him, planning to roll him over so she could straddle him and take him into her.

* * *

Carl had other plans. He grasped her legs, urging them up until they opened her like a flower waiting for a bee.

And like a bee, he plunged toward the nectar.

Danielle was a wildcat beneath him, bucking as he brought toward her as if trying to swallow all of him into herself.

He'd almost lost control when she'd grasped him. But his continual battle for control of the wolf gave him more endurance than he had ever had.

She groaned as the tip of his penis brushed against her lips, then moaned as he entered her.

She was tight.

Even with her legs pressed up near her chest, even with her moisture flowing rich and lubricating, he had to bear down to enter into her.

But she pressed back, welcoming that entry.

"Oh, yeah. Give it all to me," she whispered.

He slid his length into her. Slowly, enjoying and savoring the sensation of velvet-cloaked muscle clamping down on him, holding him into her.

He'd fantasized about this moment from when he'd first seen Danielle, all formal and stiff in her warder uniform but still looking like an angel of pure sexuality. Even his fantasies hadn't prepared him for her responsiveness, the need in her that matched his own.

He balanced his weight on his hands and knees to avoid crushing her beneath him, but Danielle reached her arms around him, pressing him to her.

"I want it all," she groaned as he thrust deeply into her. "Don't hold back."

He'd intended to do just that. To make their first time special, lingering, emotional. But Danielle's need ignited a matching fire within him.

He forgot the tricks that a dozen girlfriends had taught him and thought only about Danielle, about her body beneath and around him, about the way she clenched him, and about the way she lit his day simply by being there.

Danielle pressed up against him, pushing him to a faster and faster

71

pace, her breath short, a pulse in her neck vibrating at a rate that would have been dangerous on anyone less fit than she.

They both strained at control, found a rhythm that kept them close as they pressed their bodies together. Carl's breathing was harsh in his own ears, the scent of sex and clean sweat filled his nostrils.

Danielle's face flushed beneath his. She smiled, then reached up and sank her teeth into the side of his neck and raked her fingernails into his back.

There was no pain, only an impossible increase in intensity.

Then it was too much. He clamped down on his control, desperate not to complete before Danielle reached her own climax, but knowing it was hopeless.

Just when he lost control, as his throat readied for a cry of satisfaction, Danielle's moan and the sudden tightening of her inner muscles told him that she too had achieved completion.

A few hard surges pushed him over the edge. He spilled himself into her, then gently kissed her on the lips.

"That was incredible," she told him.

He wanted to linger in her, to share the afterglow of a moment that he would remember for the rest of his life. Until he felt it.

The change.

* * *

Danielle closed her eyes and savored the feeling of a man, swollen inside of her.

She wasn't the most experienced woman in the world, but she had been around enough to know that she'd just enjoyed something extraordinary, something that would change her life. Exactly how it would change things, and whether how she'd deal with the differences, was an open question.

She closed her eyes to better focus on sensation: Carl's male scent mixed with the scents of sex; the rough texture of his stubble, now hours from its latest shave against her face; and the weight of his body on her own.

Abruptly, he pulled away.

She groaned in protest, reached to stop his retreat.

Her hand caught at a tuft of Carl's hair and she used that to tug him gently back to her embrace.

Except, Carl didn't have hairy shoulders.

She opened her eyes hoping that her fears were unjustified.

A huge wolf crouched on the bed next to her, tugging to free itself of her grip.

"Carl?" As if she needed to ask the question.

His howl was a mournful cry into the deepening night.

From outside, more howls answered. The moon was full and the beasts of the night were at their work.

Her leash was somewhere on the floor, mixed with her clothes and Carl's. She was naked, alone with a wolf.

She hadn't been so frightened since the moment she'd walked in on her mother and stepfather. Then, she'd screamed. Now, she kicked wildly at him and scrambled for a weapon.

The kick connected, but did no damage. His wolf grin seemed to mock her.

Her hands connected with something—Carl's belt—and she wrapped it around her fists and punched at him.

He backed off.

"Out," she demanded, irrationally. As if a wolf could understand English.

The *Were* slunk out, his tail between his legs.

Danielle waited until he'd left, then locked and barred the door behind him and buried her head in her pillow.

She had no one but herself to blame for what had happened. She knew better than to sleep with an impaired. Still, she felt empty, deserted. Despite what she'd seen, despite her memories of her mother and stepfather, a part of her wanted to call Carl back. Another part of her wanted to jump in the shower and scrub until every trace of Carl had been washed away.

Carl's scent remained behind him, in the pillow she held to her face, on her body, in the sheets.

She got up, threw the sheets, pillowcase, comforter, and even the pillows into the washing machine, then went to stand in the shower. As if soap and water could wash away her mistake.

* * *

"The Tigers are planning a breakout," Arenesol told Carl.

Danielle had thrown herself back into her work after making her mistake with Carl. She was in her office, writing a report to Joe, when she heard the elf's voice over the microphone she'd planted in Carl's office. Arenesol hadn't been on Carl's appointment list and she'd tagged him as a dangerous element.

"A breakout is insane." Carl's voice was low and reasoned. And sexy. Despite everything, Danielle still responded to it.

"We need it."

"The minefields would tear you to shreds. And the warders would slaughter anyone left. Besides, where would you go?"

Where indeed. The morning after she'd fallen to Carl's attraction, Danielle had gone back to the river. The bodies of two little brownies had washed up on the shore.

"Elves can move swiftly and silently in the dark," Arenesol reminded Carl. "Some have escaped before. They've shown us the way."

"A few, maybe. But a whole gang? With children?"

"They are killing us here in the zone, Carl. We'll head south, toward one of the abandoned cities. Maybe Houston, or San Antonio. But we need you to help--to arrange a diversion."

Danielle held her breath. It wasn't too late for Carl to save himself. All he had to do was tell Arenesol that he was too busy, that he couldn't betray his mission.

"Once we find the cure, everything can go back to normal, Arenesol. Can't you just wait a few more months?"

"For us, life outside is a distant memory. But it's a memory of a golden age. We want it back. And we aren't going to wait for some miracle cure. Besides, not everyone thinks of it as a cure. We're elves now. Not many would be willing to sacrifice who we've become and go back to being merely normal."

"What?" Carl's voice sounded as shocked as Danielle felt.

"Maybe it would be different if I was a zombie or a brownie. But I'm an elf. I can see in the dark. I'm graceful. I used to be a klutz but now I can walk across wet concrete without leaving a mark and carry bottles of nitroglycerin without worrying about exploding myself.

"I've learned five languages since I got my talent. Before, I failed high school English. So, why would I go back? Should I throw away the best thing that ever happened to me just because of the prejudices of a bunch of freaking normals?"

"But it's a disease."

"It's no disease, it's who we are. Think about it, *Were.* Would you give it up? You'd have to surrender your added senses, your ability to recover from injury, your near-immunity to disease. It would be like ripping out an eye, wouldn't it?"

"I'd give it up in a minute."

Arenesol paused. "Well, not everyone feels that way. Besides, you haven't finished your cure and there's no certainty that you ever will. We want to create an elf community, for ourselves. There's a lot of open territory in south Texas where it's gotten so hot and so disease-ridden that all the normals have moved out. It wouldn't hurt anyone."

"I think you're making a terrible mistake."

"Maybe. But it's our mistake to make. All we're asking you for is a distraction."

Carl paused and Danielle crossed her fingers. It was his last chance to back out, his last chance to save his life. "What sort of distraction do you have in mind?"

Danielle put her head in her hands. Watching Carl turn into a *Were* had seemed like the ultimate blow. But this betrayal was worse because it was conscious. There was no way she could justify his decision. She'd have to report this. And she'd have to terminate him.

"Well, we figure another riot would be perfect," Arenesol said. "They plan their riots, you know. But sometimes they happen off schedule. And when they do, the warders go crazy. They'd have to pull warders off the border watch.

"In the confusion, the Tigers, a couple of hundred elves strong, break out. We've already mapped the minefields and we've got their electronic surveillance systems hacked. And if a bunch of elves can't sneak past a squad of distracted normals, they don't deserve to be called elves anyway."

"A riot won't be enough. It'd still be suicide."

"It may be suicide, boss, but it's our choice. The Tigers put it to a vote. Every single one of us voted to make the break."

"Give me a month and I'll give you a distraction you won't be able to believe."

Danielle removed her headphone and stared at it. Carl had completely thrown in his lot with the impaired.

She had thought his plans to reconcile normals and the impaired to be honest and even noble. Understood in that light, making love with her could be almost acceptable. After all, if he really did find a cure, they'd all be normal again. But she'd been wrong. In fact, she'd fallen for the oldest trick on earth. Carl was one of them. He'd co-opted her, used his physical charm to suck her in like an anxious puppy, and betrayed her and everyone who counted on her.

And for what? Even a *Were* should know it would be kinder to turn the Tigers in, let the warders arrest their leaders and let the remainder survive in the zone where they could be protected and where normals could be protected from them.

She wouldn't have believed Carl was capable of betraying humanity if she hadn't heard the words herself.

She switched on the encryption mode on her cell phone and called Joe.

Joe was incredulous, at first. None of his informants had brought him any word of a major planned operation by any impaired mob. He assured her that the minefields and electronic security were unbreachable. Arenesol's promise that the Tigers had broken security didn't provide much guidance toward solving the problem.

Still, Joe agreed to reinforce the south-side barriers. Unlike the north, the south lacked the natural barrier of the river and opened up to largely deserted suburbs and semi-rural areas. A strong warder showing would persuade the Tigers to give up their efforts without anyone getting hurt, he promised.

"Any orders for me?" Danielle asked when Joe stopped fuming.

He paused for a moment. "Yeah," he finally said. "When the distraction finally happens, I want you to make sure there's one extra victim. Carl Harriman is too disruptive. Terminate him. Wait until the breakout attempt and don't make it obvious. After all, he is a federal cause."

"You sure we'll be okay if he doesn't finish the research?"

"You've done a good job getting the information out, Danielle," Joe assured her. "Let me do my job protecting you from the Feds."

"But—"

"You've got your orders, Warder Goodman. Carry them out."

Danielle signed off and powered down her cell.

She'd expected the order and thought she'd been mentally prepared for it. If Joe had told her to terminate Carl immediately, it would have been difficult enough. But how could she work with him, surround herself with his charisma and pure sex appeal, and then gun him down in cold blood?

She made herself call up the mental image of her mother, bleeding in her stepfather's arms. It had sustained her through the Warder Academy when so many of her peers had bailed. The impaired really were evil. And Carl was just one of them.

Carl was a dead man, or rather, a dead *Were*. The only questions left were where, when, and how.

* * *

"This isn't a good idea." Danielle had gotten a sore throat explaining her opinion to Carl. And he'd ignored everything she'd said about his so-called Olympiad. It didn't take four years in the Warder Academy to recognize it as a key part of the diversion Carl had promised Arenesol.

"I've got money. Why not spend it?"

"An athletic contest between normals and impaired? I mean, come on. You know it's going to cause problems."

Carl shook his head. "Humans have used athletic contests to bring

76

people together peacefully for thousands of years. No reason why this should be different."

There were plenty of reasons why this would be different and Carl knew it as well as she did.

"It's going to be a joke, you know. At a million dollars prize money per event, the normals are going to send their best. All you have is a bunch of hungry impaired who haven't trained in years, if ever. It'll be a slaughter."

Her word choice was unfortunate. If she didn't persuade Carl to back off, she'd have to slaughter him. But that wasn't her only reason for objecting. Whatever distraction Carl was planning would result in impaired deaths. Maybe even normal deaths. Carl had, arguably, asked for it with his treason against the state. The others were innocent.

The weeks she'd spent living among the impaired had been eye opening for Danielle. It was harder and harder for her to summon her anger, to see all of the impaired as brutal killers. Many, maybe even most, seemed to be ordinary people trying to get on with their lives.

Sure they were different. The pointed ears, long teeth, and annoying habits of transforming into a wolf at inappropriate moments continued to unsettle her. Still, familiarity had, at least, made her think of them as people worth saving. The less slaughter she could ensure while protecting her own kind, the better.

Carl shook his head. "We impaired will just have to do the best we can, then. At any rate, it's too late to back out now."

Danielle hated it when people patronized her. She reminded herself that Carl wasn't really talking down to her, he was covering up. Covering up his real plans to betray humanity. It was odd that she would rather think of Carl as betraying his former species than belittling her, but then again, this business had been odd from the moment she'd come back to Dallas.

She sighed. "All right, you won't cancel the games. There's still no way I can get you permission to bring dozens of impaired out of the zone to the Cotton Bowl. Even if this were a good idea, which it isn't, it would take months to process the paperwork. And it would still get turned down by headquarters."

Carl's anguished look would have fooled most people. But Danielle wasn't most people. She was a warder. She was also a woman who had made love with this man. She knew him at a level he probably didn't know himself. He'd known this objection was coming--and had been counting on it.

"We don't have the facilities we need here in the zone," he reminded her. "Everything would be better if we could use the Cotton Bowl." A token protest if she'd ever heard one.

She was almost tempted to ruin all of his plans and approve the permits. Give him the Cotton Bowl, out of the zone, and he'd have a hard time doing anything for the Tigers.

Except she couldn't. She'd already run Carl's request by Joe, assuring him that they could head off whatever plans Carl was making by granting that special permission. Besides, Carl had probably developed an alternate plan. And, as Joe had forcefully reminded her, thousands of impaired running loose outside the zone was exactly the danger that had led to the creation of the Warders in the first place.

"You didn't ask my advice in creating this crazy plan, Carl. So don't go looking for me to fix it."

He nodded abruptly, defeat radiating from every lying pore of his body. "I guess we'll have to put contingency plans in place."

"If that's what you want to call them." She didn't see the harm in letting him know that she saw through his posturing.

"I was hoping you would help judge the martial arts contest," he continued as if she hadn't said anything. "They're a bit more subjective than running or throwing events. And all of my people know that you can be trusted to be fair."

His people. That word choice rocked her. "No can do. I got orders from the regional office. I'm going to be a contestant."

A hint of a smile played across Carl's face. "Really? I thought you didn't approve of the games."

"The region decided that a Warder should be perfect at fighting the impaired and assigned the job to me." She didn't need to mention that Joe thought it could be a recruiting plus to have her kicking impaired tail on the tube.

"Great. I always like to see you work."

Carl's whisper of a smile hinted that there was something he wasn't saying here. Well, he wasn't the only one with a hidden agenda. And she'd be damned before she gave him the pleasure of begging for whatever he was holding back.

"What will you do with the money if you win?" he asked.

She hadn't thought of that. A million was more than she'd ever imagined having at one time. Then reality set in. "It would make a big dent in my student loans," she told him.

Carl frowned. "That's about the most boring thing I've ever heard. Why not trips to Paris or new wardrobes or a car of your own?"

She shrugged. "I see plenty of impaired here in the good old U.S.A.,

I don't need to fly to foreign countries for more. Besides, I don't want the money because I don't want the games to happen. I'm going to urge you one more time. Call the whole thing off, Carl. It's insane, it's a distraction from your job, and it'll only make things more difficult for those on both sides of the zone barrier."

It might be too late for Carl, but it wasn't too late for the dozens of Tiger children he was sending to their deaths. Unfortunately, Carl ignored even the least subtle of her warnings. Each day that passed was another day closer to when she'd have to terminate Carl. Like a car that had lost its brakes, she was careening toward a conflict she didn't want, but couldn't avoid.

Lesson Two in warder school is that, sooner or later, someone you love will turn against you. The trick was to make sure you have no attachment so deep that you can't sever it with a knife or gun.

Right now, she wasn't very happy with Lesson Two. Of course she wasn't in love with Carl. All she had to do was think about that wolf on the bed next to her and her skin crawled with horror. Still, she couldn't deny that she admired him, liked him, and, in weak moments, still felt the physical attraction. Now that she'd had time to cool down, she simply didn't want to kill him.

Carl reached out a hand, almost touched her arm, then pulled back. "I know you think this is a mistake, Danielle. Maybe you're right. But I have to do it. Either normals and the magical can find a way to live together or we can't. For me, the games will be an experiment. Even a failed experiment isn't a mistake, it's just an experiment that generated results you weren't expecting."

"But--"

"Trust me, honey. I've made a lot of mistakes. I'll make a lot more before I'm done. None of them has killed me yet."

<u>No, Carl. Not yet</u>. She couldn't say those words, but she couldn't help thinking them.

Chapter 7

Carl stepped onto the field of the old Sunset High School stadium, smiled at the pretty camerawoman from the normal part of town, and held up the lighted ignition device signaling the start of the First All-Sapient Games.

Danielle guessed her own smile was more than a little frayed, but she stood with her fellow normal athletes, waiting for their moment of glory—and big bucks. Amongst the normals, the mood was upbeat. But their competitors looked confident as well. Like they knew something Danielle didn't.

Carl thrust his ignition device deeply into the ceremonial torch, then stepped back as the games torch burst into flame. With loud cheers from the mixed crowd, the games were under way.

The crowd's seating was strictly segregated, of course. The normals had been assigned the western side of the stadium, giving them some protection from the hot Texas sun. The impaired got along with what was left.

Carl strode off the field toward the east side of the stadium. Even as the games' founder, he wouldn't be welcomed by the normals. Since Danielle's event was the last of the day, she joined him there. He was still her herd and she intended to protect him—until she needed to terminate him.

Carl's All-Sapient Games were nothing compared to the weeklong pageantry of the pre-return Olympics, or even compared to the large track-and-field meets that some old-style normal colleges still held. Between the money he had available and the limited resources from the third-rate television network that had agreed to broadcast, he had limited the contest to ten events. Still, a million dollars per event—essentially all the money he had left--created an atmosphere of excitement and anticipation beyond what Danielle remembered from her childhood.

She thought people would watch the TV show. Carl seemed a bit worried about it, about whether he'd have any money left after the event. She couldn't bring herself to warn him that it didn't matter. Dead men don't spend money.

The first event was the hundred-meter run—popularly known as the event that defined the world's fastest human.

Danielle didn't think the normals would lose any of the events, but she was absolutely certain about this one. Three normals, two of them former record holders and one a college hurdler who had recently signed with the Dallas Cowboys as a wide receiver, had entered. Representing the magical world was a long-legged elf and a *Were*. From Danielle's research, neither of them had run anything for more than a decade. They were hopelessly outclassed.

A well-known television commentator--representing another hundred thousand of Carl's dollars--fired the starting pistol and the runners were off.

Mike the Vampire edged next to Danielle. "Carl asked me to pick the contestants. I think it'll be interesting."

Danielle though he should have picked a troll rather than an elf. Sprints require strength, not grace. "If getting slaughtered is interesting it will be."

"Watch."

For a moment, it looked like Mike had been a genius. The elf reacted fastest to the pistol and was out of the blocks two full steps before the normals reacted to the shot.

A collective gasp went up from the crowd, and then a hubbub of conversation as the normals recovered from their late start and pulled ahead.

The *Were* lagged behind, obviously outclassed as he struggled forward, his legs churning but without the grace of the elf or the power of the normal runners.

Until he shifted.

A black wolf charged down the track rapidly closing the distance to the panicked normals. A murmur went up from the crowd. An ugly murmur from the normal side of the stadium.

Could this be the beginning of Carl's distraction? "Isn't that cheating?" Danielle demanded.

Carl had somehow joined them. "Everybody knew that these games were to pit normals against the magical. Nobody said the magical couldn't use all four feet."

The wolf's final burst brought him even to the pack as they crossed the finish line. From where Danielle sat, it was impossible to determine who had won.

The crowd's murmurs grew louder and uglier as everyone waited for the official results to be posted.

Carl was grinning. A photo finish was exactly the type of result he had been hoping for. By now, phone calls and instant messages would be flashing through the normal world telling non-watchers to tune into the games, that something unique and exciting was happening.

A huge display, rented by Carl for exactly this purpose, displayed the photo finish. The young hurdler, hugely popular in sports-crazy Dallas, had edged out the wolf by a fraction of an inch.

A roar of approval went up from the normal side of the stadium. Their man had won and charges of cheating were quickly forgotten.

"That won't work in the martial arts competition," Danielle remarked. "Anyone who transforms or uses their teeth will be disqualified."

"Of course, Carl agreed, almost too easily. "We all want to follow the rules."

Danielle's phone rang and she checked the calling line I.D. It was Joe Smealy, of course.

"Warder Goodman."

"What the hell is going on there, Danielle? That animal nearly won against a human."

"There is nothing in the rules prohibiting use of magical impairments," Danielle said. She'd run those rules past Joe before approving them so he should know that.

"Tough. There's a rule now."

She didn't like it. The football stud had won without the need for special advantages and she liked to think that the other normals could as well. "Is that really fair, sir?"

"Do we care about being fair to the impaired, Warder? Did they ask your mother if it was fair before they killed her?"

He was hitting below the belt and she didn't like it. "I'll notify Carl that the rules have been amended."

"Tell him…" Joe detailed his new orders.

The Marathon started second, although it would be among the last to finish. The runners would leave the stadium, circle around the outskirts of the zone, and finally return to the stadium after the field events had been completed. Carl had planned the route to give the normals a chance to see how the magical lived--their crushing poverty and human suffering.

"Warder headquarters says that if any *Were* run the marathon in animal form, they'll be shot as attempted escapees any time they near one of the warder posts. You'd better pull them from the marathon," Danielle said.

Carl shook his head. "Let them run. Mike will tell them not to shift."

After a brief delay to notify the field about the rules change, and another to allow sponsors to get their message out, the marathon started.

One of the network executives gave Carl thumbs up as the runners circled the field and headed out the stadium gates. Which meant he'd been right about the economic viability of his games. Viewers were tuning in. Danielle wondered who would get the money once this was over. Probably Warder Headquarters.

Once the marathon runners were gone, the field events opened, beginning with the hammer throw.

Four normals and a single dwarf lined up. The normals stood head and shoulders above the squat dwarf; one of the normals, grinning broadly, rested his elbow on top of Willie's head.

The flood of mirth from the normal side of the stadium was matched by an ugly growl from the impaired side. Not that many of the magical liked dwarves—their surly personality made that difficult. Still, Willie stood for all of them.

Could this be Carl's distraction? A riot now would send angry impaired burning and looting through the streets of the zone and dozens of normals could be hurt despite the heavy warder guard surrounding their sections in the bleachers.

Carl glared at Willie and shook his head slowly.

Willie's eyes shined black with anger, but he kept his back straight and didn't strike out at his tormentor.

The normals stretched, whirled around with their hammers, and generally looked like serious athletes. Willie, in contrast, stood and sipped on a cup of coffee.

Danielle wondered if allowing the coffee into the stadium was a good idea. Willie had assured them that he could control himself, that the coffee would merely enhance his reactions. When Mike had backed the dwarf up, Carl had agreed. But Danielle had heard too much about dwarves and coffee. Nothing of what she'd heard had been good.

The judges explained the rules to the contestants, their voices carried by loudspeaker to the bleachers and to the viewers on the network. Each would have three throws. Only the longest throw would count. Any touch outside of the circle would disqualify that throw.

One of the normals was first to compete.

He crouched low, then gradually began to spin around letting the hammer gather speed as he edged closer to the foul line.

The heavy hammer, when released, seemed to float into the air, drifting meter after meter, until it finally slammed into the ground.

Wild cheers from the normal side and waving of the American flag accompanied the network sports anchor's claim that the eighty-eight meter throw was close to the American record.

The normal smirked at Willie and dusted his hands with chalk. He did not, however, renew his attempt to use Willie as an elbow rest. Danielle was just as happy the microphones hadn't picked up whatever Willie had muttered at the normal.

Willie stood up second. He picked up one of the hammers, stepped to the foul line, and simply threw it like he'd have thrown a baseball.

The hammer slammed into the ground about three feet in front of him.

Howls of laughter shook the stadium.

"Damned coffee. I told him not to show off," Mike the Vampire whispered in Danielle's ear. "I told him that those normals were good and that he'd have to give it his all if he wanted a chance."

"Looks like he didn't listen," Danielle replied.

"He is a dwarf," Mike admitted. "Listening isn't what he does best."

In that case, why were they letting him compete? Carl asked Mike before Danielle could get the words out.

"Same answer. Because he's a dwarf," Mike explained. "I asked the dwarves who could throw the farthest and they told me to go with Willie. It seemed reasonable at the time."

* * *

Danielle sighed. She'd been right about these games.

The 100-meter had been a fluke, arguably a cheat. But Willie's poor throw was the kind of joke she would have expected in a contest between poorly fed impaired amateurs and the professional athletes representing the normals.

She shot a glance at Carl, wondering if he was devastated, then wished she hadn't. What did she care how he felt? She had orders to kill him. The game was hardly important.

Willie's second throw was even worse than the first.

He'd clearly been watching the normals and this time he aped their technique, spinning around like a top and whirling the hammer until it became a blur.

When he let go, the hammer had climbed straight into the sky and plunged down, digging a second crater only inches from the dwarf's hard head.

If he hadn't gotten dizzy and staggered away from where he'd started, it might have killed him.

She could imagine viewers turning off the games in disgust at Willie's poor performance.

Again, the normal side of the stadium rocked with laughter. Even some of the impaired, she noticed, were laughing.

Well, she shouldn't be surprised. The impaired were notorious for laughing at almost anything. Danielle couldn't remember the last time she'd had a good laugh. These days, she didn't find much funny.

Snori the troll handed her an ice cream cone. She took it without thinking, then set it aside. It wasn't that she didn't trust him, exactly, but everyone knew that the impaired were sneaky. She was scheduled to compete in a couple of hours. Who knew what sort of drugs they might try to get into her first? Danielle didn't intend to be the only normal to lose that day.

"What's the matter? Not hungry?"

She hadn't thought about offending the poor troll. After all, she didn't know they were trying to poison her. Even if someone was, Snori wouldn't know about it. She trusted him. Besides, the troll's emotions couldn't have been easier to read if they'd been close-captioned.

"Sorry, Snori. I'm scheduled to represent the normals in a martial arts competition in a couple of hours. I need to watch what I put in my stomach."

"I heard about that. I'm looking forward to seeing you there. But you should eat your ice cream. Don't want to get overheated," he told her. "Got to save that for your event."

She wasn't sure what that was supposed to mean, but she didn't have time to ask because the crowd chose that moment to erupt into a fit of screams.

Willie scratched his rear while the first hammer thrower wound up for his final throw.

That wouldn't have been especially serious or create any particular stir in the audience, except that he'd decided to drop his trousers before doing so.

The normal was so distracted that he stepped over the foul line before completing his throw. Which hardly mattered. His throw barely cleared the ten meter line.

Danielle had never seen a dwarf butt before. She hoped she never would again. It was as hairy as a bear's, as wide as an elephant's, and bright red like one of those monkeys in the zoo.

Hilarity from both sides of the stadium drowned out the angry contestant's complaints.

The normal, the same one who had leaned his elbow on Willie's head to start the event, picked up another hammer and started toward Willie and the judges ran to intervene.

Willie ignored the charging normal and bent over to tie his shoe, again strategically presenting his hairy butt to the enraged athlete.

The normal screamed with rage and threw his hammer directly at the dwarf's rear.

With their short legs, dwarves would never be great runners, but that didn't make them slow.

Willie whirled around, caught the hammer in one hand, and tossed it back.

It didn't look like much of a toss but it staggered the normal. That moment of distraction was enough for the judges to insert themselves between the angry normal and the placid dwarf.

"Guess he got that jerk back for leaning on him," Snori told Danielle.

Trolls and dwarves were rarely friendly so Danielle didn't know what to make of this moment of solidarity among the impaired. She toyed with the idea that, somehow, this was part of Carl's plan--that he was trying to create some sort of unity among the impaired overcoming the differences that kept them at one another's throats and ready to betray each other to the warders.

She shook her head. Maybe he was. She had underestimated Carl before. But that didn't matter any more. None of his plans mattered. By midnight, he would be dead. And she would be his killer.

"I guess since he can't throw, he's just getting his revenge another way," she said to Snori.

"Can't throw. Are you kidding? He's a dwarf."

Snori wasn't the brightest bulb, but he didn't have to be completely oblivious.

"He's already blown two throws, Snori. Face it, he doesn't have a chance and he knows it. That's why he's playing these games. He knows that's the only way he can make a statement."

"I'd never disagree with a sixth-degree black belt," Snori said, sounding like he completely disagreed with her and was waiting for her to get her comeuppance.

Which left her wondering if she could be missing something.

After listening to the judges through a five-minute lecture that was broadcast nationwide but seemed to be made up mostly of words that the sensors bleeped out, Willie nodded firmly and stuck out his hand in a gesture of shaking with his opponent.

The normal backed away with even more than the average reaction to the impaired. Since Willie was offering the same hand he'd used, moments before, to scratch his hairy butt, Danielle wasn't too surprised by his reaction.

Snori's hooting laughter let her know that Willie's gesture hadn't passed him by either.

"Guess they just won't be shaking," Snori suggested.

"Probably not."

The judges let the other two normals throw, then let the first repeat his disqualified throw despite Mike the Vampire's complaints.

None of these throws were spectacular, but then, they didn't have to be. Each of the three normals had already posted near-record throws while Willie hadn't cleared a meter. Things were looking bad for the impaired, just as Danielle had warned Carl to expect.

After another lecture from the judges and a quick word, mercifully not broadcast, from Mike the Vampire, Willie took the field for his third throw.

He stepped up to the line, reared back, and heaved the hammer on a flat trajectory.

The heavy device spun like a football, its head pointing straight forward as it drilled down the field, only ending its trajectory when it smashed a hole in the concrete retaining wall behind the football goal posts.

"Guess that means Willie wins after all," Snori deadpanned.

Oh, shit, Danielle thought. Carl did have a plan. Letting the normals win the first event, but barely, would increase viewership, letting everyone see the impaired clean up in the hammer throw. Maybe Willie's antics would get more people watching, just in time to see an impaired do what no normal could ever hope to achieve.

She shouldn't have been surprised by anything Carl did. Even if she'd slept through the lectures at the Academy, personal experience had prepared her for constant betrayal by the impaired. Still, Carl's deception hurt her.

With another eight events coming up, she wondered what other surprises Carl and Mike the Vampire might have.

The crowd hesitated for a moment, as if in disbelief, when Willie's toss had carved a crater into the reinforced concrete, but then went wild. The uproar continued even as Danielle made her way through the stands back to the platform where Carl and Mike sat.

Although the whole impaired side of the stadium was celebrating, only Danielle seemed especially surprised by the results. It was as if all of the impaired, like Snori, had known that Willie was showboating.

The normal side, on the other hand, was shell-shocked. To see their champions not only beaten but humiliated by a mere dwarf seemed impossible and unfair. That he'd mooned them first only added to the aggravation.

Her cell rang before she'd made it to Carl's box. "Warder Goodman," she said.

"Goodman, what the devil are you doing?" Joe never called her by her last name.

"Getting ready for my event, sir."

"Damn it, I thought I made myself clear. You've got to stop this nonsense. An impaired just beat some of America's best. What's that going to do for morale?"

"I don't know, sir."

"Well, it stinks. So fix it."

"But you agreed to let the games go on, sir. I warned you to stop them."

"I'm giving you an order, Goodman. The impaired are to lose this contest, and they're to lose it in a rout."

Danielle nodded miserably. "Yes, sir."

She headed over toward Carl and Mike the Vampire. She wasn't going to like doing this, but she was a soldier in a war and she was going to follow orders.

All right, Willie's performance had been lowbrow and disgusting. Still, Carl was laughing like it was the funniest thing he'd ever seen.

"If that jerk hadn't decided to show off his height by leaning on Willie's head, Willie would have just thrown the damned hammer," Carl whispered when he got his breath together.

Danielle shook her head. "Headquarters is not happy."

A junior network exec interrupted her, speaking to Carl with complete respect. "We've moved up another four points, sir. Right now we're second behind *Another Hospital.*"

Nobody competed with the soaps on the normal side of the zone— the only side that was measured by ratings since impaired didn't have money to spend on advertiser products.

"That means we've up to ten million," Carl said. "From now on, everything is pure gravy."

Gravy for somebody, anyway. Joe was still squawking in her ear.

"What's the next event?" she demanded.

Carl consulted his program. "Broad jump."

"Who do you have entered?"

Mike answered for him. "An elf, a troll, and two fairies."

She repeated the list into the phone.

"Are you kidding?" Joe screamed. "Fairies have wings."

"The fairies are disqualified," she told Carl.

"Mike hasn't disqualified any of the normal athletes."

"Flying would be a different event entirely."

This was too painful. Rather than argue about each event, she grabbed the list of contestants from Mike's hand and went through it with Joe, striking half the entrants from the magical side of the list.

"If I didn't know better, I'd say that you normals don't want real competition," Carl said.

"If I didn't know better, I would think you were trying to create a massacre here, Carl," she fired back. "Don't you see that you're playing with fire? I mean, flying creatures in jumping events? How fair is that? Normals won't stand for it and you know it. Hell, you wouldn't have stood for it a year ago."

She didn't bother with the martial arts list. She'd vetted the rules and that was enough. She figured she might face trolls or vampires. They could be tough, but normals could fight, maim, and kill as well as any impaired. As long as the impaired followed the rules.

Once she'd finished, she took the revised participant list to the television announcer and had him list the disqualifications over the cable and to the stadium.

The result was stunned silence from both sides. Even the normals seemed a little disturbed that so many of the magical were being eliminated. They had come to watch a triumph, not to be handed a victory through cheating.

Danielle tried not to notice the reaction. She kept her phone to her ear, reporting what she'd done back to Joe, and plowed through the resistance coming from the network and from Mike the Vampire.

Mike tried to convince Carl to withdraw in protest. Carl's money had funded this event. Carl and Mike had lined up the network despite the problems in getting anyone interested in anything having to do with the magical. The normal entrants had known they would be competing with the impaired before entering. Even the contestant lists had been given to the normals. They could have objected or stayed home if they weren't happy with the rules. So what business did the warders have in changing everything at the last minute?

Danielle hoped that Carl would listen to Mike on this one. If he would just go back to his lab, Danielle had a chance to persuade Joe to give him another chance. But he insisted on pushing ahead. As if Arenesol's distraction was more important than his responsibilities to the normals and more important than anything he owed Danielle.

"We're going to send a message that would be heard in every zone across America," Carl said. "We aren't losers, condemned to incompetence and second-class status. I can't stop this, Danielle. I owe it to my fellow magics."

"Impaired," she insisted.

"I'm not sure magic is an impairment after all."

Joe's voice crackled over the phone. "Proceed as planned, Danielle. Just make sure no more of those stinking impaired win."

Even after Danielle's decimation of the magical contestants, the magical put up a pretty good, if losing, show in the broad jump. An athletic elf pole-vaulted into an early lead and only a superlative effort by the world champion inched her ahead. A troll won the caber toss, but nobody cared since even the supposedly normal contestants all looked pretty much like trolls in that Scottish tree-throwing event.

With the Marathon and the martial arts competition left to go, the normals were up five to three in golds and seven to two in silvers.

Danielle decided it was time to limber up. She'd win her event and it would be a normal rout. The few impaired successes could be written off as unfair advantages and no normal egos would be threatened.

Chapter 8

Danielle met briefly with the other normal contestants in her event. There were two men and another woman. All were senior black belts, and all moved with the type of assurance that comes from years of training. None, she saw, were likely to be intimidated because they had to face a troll or even a vampire.

"You've been working with them," the female contestant said. "Anything special we should be looking for?" She was a tall African-American woman with brown eyes so dark that there seemed to be no line between iris and pupil. Her musculature was as highly developed as a professional body-builder's, but even if Lina Kildock hadn't been something of a legend in the Full Contact Karate world, the seven stripes on the black belt around her waist would have assured Danielle that this woman was the real thing. Although she hadn't fought impaired before, she would adapt quickly.

"Elves and vampires are fast," Danielle said. "You'd expect that. They can take some abuse, but neither group likes getting hit. Vampires are especially sensitive about their teeth.

"The elves are also flexible. Don't bother trying grappling techniques with them, they'll roll out or let you bend their joints in any direction you like while they continue to strike.

"As for the trolls, they don't even notice pain. And they'll shake off most strikes. Go for joints."

"What about the *Were*?" one of the men asked. "My trainer made me get a rabies shot, but I don't know how to fight a wolf."

"Any *Were* who transforms is automatically eliminated from the competition," Danielle reminded them. "They must fight in human form, or as close as they can get to it."

"Any dwarves fighting?" The other man must have been watching Willie. His voice showed nothing but respect for a class of impaired that most of the world held in contempt. Of course a martial artist doesn't progress if she doesn't respect any possible opponent.

"I didn't double-check the program, but it's supposed to be one *Were*, one vampire, one elf, and a troll. No dwarves."

Lina laughed. "Good. Wouldn't want anything like that dwarf's rear-end near me. Wooo. I could practically smell it halfway across the stadium."

Dwarves aren't known for their hygiene, but Danielle suspected that anything Lina had smelled would have come from the normals around her. The turnout here at the stadium didn't include the best elements of normal society.

"Willie thinks he's funnier than he is," she admitted.

"He must think he's hysterical, then" the male who'd asked about dwarves stated. "Because he sure cracked me up out there. That big red butt." He was laughing so hard he could barely get the words out. "I've never seen anything so ugly. But can you imagine being a prima donna like that hammer thrower who couldn't even deal with a little distraction? Served him right."

One of the first things any martial artist learns is to cultivate stillness within oneself. Being distracted in a sparring match means losing points. Being distracted in a real fight means injury or death.

Danielle knew the impaired would count on their differences to give them the advantage of surprise and distraction. Against this group, they would be disappointed.

"First round, each of us lines up with one of the impaired. After that, I suspect we'll be fighting mainly with each other," Lina told the normals. "So let's keep it clean. I've only lost two teeth so far and I don't want to lose any more today. Anyone have problems with that?"

Danielle didn't think anyone would have problems with anything Lina said and she was right. Lina got nothing but quick nods in response.

"Then lets go kick some impaired butt," Lina ordered.

They marched from the dressing room into the stadium, Lina waving a big American flag.

While they'd been dressing and stretching, Carl's staff had covered the field with thin mats. Large circles drawn on the mats gave boundaries for the fights. Any contestant who stepped beyond the boundary would be disqualified.

Danielle didn't plan on being disqualified.

A huge cheer went up from the impaired side of the stadium, surprising Danielle and the others. Then she saw it wasn't for them. It wasn't for the impaired martial artists, either. The marathon runners, or at least some of them, chose that moment to make their entrance into the stadium.

Three elves ran in, chatting lightly among themselves. Neither the *Were* nor the normals were anywhere in sight. None of the elves were even breathing heavily.

Danielle glanced at the official clock, then looked again in a huge double-take. It was impossible. Everything had happened in an hour and thirty-three minutes. Three elves that no one had ever heard of had smashed the world Marathon record by half an hour. In a sport where tenths of a second made the difference between champions and the middle of the pack, a thirty-minute victory was close to a miracle.

"Guess it's up to us," Lina whispered to Danielle, her voice grim. "We don't win this one, the impaired tie us. Now that would be a pretty scene."

* * *

She should have suspected it.

Carl, wearing his three-striped black belt, stood with an elf she didn't know, a vampire woman she vaguely recognized, and Snori.

Snori, she noted, had looped a worn black belt around his huge girth. Five stripes indicated he'd achieved some serious rank. He'd only made green belt in her school so she guessed he'd been sandbagging. Had Carl put him up to this?

She didn't teach her green belts anything that they couldn't have learned at a thousand martial arts schools around the country, but she still felt that Carl had betrayed her by sending the troll to spy.

It doesn't matter, she reminded herself. She was going to terminate Carl. She didn't have to trust him. Her assurance didn't make her feel better at all.

The eight martial artists bowed to the judges, then bowed to one another.

Danielle drew the vampire.

Female against female fights do well in the ratings: something having to do with most male's prurient interests. But Danielle didn't have time to think about that now.

The vampire wore a black belt with only one stripe. Danielle didn't let that fool her. The female's smooth movement made it clear that she was a deadly opponent. Besides, she was a vampire, which meant more strength than human physics could explain packed into a compact figure.

She took the advice she'd given the others, mixing hard straight punches with brutal thrust kicks the torso and head to keep the vampire off balance and to neutralize the magic-enhanced strength the female could employ if Danielle let her close the distance and grapple. She'd save her blur for when she really needed it.

The vampire blocked most of what Danielle sent her way, and shrugged off what licks she took, dishing back effective counters.

And Danielle realized she was in a real fight. This vampire could

95

finish her off now and eliminate her from the contest. Joe would kill her.

Danielle blurred. She needed to win the contest, not just the match. If her body took too much abuse now, she wouldn't be as effective in the next two matches.

At high speed, Danielle could see the vampire's muscles twitch a fractional second before she began her movement. The female hadn't fully integrated her martial art into her essence. Like many first degree black belts, her techniques were flawless, but she still thought rather than letting her mind and body work as one. Against most opponents, it wouldn't have made any difference.

Against Danielle and the blur, it made the contest a walkover.

Danielle blocked a kick with an elbow placed next to her own ribs, but oofed as if it had gotten through and reeled back. She suspected that the vampire would believe the evidence of her eyes rather than of her body. Eyes lie.

The vampire's pupils dilated and she charged after Danielle, obviously intending to finish her off.

Danielle parried the vampire's punch, then grasped her and rolled to the ground, bringing both of her feet into the vampire's abdomen and thrusting straight up and over.

The vampire didn't fall outside the line as Danielle had intended. But only because she transformed into a bat, flapping desperately to avoid Danielle's strikes.

The judge pulled the red disqualification flag and it was over. Danielle had won her first match.

Lina had already dispatched her opponent, so Danielle didn't have a chance to see her work. To her surprise, though, the other two matches were still under way.

Snori left his body open, taking blow after blow on a stomach that Danielle knew was as hard as a rock, but protecting his only slightly less rock-like head.

His opponent was in great shape, but kicking a rock will eventually wear anyone out and Snori waited for his moment, then caught a leg that the normal hadn't retracted quickly enough, brought him in, and squeezed a submission hold.

The normal tried a couple of escapes, then tapped out as Snori clamped down, threatening to snap his leg off.

By this time, Carl had won as well.

It was up to Danielle and Lina to win for the normals.

"Never send a man to do a woman's work," Lina whispered to Danielle.

Danielle smiled politely. If anything positive had come from the return of magic, it was the elimination of old beliefs that women were inferior. With so many people called into guard service or impaired, women had stepped up to do anything men could do, often better. Which was why Carl's contest didn't bother with old-fashioned male and female categories.

Admittedly, women were at a disadvantage in the caber throw, but then, men were at a disadvantage at anything that required endurance or intelligence. Like martial arts.

* * *

Danielle didn't bother with body shots. Instead, she worked Snori's joints. The troll probably weighed over four hundred pounds, which meant a lot of weight supported on the sinew and cartilage in the knee, ankle, and hip.

In old-style martial arts, these targets would have been fouls. Modern Free-style anything-goes competition, together with improvements in medical technology that let joint injuries be easily repaired, had shifted the emphasis from the stylized sparring of an earlier era toward the far more practical—and deadly. Four years in the Academy on top of a lifetime in a dojo, made Danielle the master of practical.

Of course, practical didn't mean perfect. Snori landed one punch to her ribs that knocked her wind out and made her wheel away from him, struggling to find oxygen and to avoid the type of hold that Snori had used to end his last fight.

She finally slowed him down with a solid kick to one knee.

Snori tried to face her balanced on only one good leg; he wasn't able to avoid her follow-up. He reeled out of the ring to protect himself from serious harm.

Unfortunately, her victory had taken a while—her head felt woozy from overuse of the blur.

Two down. One to go.

That one, though, was Carl.

She couldn't believe that Carl had gotten past Lina. The woman was a legend. Danielle hadn't looked forward to facing Lina herself. She would have given any odds that Lina would have no problems with Carl, third-degree black belt or not.

Carl wiped blood from his lip and sported an already impressive black eye, but he didn't look like he'd taken serious damage. Lina had underestimated Carl and Danielle knew she'd underestimated him as well. Well, she wouldn't do that again.

He bowed to her.

Watching him carefully, she returned the favor.

She considered terminating him during their match, as an apparent accident. People did die in the ring, just as they did in football games or hockey games.

But children would be watching. The benefits of any moral lesson would be offset by the violence. She wasn't making up excuses to delay the inevitable. She almost persuaded herself of it. A judge rang the bell that began the match and Carl moved toward her.

She feinted at him, trying to assess his reactions.

Carl shifted his body slightly, letting her strike miss without even a need for him to block.

She nodded grimly. Two could play at this game. She put herself in guard, upped her blur to the maximum, and waited for him to make a mistake.

He smiled, then did nothing for a full ten seconds. It felt like twenty minutes to Danielle in blur mode, every second took its toll on her body's reserves; still, she made herself wait it out. She wouldn't let impatience force a mistake. If Carl could beat Lina, one mistake by Danielle could give him the match and give the impaired the tie that the SAIC had ordered her to prevent.

When Carl finally moved, he seemed to be operating in slow motion. That was partly a result of the blur, but partly also of his technique. She recognized old moves that blended kung fu with t'ai chi. Recognized them from ancient textbooks. She didn't think anyone had actually practiced some of those moves for nearly two centuries, going back to the Chinese Empire.

Maybe Carl thought he'd confuse Danielle with techniques she'd only read about, making her think rather than let her body operate.

Well, Carl was a scientist--no one, least of all Danielle, should be surprised if he tried something intellectual or clever. Danielle was the practical one. She decided a spinning triple roundhouse kick followed by a backfist to his already injured eye would put a practical end to his experiment.

Except her foot got tangled up in hands that seemed to be moving too slowly to be a possible threat but were always exactly where they needed to be.

She leaned into his grip and jumped, driving an axe kick to the top of his head.

That kick too ended up entangled.

She turned a somersault in the air, landing on her feet and facing

Carl with a new respect.

Carl knew what he was doing. He didn't need to shift to wolf form to be dangerous.

It made her wish that they could be allies rather than enemies. That there was a way to save the good in Carl rather than let it rot in his grave.

Danielle forced down the thoughts, all thoughts. Thinking is the enemy in the martial arts.

Carl advanced on her slowly, giving her time to catch her breath, breath deeply, focus on the now, let her body and mind become one.

He was watching her eyes, looking for that momentary sign when she made up her mind and decided to act.

She clamped down on her physiological responses. She wasn't going to telegraph anything.

Danielle faked another kick, let Carl catch her up in his sticky hand technique, and drove her foot down into his instep.

He avoided her strike, but barely. His eyes narrowed. He hadn't been expecting that.

Well, she had. She'd also expected that her first strike would miss. But she was in close now. Her blur gave her the advantage of speed and she used it, slamming elbows, fists, palm, and knife-hand into soft targets.

Carl managed to avoid most of them, but one backfist snuck through to his already swollen eye and a knee connected with his groin.

Which should have ended it. Everyone knows that men were complete weenies when it comes to a groin strike.

But it didn't. And Carl was away from her.

She had been confident that the fight was over--that she could press after him, taking a few strikes, perhaps, but dealing out three for every one she took. Except she had no idea how he'd gotten away.

Still, she had achieved two effective strikes. So far Carl had done nothing but block.

Although she was breathing easily, she knew that she was overusing the blur. It was great for a minute or two at most. Counting the earlier matches against Snori and the vampire, she'd already used it for close to twenty.

She needed to finish Carl off quickly because if she didn't, she would slow down. And if she slowed down, Carl was going to have her for lunch.

* * *

She was good.

Without his wolf reflexes, Carl knew he'd be finished by now. Even with them, he was getting beat.

Danielle moved more quickly than any normal he'd ever seen. Television programs made a big deal about the warder blur, taught to an elite group of warders in their academy in Los Angeles. But television, and even the time she'd attacked him when he accidentally took wolf form, hadn't prepared him for the fighting machine that Danielle became.

He backed away from another attack, relying strictly on defense and counterstrikes, refusing to commit himself to something that could put him in trouble. Danielle's techniques were picture-perfect, but she wasn't completely scientific. If he could stay in the fight long enough, he could analyze her weaknesses and strike.

Of course, staying in the fight was the key challenge.

She double-feinted, then tried a risky sweep.

He leapt over her leg, then saw that she had anticipated his reaction and was moving in to finish him.

Somehow, however, her strike was a fraction of a second too slow, hundredths of a second being the difference between a crippling strike and a somewhat painful blow to his thigh.

He chopped at her arm reflexively, knowing that he would never connect. Except he did.

Danielle winced, pulled back in disengage.

Then he saw it. She was slowing and clearly was not used to backing away from a fight.

Those were the weaknesses he'd been searching for. He closed in, letting her strike at his body but protecting his head and joints, and started pounding out his own attack.

Danielle scored again and again, managing to avoid most of his strikes, but he was determined that this match would not be decided by points but by whichever fighter remained standing. Danielle had overused the warder-trained resources she called on and underestimated his *Were*-enhanced ability to absorb punishment and keep on coming. He didn't like it, felt guilty about it, but he intended to make her pay for that misjudgment.

A hint of concern crossed her eyes so quickly that he would have missed it if those eyes hadn't fascinated him for weeks.

He smiled, ever so faintly, hoping that she'd use too much of her precious energy to wipe it from his face.

Danielle hammered fists into his stomach, the pain sharp and nearly incapacitating. Nearly, but not quite. He made himself grin through the agony.

She hit harder, clearly thinking she was winning, not analyzing, as he had done, the relative costs of her strikes against her ability to continue.

Finally, just as he was beginning to wonder if he'd made a terrible miscalculation, Carl saw her blur fail, restart, then fail again.

He struck as she was trying to recoup it.

No martial arts textbook would suggest a turning roundhouse against an opponent of Danielle's speed. But Carl pivoted, using the momentum of his turn to power his foot into Danielle's belly.

She froze, caught him with a look that would forever haunt his dreams, and collapsed.

The crowd went wild.

The impaired fans swarmed into the field, clapping, shouting, and celebrating. The normals hung back for a moment, then surged themselves.

But they weren't celebrating. Many of them pulled out concealed weapons. They waded into the crowd of the magical like reapers cutting wheat.

Carl fought back a curse. He'd counted on drunken normals who wanted to break windows for Arenesol's diversion. He hadn't expected them to be prepared with clubs, brass knuckles, and sawed off shotguns. As if they'd known that something was going to happen—had been planning to riot whatever the event's outcome.

With practically no delay, black warder helicopters shook the darkening sky. Their searchlights circled around, hunting for pockets of the magical, pointing them out to groups of sullen normals.

Carl sighed. Arenesol had been right. The warders did participate in riots. Well, this wasn't what he'd had in mind, but it looked like the Tigers were getting their distraction.

He grabbed Danielle from where she lay, still moaning on the ground, slung her over a shoulder, and headed for the locker rooms and the back exit from the stadium. Time to get back to his experiments. He'd certainly proven his failure as a reformer. The money he'd made from television sponsors suddenly felt empty.

Chapter 9

Danielle swam across an endless gray sea.

The waves tossed her body around, oblivious to her struggles. And around her, the horizon stretched endlessly. It was a sea of nothingness.

Gradually, sensation returned.

Pain came first.

Her ribs ached where Snori had scored. Her arms ached from hard blocks. Her head throbbed from who knew what contact.

She couldn't remember what had hit her, but she was pretty sure she'd lost.

Joe wouldn't be happy.

She almost jerked at that thought. Time was passing and she had a job to do.

The gentle rocking of waves against her body resolved themselves not into swimming, but deliberate movement. She was being carried.

She inhaled deeply and caught the scent of Carl--clean, male, and sexy.

He must be carrying her. Which meant that she hadn't missed her chance to finish her job.

She ignored the sick feeling that thought created and risked opening one eye.

Carl was jogging easily despite a hundred and twenty pounds of woman in his arms. A small group of impaired had gathered around him. Several, she noted, carried clubs. One of the *Were* had transformed and was running ahead, sniffing at doors, his ears perked straight up and alert.

Smoke stung her eyes, warred with the clean scent of Carl in her nostrils.

A squawk of radio static was followed by a burst of voice that Danielle's muddled mind could make no sense of.

"The Tigers ran directly into a reinforced group of warders," Mike the Vampire reported to Carl. "Most were killed. The rest retreated back into the zone. The word they're using is treachery."

"Meaning what?" She'd never heard that hard tone in Carl's voice. Even when he'd been angry with her, he'd always held a streak of humanity that shone like a beacon.

"Hey, boss, I'm just reporting what they're saying."

"And just what are they saying?"

"That you let your pet warder find out about the plan and she squealed."

All through her body, Danielle sensed Carl's muscles tense. In moments of crisis, his wolf-self fought to assert itself. Would he lose it now and tear into the vampire?

She didn't miss the irony that Carl's wolf-self wanted to protect her when she had already betrayed him and now was going to be forced to terminate him.

"Somebody talked."

Danielle hadn't sensed Arenesol, but his distinctive voice rang with certainty. "You know that no elf would betray the breakout."

Arenesol was right. The warders had tens of thousands of informants in every zone in America. Not one was an elf.

"Who else knew?"

"You are the only non-elf we told," Arenesol said. "You figure it out from there."

Arenesol's words hung in the air like the smoke.

Carl continued his jog, seemingly oblivious to Danielle's weight, and his gang ran alongside, ducking through filth-covered alleys, cutting through uninhabited homes and deserted strip malls, and dashing across the few major streets that they could not avoid.

The roar of black warder helicopters split the sky, their searchlights cutting through the evening darkness.

"She must have wired my lab," Carl said. "I should have guessed."

"My wife, my brother, my beautiful daughters. All killed. The warders trapped them and slaughtered them like sheep." Arenesol sounded like he'd been hollowed out from the inside, left with nothing to live for.

Danielle couldn't blame him. The elf might be impaired and crooked. Still, she had met his little girls. They had been precious things with their pointy little ears and tiny bodies. The older had been thirteen, just passing from child to womanhood. She would never make that passage now. Both girls had been innocent of anything but wanting to live their lives in freedom.

And Arenesol was right. By informing on Carl, Danielle had killed those little girls as surely as if she'd yanked their pretend swords from their hands and thrust through their hearts.

Joe had lied to her. He'd promised to simply block the Tiger escape. Joe had been the rock she'd built her world on after her mother's death. If he lied about this, Danielle had to question everything he'd ever told her. Everything she'd learned from the day she decided to become a warder.

She swallowed hard.

Carl set her down on the ground. Around him, the mixed party of elves, dwarves, vampires, trolls, and *Were* milled. The two trolls leaned against a freestanding wall, the remains of a long-deserted brick home, gasping for breath.

"We can't go back to the lab," Carl stated. "If they knew about the breakout, they'll be looking for us there."

"What about the warder?" Arenesol wasn't letting up. "If you don't kill her now, she'll betray us again."

"She was doing her job," Carl argued.

Arenesol spat on the ground. "Those murderers who slaughtered my precious daughters were doing their job, too. Nobody held a gun to her head and forced her to join the warders."

He squared up against Carl, almost pressing his narrow elf-chest against the breadth of Carl's muscular torso. "Plenty of normals either ignore the magical or cooperate with us. So don't give me any crap about just doing her job. She killed my daughters and fifty of my kinsmen as sure as if she'd slit their throats with a silver blade."

The elf backed off abruptly at Carl's wolf-like growl.

Arenesol put up a hand. "Damn it, Carl, listen to me. I've got a lot of respect for you. You came into the zone and made things happen. A lot of folks figured you were just a crazy scientist puttering away with your chemicals and test tubes. But that's not it. We've done more building in the zone since you got here than we did in the decade before you arrived. I know you're smart, and not just with the I.Q."

The elf kicked the ground and, for the first time, seemed to search for words. Finally he continued. "So why don't you show some of that intelligence and think this through? You don't seriously think the warder is going to owe you for keeping her alive, do you? Because, like as not, she's already got orders to terminate you. The warders don't put up with magical who try to make things better."

"That's just not true," Carl argued. His voice almost shook with surprise. "They let me out of jail so I could do my research."

Arenesol laughed. "Yeah, but what happens when you find your cure? You already know that most of us won't take it. Don't you think they know that?"

"I don't--"

"You hadn't thought about that, right? They'll use it on any magical who steps out of line. Cure him, as they'll call it. Except they won't let them rejoin normal society. They'll just classify him as latent and leave him here. Surrounded by the talented. Laden with memories of being something beyond merely human, but forever stripped of those abilities. It'll be like giving a man sight, then yanking out his eyes."

Carl slammed a fist into the brick wall. "That's not what I intend, Arenesol, and you know it."

"What you intend may not have a lot to do with anything, Carl. They'll use what you bring them and then spit you out like a watermelon seed."

"Maybe you're right," Carl stated softly. "What do you think, Danielle?"

She'd been certain Carl thought she was still unconscious. She'd modulated her breathing, even her heartrate to keep her secret.

Obviously, he'd seen through her best efforts. Equally obviously, she was about to die.

In the Warder Academy, she'd learned to lie. To keep her composure when telling the most outrageous story, and to make even herself believe it. She couldn't imagine a lie that would fool anyone now. Besides, she was tired of lying, emotionally drained by the lies that Joe Smealy, the man she had trusted more than anyone else, had used against her.

After Joe's betrayal, trust was hard. But it didn't matter. Danielle threw away all of her training, all of what she'd been taught about the impaired. She decided to trust Carl.

She struggled to her feet, unwilling to face her death lying down.

"If the warders want to use your invention as a weapon, they never told me."

"And you just thought they would let millions of supposedly cured talented integrate back into normal society." Arenesol's sarcastic voice cut through the night.

She shrugged. "My job was to herd Carl. Keep him doing his job."

"Is that right? And how did you do?"

She hoped that the darkness of the night, lit only by distant fires as parts of the zone burned, would hide the flush on her face. She had been a terrible herder. She'd had sex with her herd, failed to follow through on a termination order, and let him create a gang in the zone. Even though she had headed off a dangerous breakout, she could hardly claim any great success, even for that.

"That's between me and the Special Agent in Charge."

"I don't imagine Joe Smealy will be very happy when he finds out that you didn't terminate Carl. Or are you counting on us doing that for you?"

The question was transparent. Arenesol was trying to get her to admit to something he had no evidence about. Unfortunately, they could find evidence of her bugs if they looked for them.

"Why are you listening to him?" she demanded of Carl, trying to take the offensive even though her heart wasn't really in it. "He's a creepy elf who deals in drugs, explosives, and blackmail."

For a moment, Carl's eyes softened and she thought she was getting through.

Then he shook his head slowly. "We're going to have to talk about this, Danielle. But not tonight."

Danielle shrugged. He thought there might actually be a later. If only that was a possibility.

"We've got a backup compound just down Bishop Street," he told her. "I don't think your bugs would have picked up any discussion of it so it should be safe. I'd like you to go there with Snori. We need some time apart."

"You can't send me away like this, Carl. I'm your herder."

He shook his head. "Not any more, Danielle. After what you did, and after what the warders did, I don't owe you anything. But I owe Arenesol and the Tigers payback. So tonight, I'm going hunting."

He transformed as she watched, his torso lengthening, his nose and mouth growing together into the wolf's grinning face.

The wolf glanced at Arenesol, caught a sign that even Danielle's warder-trained senses missed, and slipped around the corner.

"Let's go, Mistress Goodman," Snori suggested.

"I'm going after Carl. And if you think you can drag me off to some safe house, you're just looking for trouble."

"Damn right," the troll told her. "Just because I have a bum leg doesn't mean that I'm going to hole up in some little cave somewhere and let other people take care of business."

She realized she hadn't thought about Snori's leg since she'd taken out his knee.

"I'm sorry about that kick," she told him.

"Hey, it was legal. You were trying to win. Same as me," Snori said. "Course if I'd hurt you any, the boss would have really let me have it."

"You knew he was good, didn't you?"

Snori shrugged. "We trained together a couple of times. Never fought anyone like him before. He's so, well, peaceful. But he's just where he needs to be."

"Right. Especially if he knows your tricks, you little spy. I can't believe you were pretending to be a green belt."

Snori gave her a shy smile that looked hopelessly out of place on that massive pitted face. "I always start as a white belt in a new dojo. Shows respect."

For the first time in days, Danielle felt the hint of a smile on her lips. "I guess so." Changing the subject suddenly, she said, "So, what are we going to do tonight?"

Snori stretched his hands before him, the knuckles cracking nearly as loud as gunshots. "Well, the normals are rioting again. I think it's time we taught them that not all of the magical are patsies. And there's something else."

Danielle's blood chilled. Her job was to protect normals, even lowlife normals who decided to riot. "Yeah? What else, Snori?"

"Maybe I'm misjudging you, Danielle, but it seems to me that you've got some sense. You're not one of those who hates people because they're different. If I'm right, I think you should see some of your brother warders at work."

Danielle knew what warders did--she'd spent four years in the Academy including six months as an intern in the Los Angeles zone protective force. Still, she needed to stay close to Carl if she was going to do her duty. Humoring Snori seemed a lot easier than fighting him. "All right I'd be interested in that. But I'm not going to let you attack normals. You know protecting normals is the prime directive for all warders."

Snori laughed. "That may be what they taught you in the Academy, Danielle, but it just ain't so. Come on. You've got things to learn."

The troll moved remarkably silently for a four-hundred-pound mountain of muscle and bone. He sniffed the air occasionally, using his magically enhanced senses to track Carl and his mob.

Danielle trotted alongside and used her control over her body functions to flush the damage from her system. Whatever happened, she'd need to be one hundred percent.

The night air hung oppressively over the Dallas zone, moist with the humidity from the encroaching Gulf of Mexico, rank with the scent of fire, and filled with distant shouts, screams, and the crackle of gunfire.

Twice Snori pulled her aside and hid in the shadows as warder armored personnel carriers tore past. One sent a burst of automatic weaponry into a nearby apartment, phosphate tracers igniting a blaze that continued despite the efforts of a bucket brigade that formed after the warder vehicle had moved on.

"The warders must have had information about that apartment,"

Danielle said. She wasn't sure whether she was trying to convince herself or Snori.

The troll just laughed. "Do you know why you lost your match against Carl?"

She shook her head, halfway angry at the change of subject and halfway intrigued. She did want to know.

"It's because you refuse to see what's there in front of you. Just like now."

"I don't know what you're talking about."

"You put a lot of energy into that ignorance. In your fight, you believed that Carl would fold, would turn wolf. You depended on it, even when you could see he wasn't going to. You dug deeper and deeper into your energy levels to push him over the edge, but here's what you were missing. Carl wasn't your enemy there. You were.

"And now, you're still at it, using all your energies to sustain a fantasy that just can't bear the weight. Those warders didn't have information about that apartment. They had a machine gun and a trigger-happy gunman. That's all."

As if to punctuate his words, another burst of heavy machine gun fire cut through the night.

Danielle shook her head. Snori's five-cent philosophizing had to be wrong, but she found it disturbing nonetheless.

"Let's keep moving," Snori said.

* * *

An army of warders and warder-led punks swarmed across the zone barrier, torches and firearms clasped in their hands.

Carl put down his binoculars and sighed. "You say they do this fairly often?"

Mike the Vampire shrugged. "This riot is bigger than most. But not a year goes by that we don't have a big organized affair. Takes a while for their informants to sniff out enough loot to make a good riot worthwhile."

The warder guards did nothing to stem the flow of normals into the zone. They did slow the return flow--mostly young men carrying televisions, food, and alcohol they'd looted from the zone. The goal, it seemed, was to ensure that the warders got a cut of the loot.

One of the men carried a wiggling sack over his shoulder.

At a warder's request, he set it down and opened the bag.

A teenaged elf girl shook herself out of the hampering material and made a dash for freedom--and was caught by the warder's bullet between her shoulder blades.

"They don't mind a little rape within the zone, but frown on bringing it outside," Mike observed.

At his side, Arenesol hissed. Well, Carl couldn't blame him. He'd lost two daughters tonight. Seeing that child murdered would only freshen those memories.

Carl swallowed, tried to keep control, but failed. He spewed the contents of his stomach over the ground. However long he lived, that elf girl's expression, and the explosion of flesh and blood when it emerged from her tiny chest would be seared indelibly into his memory.

He didn't know which was worse. The warder's casual contempt in shooting down the child, or the redneck's decision to bring a girl home as a sex souvenir from the riot. Neither was acceptable.

He forced himself to stand. He couldn't run away from this, couldn't tell himself that this was someone else's problem. His games might have set this riot into motion, but he couldn't blame himself. He hadn't made the warders and their allies riot. They had decided to do it themselves. He had simply provided a pretext. Still, just because it wasn't his fault didn't mean that he wouldn't try to fix it.

In college, he had read about the Russian pogroms against the Jewish ghettos. At the time, he'd assured himself that those were ancient history, that contemporary America was far removed from that blot on humanity. He'd been wrong.

"That warder was just doing his job." Arenesol fed Carl's own words back to him.

"And I'm going to do mine," Carl replied.

He welcomed his body's shift back from human to wolf form. Joyed in the play of muscle and sinew, the heightened senses of smell and hearing.

"They'll shoot you down before you get within a hundred feet," Mike warned him.

In his *Were* form, his mind was a little less logical, a bit more driven by emotion and primal needs. That didn't mean he was an idiot. Getting shot in the streets wouldn't do anything to avenge that poor elf-girl or end the warder injustices.

"Diversion." His wolf vocal cords mangled the word, but Mike and Arenesol nodded their understanding.

"Give us five minutes," Arenesol told him.

The elf's calm demeanor would have fooled him if Carl had still been in human form. His wolf self was more attuned to subtle signs of emotion, even emotions hidden by the famously stoical elves. To him, Arenesol glowed with suppressed fury.

"Be careful," he growled. The last thing he needed was for the elf to take unnecessary chances.

"Just be in position in five minutes and let me worry about myself."

Carl nodded, then loped into the darkness.

He circled around, cutting through deserted alleys. When he had to pass in front of one of the many burning buildings, he hunkered low to minimize his profile.

No sober warder would mistake him for a stray dog, but some of their freelance assistants might. He intended to give them every chance to make a mistake.

The warders had cleared away all structures within a hundred feet of their guardpost, creating a fire zone that would normally be lit by searchlights.

Now, though, the searchlights were stationary, focused on the crowd of returning rioters and their collections of loot.

It made sense, Carl realized. Like himself in human form, many magical could pass for normal. If they could just mix with the returning rioters, they could escape the zone. At least, that seemed to be the warder's fear.

He waited, counting down the seconds in Arenesol's five minutes.

The diversion came exactly on schedule. A shot kicked up dust near one of the warders, the sharp snap of rifle fire sounding a fraction of an instant later. Rioters seethed like disturbed ants, some firing blindly into the night, and some gathering their collected loot more closely.

From the warder tower, the searchlights moved, zooming into the darkness. Tracer bullets from a machine gun cut a deep hole into the area from which that single shot had emerged. Overhead, a helicopter gunship swung by, its lights adding to the glow, its phosphorous-packing Gatling gun adding firepower to the river of destruction.

One of the rioters panicked, made a sudden dash through the gateway that separated the zone from normal territory.

The warder reached out and touched the man as he ran past. An electric snap sounded nearly as loud as the gun's retort and the panicking man collapsed.

Unlike the elf girl, the normal wasn't damaged. He moaned, then struggled back to his feet.

Carl gritted his teeth and dashed across the hundred feet of open space.

Normal human eyes can see movement hundreds of times more easily than they can see the stationary. Carl had to hope that the warders in the watchtower would be blinded by their own searchlights and by the glow of their tracer bullets. Now was his only chance if he was to accomplish anything.

By what he had done to the normal, the warder had shown that he could have stopped the elf girl without shooting her. He simply hadn't bothered.

Anger about Danielle's betrayal, about the Tiger ambush, and about the elf-girl burned into a single sharp focus in Carl's mind. This warder had to pay for all warder sins.

That Carl was unlikely to survive his attack didn't weigh heavily on him. He'd felt an emptiness inside ever since he'd realized that his own trust in Danielle had been responsible for betraying the Tigers. He would die here, but he could take out the warder who had shot that poor girl.

Maybe this insane attack was just a way of running away from his problems. Maybe he should stay and fight injustice and stupidity another way. But a wolf wasn't that great with abstract logic. As wolf, he looked at evil and knew that he had to destroy it.

Carl closed the last few yards of open space, wiggled his way into the shaded area beneath the machine-gun tower and caught his breath.

No further gunshots came. The normals gradually regained their calm and the warder started processing the loot again.

Carl crouched and waited for his opportunity. He was on his own now. Mike and Arenesol had delivered their diversion. If they had survived the brutal fire from guard tower and helicopter, they would be scurrying for safety somewhere deep in the zone. He hoped that they were. Those two, perhaps more than any of the other magical beings he had met since living in the zone, had taught him about himself, about the realities of the zone, and about the way that humanity doesn't have to express itself in a normal human form for it to be real and true.

* * *

Mike's pale face writhed with pain.

He stumbled into Snori, then began a slow collapse.

The troll picked him up as lightly as if he had been a baby and moved into the shadow of a long burnt-out Lock-and-Store storage center.

"Almost got away," the vampire breathed.

"Come on, buddy," Snori urged. "You'll be fine."

The vampire shook his head. "Didn't expect the helicopter. It caught me in the open as I ran."

Danielle had thought Mike's rumpled shirt was merely the result of a long evening. She looked more closely now and saw that it was torn, shredded and singed. Part of what she'd thought were ragged edges was really his vampire flesh, exposed and raw.

Her warder instructors had never imagined that she would use her first-aid training for an impaired. Danielle herself would have bet money that she would only laugh if she ever saw a vampire in pain.

Still, her hands moved without conscious thought, cutting away at the filthy torn fabric to fully expose terrible wounds on Mike's chest.

Silver bullets had pierced the vampire leaving wounds large enough for her to put her hand through. The worst of the damage, though, was from fire.

The left side of his chest, where his heart would be if he'd had one, was a blackened pit. A fiery bullet had nearly consumed him from within.

Danielle swallowed hard, then pulled off the karate gi she still wore and ripped long strips from it.

"Help me wrap this around him," she told the troll. "We've got to stop the bleeding."

The vampire might be dying, but he still laughed. "Bleeding? You can't get blood from a vampire."

"Let me take care of this," the troll told her.

"But--"

"Danielle, quiet."

She was so used to Snori's placid behavior that she hardly recognized the harsh voice.

The troll pried open the vampire's mouth, set his own neck beside the sharp teeth, then shoved.

Snori gasped in pain as he forced the vampire's teeth into his own carotid artery.

Blood, powered by a massive troll heart, shot from the deep wound.

Only a fraction of that blood reached the vampire's mouth.

Still, he swallowed.

"You don't have to watch this." The troll gasped the words.

Beneath him, the vampire sighed, then swallowed again.

Every instinct told Danielle to attack, to protect her friend from the vampire that was sucking out his life-blood in such huge gulps.

Her mind superimposed the scenario before her with that of her childhood, of her stepfather drinking deeply from her mother's still twitching body, of countless pictures and videos she had studied in the Warder Academy.

Her hands bunched in fists and she was halfway into a fighting crouch when Snori opened his eyes.

"I'll be--" he gasped as the vampire took another swallow, then adjusted his teeth more deeply into the troll's neck.

"Don't worry about me," he concluded. "I'll take care of Mike. You go find Carl."

Chapter 10

Danielle didn't need magically enhanced senses to follow the path Mike had left. Bits of vampire flesh, scraps of smoldering clothing, and the scent of fire left a clear trail.

The spot where Mike had been hit was a scene of absolute destruction. Tens of thousands of high-powered shells had left a lunar surface of craters, dust, and loose rubble. What had once been a wedding dress shop was now a flattened parking lot.

She crouched amongst the rubble and scanned for any sign of Carl and Arenesol.

Drunken laughter drew her attention like a magnet.

Despite her need to find Carl, she crept toward the sound.

In Los Angeles, Danielle had been on duty during one of the riots. Like the other warders, she'd headed toward the zone expecting to be put to work protecting normals from impaired attacks. Instead, she had been politely informed that the more senior warders had inside guard duty. She had ridden patrol outside the zone looking for any escapees.

At the time, she'd assumed that this had been to protect an inexperienced intern. Now, she saw the truth.

Warders were collecting a share of the loot from the rioters.

One of the rioters displayed a long string of ears he'd evidently collected from his victims. Tiny ones from brownies and fairies, pointed ones from elves, a couple of large ones--troll. Several looked perfectly normal. Danielle barely contained her disgust as he and a warder haggled over what fraction of the ears he would leave as toll and whether a brownie ear was worth as much as a troll's.

As she watched, Danielle picked up a hint of movement directly under the guard tower.

Too low and slinky to be a human, she first mistook it for a stray dog.

Her heart almost stopped when she realized it was a werewolf. Carl.

It was her duty to shout out a warning, to protect her fellow warders from an impaired attack. She opened her mouth and found herself unable to force out a sound.

The amount of wealth the looters carried with them astounded Danielle. Fine carpets, antique furniture, paintings, pouches of long hoarded gold coins, and large supplies of food and alcohol were in evidence.

A little elf girl lay dead, piled amongst the loot. They'd slaughtered her as if she was a bothersome mosquito rather than the precious child she was.

Danielle had spent months in the zone and had never seen a hint of this kind of wealth. Which meant one of two things. Either the impaired were hiding it from her and had far more assets than they let on, or that the rioters were not merely random looters. That they'd targeted their victims. Danielle didn't think the zone was wealthy.

The only deduction that made sense was that someone had equipped the rioters with directions to the wealth of the zone. Only her fellow warders, and the network of spies that they maintained in every zone, had the capabilities for that.

Maybe Carl had hit her harder than she'd realized, but Danielle's world-view turned on its head. She'd been taught that normals need protection from the impaired. Even when he'd lied about the elf breakout, she'd thought Joe Smealy really wanted to protect the normals. But that too had been a lie. The warders were attacking, not defending. They were the problem, not the solution. And she was part of it.

Despite the two hundred yards that separated them and the dark shadows of the gun tower under which he crouched, Danielle recognized the bunching of Carl's muscles. He was getting ready to attack.

A decade of training kicked in. She opened her mouth to shout a warning, and then shut it firmly. These warders weren't her friends. And they had betrayed everything Danielle believed in.

Carl seized one of the warders--the one still admiring the collection of ears he'd taxed from the looter--and flung him to the ground.

The looters were tough, armed to the teeth and already filled with the flush of successful battles against the impaired. Carl should have been an easy target for them.

But they were lulled by the nearness of the zone border, drunk on ransacked alcohol, and laden with plunder. Instead of a quick and deadly response, the result was chaos.

Some ran. Some stood and stared. A few turned and attacked Carl with their bare hands.

If Carl had been in human form, the half-dozen assailants might have scored hits. In wolf form, he couldn't be touched. He darted between them, contemptuously knocking down anyone who got too close.

He ripped open the bags of plunder, knocked over bottles of spirits, and tossed the string of ears into the nearby river.

Oddly, he didn't seem interested in killing. Instead, he created havoc, destroying the carefully planned looting of the Dallas zone.

A machine gun in the guard tower chattered briefly, then stopped. The gunners couldn't depress the weapon low enough to target Carl while he remained in its shadow, and ricochets stung several in the mob without affecting Carl at all.

The wolf laughed, whirled to avoid another normal attacker, then howled a challenge to the world.

He knew this was his last stand.

If Danielle hadn't experienced Joe's lies, she would have been relieved that someone else would handle terminating Carl. Now, though, things had changed. Carl was the only hope for reconciliation between the normals and the impaired. She needed him alive.

And he was going to die. The protection offered by the gun tower's poor design wouldn't last. Sooner or later, the normals would regroup. Carl was dancing his last dance.

She felt only a terrible emptiness.

A trap door opened at the base of the gun platform and three warders, grim-faced, descended. One carried a silver herder whip. Two bore assault rifles.

From the way they climbed down the ladder, Danielle could tell they were professionals, possibly even fellow graduates from the Academy.

Carl was finished.

He turned toward the descending warders, seeming to recognize and welcome the end.

His howl split the night air, long, high-pitched, and filled with a sorrow that put a lump in Danielle's throat that no swallowing could dislodge.

His body flickered from wolf form to human, then back to wolf.

That brief glimpse of his beautiful human body left Danielle gasping for air. It didn't seem right that it be destroyed. She wished that she had ignored Carl's plot, forgotten her job, and done nothing but make love to him. Now that he was as good as dead, even his habit of turning into a wolf seemed forgivable.

The warders were halfway down the ladder when the lowest of them, the one with the whip, stopped, pointed, and shouted something indistinguishable over Carl's howl.

Danielle followed the warder's gesture and saw Arenesol

approaching.

The elf looked like he was walking in a dream. His eyes never wavered from the guard tower. His always-smooth gait almost floated him toward the conflict.

Holding onto the ladder with one hand, a warder fired a burst toward the elf.

Arenesol staggered, then smiled and continued his approach.

His was a brave but pointless gesture. Even if he made it to the tower, he'd be in no condition to help Carl. So why was he doing it? And why, now that he could see he couldn't help, didn't he turn and run? As Mike the Vampire had shown only a few minutes earlier, the magical could sometimes recover from wounds that would destroy a normal. Arenesol might live if he would just run away.

Danielle found herself saying those words out loud. "Run away, fool. Run away."

"Run, fool"

It seemed like an echo, but it wasn't. Over the shouts and gunfire, she heard the elf's words as distinctly as if he'd been talking directly to her.

But he wasn't talking to her--or himself. He was talking to Carl.

Which meant--oh, shit.

"Run, Carl. Bomb." She screamed the warning at the top of her lungs.

Arenesol heard her, tipped a sardonic two-fingered salute in her direction, wrapped an arm around one of the supporting legs of the tower, and smiled.

Even from two hundred feet away, the explosion's overpressure shoved her to the ground. Her ears tingled but all sound seemed distorted, distant, and buried beneath a low roar that seemed to come from within her body rather than from the outside world.

She pushed herself to her feet and looked at the crime scene.

The three warders had vanished, blown from the tower like autumn leaves from a tree. The tower remained, but it was supported only by two of its legs now. The third was simply gone. A few of the looters, protected from the explosion by the guard tower or luck, gaped in shock. The wolf had vanished.

As she watched, the damaged gun tower wobbled, straightened, then collapsed to the ground.

Danielle staggered forward. It was her duty to do something. Frankly, duty was the farthest thing from her mind. Still, she headed toward the scene of destruction.

She hadn't gone more than ten feet when she saw movement. A soft whine greeted her as she knelt beside the injured wolf.

* * *

"So what do we do now?"

Of the four of them, Mike the Vampire seemed to be in the best shape. Considering his condition the last time Danielle had seen him, that said something about both a vampire's ability to recover and about the state of the rest of them.

She had only a vague memory of carrying two hundred pounds of wolf through the streets of the Dallas zone until she'd found Snori and Mike. They'd gone underground in a prairie-style frame house, apparently abandoned because it was too close to the zone border.

Carl moaned, but said nothing.

Snori flexed a powerful arm and muttered something about stopping a few more looters.

Danielle slammed a fist into a built-in bookcase and then wished she hadn't. She hadn't recovered from the damage she'd taken in her fights. The explosion had only added to her general misery. She was just as happy there wasn't an intact mirror in the remnants of what had once been a house. She felt like a single bruise extended over her entire body.

She gave herself a moment to wince, then glared at the others.

"Oh, yeah. Going after the looters is a brilliant plan. Look where it's gotten us so far. Arenesol is dead. Carl is barely conscious. Mike would be dead if Snori hadn't opened up his own arteries and nearly bled to death himself. And what did we accomplish with all of that? We scared a couple of warders, threw some ears in the river, and blew up a guard tower. Well, big deal. The warders will come looking for revenge now, and they won't particularly care whether they find the people who did it. One impaired is as good as the next for their purposes."

A week earlier, Mike's vampire smile would have chilled her to the bone. His extended canine teeth were still discolored by traces of the troll's blood. His normally pale lips were filled with the crimson flush of life.

Even now a residual fear gibbered at the back of her mind-- Vampire.

She shook her head. A vampire had killed her mother. But that vampire had been her stepfather, not Mike. As far as she knew, Mike was as much a victim as her mother. She'd too long accepted the common wisdom that all of the impaired were evil. That none of them could be trusted. That they thought only of themselves and would sacrifice anything for continued life.

The previous night, she'd seen an impaired whom she'd believed to be purely evil sacrifice himself to save Carl. She'd seen warders indiscriminately killing and looting. She couldn't go back to her old life, but where could she go? She didn't belong with the impaired and couldn't live with the normals and their lies. Mike reached out a calming hand, then stopped when Danielle involuntarily shuddered. Intellectually she was aware that this vampire was another victim. Her gut hadn't adjusted to that reality yet and she certainly wasn't ready to let him touch her.

"You've got a point," Mike agreed. "But Snori has a point too. We've got to do something."

"You don't understand how Carl's work has transformed the zone, because you didn't see it before," the vampire continued. "For these few months, we've had hope that we could create something special and unique and wonderful. But this riot will shake that belief. Another one, and everything will be destroyed. Unless we can stop the warders and their pet rioters, there won't be anything for us. And after what happened to the Tigers, there aren't going to be a lot of volunteers to escape."

Danielle wanted to slap him down, to tell him that the rioters didn't belong to the warders. But the icy realization that she had been wrong, willfully blinding herself to the evil her own organization was doing, had descended over her. She'd dedicated her life to a lie. And now it was up to her to fix it.

"Well, we can't eliminate the normals," she reminded them.

"We could." Carl struggled to his feet, then sank into a dilapidated chair the home's owners had abandoned when they'd fled. His voice sounded like it was coming from the bottom of a well. But at least it was comprehensible and not the pained babble he'd spoken while she staggered through the streets of Dallas.

"What?" A war between normals and impaired would cause millions of casualties, but most of those casualties would be impaired. The warders had the numbers, the weapons, the training, and the strategic positioning to cripple any impaired attacks.

"We could eliminate the normals," Carl continued. His tone was neutral, as if he wasn't talking about the biggest genocide in the history of the world.

"I don't know, boss." Doubt filled the troll's voice. "Killing rioters is one thing. Slaughtering all them normals is something else. Lots of them are just kids. I don't think I could do that."

Carl's laugh rattled in his chest. "Not kill them. Just make them not normal."

"Are you talking about what I think you're talking about?" Mike the Vampire leaned closer to the *Were*. "Your cure, except in reverse?"

"We've isolated the RNA sequence of the original virus and replicated it in the lab. I've run some vector tests. I think I could come up with a way to transmit it that wouldn't involve getting every normal to come in for a shot. With a few months of mass production we could blanket the world with a second return-of-magic plague." Carl's voice grew stronger as he described a plan to eliminate violence against the zone by turning the entire world into a larger version of the zone. A world where vampires could walk freely, but where normal human life would be extinct.

But it wouldn't be right.

"That's not the answer, Carl," Danielle insisted. She had lost her naive faith in the warders, but she hadn't abandoned her belief that the world could be made better--and not by massive murder or even the controlled introduction of a plague.

Mike and Snori eyed her cautiously. She'd already beaten Snori in a fair fight. Mike hadn't even been one of the contestants in the martial arts competition. She thought she could take them both. But she didn't want to. She needed them on her side. She certainly needed Carl on her side.

"Let's go back to Carl's original plan," she urged. "We finish the cure to magic. But then we surprise everyone. We don't turn it over to the warders. We use it ourselves. Every zone in the world takes his drug at the same time. The next morning the world wakes up and finds that it was all a bad dream. The return of magic is over. We tear down the zone walls and walk out. All normal. All ready to reintegrate into normal life. It's the perfect solution."

She stopped and looked at her three colleagues, waiting for, expecting, needing some sort of affirmation, of applause. This was the obvious and best answer. Certainly Carl would second her. After all, this had been his vision from the first.

She didn't think that a vampire could pale, but Mike certainly looked as if he had. He shook his head, slowly at first, then with gathering speed. "No way, Danielle. I won't give this up. I wouldn't if I were the last magical in the universe."

Carl struggled to stand, collapsed, then tried again, this time succeeding.

"Mike is right, Danielle. My original plan was based on a paternalistic misunderstanding. The return of magic doesn't impair people, it enhances them. I've started to think that maybe the DNA is in us for a reason. The loss of magic, not it's return, was the problem. You can't ask the magical to give up the powers that make them who they are. Spreading the return of magic virus wouldn't be like a plague, it would be a gift."

"That's ridiculous. Killing and drinking blood is no special enhancement, it's a disgusting impairment." As was turning into a wolf when you made love. Danielle barely managed to hold herself back from adding that out loud, but even in her angry state, she knew that some things were best left unsaid.

"We don't have to kill to drink blood," Mike said. "You'll notice that Snori is still alive."

"Snori weighs four hundred pounds. He could probably feed a dozen vampires. But I've seen what vampires do to normals. I never want to see it again."

Mike leaned closer, deliberately putting one hand over hers. "You've got to let go of your pain, Danielle."

She fought back the urge to yank her hand away from his. "So you're some kind of blood-sucker therapist now?" she mocked.

"You know, that's kind of funny because he was a headshrinker until the magic cured him," Snori told her. "Made good money at it. 'Course everyone knows that the best shrinks are all crazy."

"It is true that there isn't much of a job for a psychiatrist amongst the magical," Mike said. "Carl's research is pretty convincing. The chemical imbalances that lead to schizophrenia and depression are simply missing in every magical being we've examined."

Danielle knew better than that. "But--"

Mike released her hand and shook his head. "You're right. A good number of magical are plain sociopaths. It turns out that the percentages are about the same as among the untalented. It's one thing that magic doesn't seem to cure."

More of the basic underpinnings of Danielle's life were being torn away. She glanced at Carl who looked back at her, his eyes filled with hope. Despite the mistakes she'd made, he still had faith in her. With so much of her life a shambles, Carl's faith and certainty meant a great deal.

"All right, that's enough talking. You two get out." She gestured toward the door. "You go rustle up some food or something. I'll take care of Carl."

Snori bristled, clearly wanting to protect the injured *Were*.

"She's not going to hurt him," the vampire told him. "Come on, I don't think Carl will thank you if you insist on staying."

Danielle watched the two magical beings step from the room. They were completely unalike. Snori had leather-dark skin, moved like a lumbering elephant, and presented to the world a face with craters that would make the moon jealous. Mike had his perfect and pale vampire facade, a build so thin he looked like he would vanish in a stiff breeze, and a walk that seemed to float over the ground rather than ever set foot in one place. Still, the two both seemed content with their magical selves. The whole thing was a mystery to her--a mystery that she needed to solve but was afraid to touch.

"I was starting to think they would never leave." Carl snagged one of her hands and pulled her toward him.

* * *

Danielle sobbed once, suppressed it, then buried her face in his chest.

Well, she had good reason to be upset.

Carl just failed to suppress his hiss of pain. What she'd meant as a comforting gesture had only caused more pain.

A part of her wanted to back out of there and hide somewhere. But she'd been hiding from reality for too long without knowing it. She intended to start doing things differently.

"What you did was brave and stupid," she said.

He nodded. "I won't disagree."

"But I think you're right."

He looked her in the eye. "What?"

"It's obvious that the impaired have been given a raw deal, and that the warders have been lying about it."

As they'd lied about so many other things.

"I'm going to fight them, Danielle." His low-spoken word held a promise harder than diamonds. "I knew Arenesol's little girls, and there's no way they deserved to die. And I'll fight you if I have to."

"We already know what happens when you and I fight." She hated to admit it, but he'd beaten her fair and square. Not that she would ever let that happen again.

"I caught you by surprise."

She shook her head. "Snori told me what I did wrong, if you can believe that. I can't believe I thought he was stupid just because he's a troll."

"He puts on a good act," Carl said. He turned his head to the wall. Tuning her out. Or trying to. Danielle didn't intend to let him get away that easy.

"Come on, Carl. You've got to talk about it."

"About what?"

She sighed, then slammed one fist against an open palm. "As if you

123

didn't know. You've never killed anyone, Carl. Right? Before now, I mean."

He shook his head slowly.

"Then let me tell you a story from back when I was an intern.

"A vampire had escaped the L.A. zone. He'd killed a couple of women and left another dying. It came down to him or me. He needed to be stopped and he'd certainly given up any right to expect mercy. But do you know what?"

He leaned closer, stared into her eyes. "Tell me."

She swallowed down the lump in her throat. This wasn't the time to get sappy. "I still see his face in my dreams. I wonder whether he had children who were waiting for him to come back. He was a killer. What Mike would call a sociopath. But he was a person and I killed him. I've wondered if there was something else I could have done. Some way to disarm him. I've had almost a year to get used to that. You've had what, six hours? You need to talk about it."

He tried to turn away again but she grasped his head and held it. "Talk."

"I didn't have to kill anyone."

"Go on."

He told her the entire story. His growing frustration. His sense of betrayal when he'd realized that Danielle had bugged him. And then the way that the warder had shot down that little elf girl, like she was a cockroach that had just skittered across his chocolate cake.

Danielle nodded, asked a few questions to keep him talking, and kept his head cradled in her arms so that he had to look at her, letting him unveil a soul nearly as tortured as her own.

He finished with his guilt at putting Mike in danger and getting Arenesol killed.

"Are Mike and Arenesol children?" she demanded.

He looked at her, confusion written on his face. "Of course not. Arenesol could have been any age since he's an elf, but he was definitely adult. Mike is probably ninety. For him, the return of magic was a literal lifesaver."

"Right. They are grown up. Which means you aren't responsible for their decisions. Arenesol decided to blow up the tower to save your life and because he didn't want to go on living. You didn't make him do it. Mike agreed to create your diversion. You both calculated that the risks were low. And he would have been fine if that helicopter hadn't happened along. So, I don't think you can wallow in your poor-pitiful-me act any more. Not about Mike and Arenesol, anyway."

Carl didn't want to be let off the hook so easily. "But I killed that warder."

"I saw that. But I'm not going to judge you for it, Carl. You saw what he'd done. No one else was going to punish him for it."

Impulsively, she bent and kissed him on his forehead.

Carl raised his face and, without thinking, without meaning, without anything but the most basic attraction between male and female, man and woman, their lips closed on one another, kissing frantically as if this were the last day of both of their lives.

Quite possibly, Danielle realized, it might be.

Chapter 11

Danielle hadn't meant to kiss him. She was confused about everything and adding emotional fuel to the fire didn't make a lot of sense. Once their lips met, though, raw need pushed rational thought aside.

Under the tattered blanket he'd wrapped around himself, Carl was already naked.

Danielle still wore the canvas pants to her Karate gi, and a sports bra that had been through far more than the manufacturer would have guessed possible. They didn't provide much coverage—certainly didn't stop the contact of body to body or the raging heat that Carl's touch generated.

Carl's hands brushed against the fabric of that bra and her breasts, sending surges of warmth and desire pulsing through her body.

She yanked the blanket away from Carl and gloried in the lean muscles of his torso. His erection stood proud and fierce, jutting from his body like a missile posed for flight.

She cupped it in both of her hands, stroking its smooth length until he shuddered with pleasure and desire.

Carl pushed himself up on one elbow and pulled her toward him, his lips greedy to kiss her again.

But Danielle couldn't miss the wince of pain that Carl had tried, and failed, to suppress.

"Let me do this, honey." She gently lowered him back to the bed, kissed him lightly on the lips, then ran her lips down his hard muscled body.

Touching him, brushing her skin against his, filled her with a drugged giddiness that let her hope that all of their problems could be overcome. She wasn't operating on logic now, but on a primitive level of intuition and emotion. Carl wasn't her herd any more, he was her pack. The alpha male to her alpha female. Sex reaffirmed their bonding. She had no idea where their lives would take them next. Whatever happened in the future, she would hold the memories of this perfect moment, this much-needed lovemaking, forever.

Carl groaned when she kissed his hardness and licked its length. She tasted his maleness, inhaled the scents of a man.

He moaned again when she slid his arousal deep into her mouth.

He hadn't resisted when she had pushed him back in his bed, but that didn't mean he was willing to simply accept her explorations passively.

A growl sounded deep in his throat as he jerked at the ties that secured her pants to her body, then yanked the pants off of her and pulled her onto the bed beside him.

Beside him, but with her head at the opposite end of the bed. Which, it turned out, was exactly what he had in mind.

His strong hands made short work of her panties, tearing them away rather than going to the trouble of sliding them off her legs.

In a moment of giddy delight, she decided that if she was going to stay with Carl, she'd look into Velcro panties. Her delight faded when she realized that staying with Carl was the least likely of futures.

For them, the future was a mystery, but a dark mystery. Its one certainty was that there was no hope for a world divided between the normal and the impaired--the magical, she reminded herself. Still, if they lacked a future, they had a present. She needed to stay grounded in the now and not get carried away in teenaged fantasies about ever-after.

With one hand, Carl traced a slow circle that led from Danielle's right knee up her inner thigh, brushed gently against the sensitive folds of her womanhood, then continued down the other thigh. With the other hand, he tugged her closer to him until she could feel his warm breath against her upper thighs.

Wherever he touched, Danielle's body tingled. Her blood pulsed behind his caress, her internal thermostat cranked up to full burn.

This wasn't fair. He was injured, barely able to sit up, yet he was taking control over their lovemaking. She opened her mouth to protest, and then shut it abruptly when his mouth pressed against her most sensitive area.

He kissed, nibbled, then found an indescribable pattern of tongue, lips, and fingers around, and inside of her.

Any idea of protest fled as indescribable pleasures pulsed from her core to the extremes of her body, then rebounded to double and triple her bliss.

Rather than resist, she wallowed in his touch. She threw back her head and shoulders, straddled him, clamped her thighs around his head and pressed herself more closely to him, urging him to bring his kisses more deeply into her welcoming body.

He responded willingly, enthusiastically. Like her, she realized, Carl was enjoying the now.

She thought about bending forward and taking his erection into her mouth again while he gave her pleasure, but Carl's caress commanded her entire attention, demanded every inch of her body.

Pressure built up inside of her like a wall of water rushing at a dam. She clamped down, letting the intensity build, but her effort at control was doomed. Orgasm washed through her entire body--a sudden explosion of sensation and pure glorious delight. Then, like an overflowing river, joying in being free when the dikes finally break, surges of orgasm continued, for seconds, minutes, forever it seemed, as wave after wave of pleasure swept over her, each more intense than the last.

All of her strength deserted her. Danielle fell forward over Carl's body, as boneless as a cat, her short hair brushing against his glorious erection.

For an eternity that lasted all of thirty seconds, Danielle wondered if she would ever move again. Her brain worked at a fever pitch but seemed disconnected from the real world. Random thoughts of love, sex, and running away with Carl to somewhere where no warder could ever find them, competed for attention.

Carl's breathing brought her back to full consciousness.

She was lying on top of him, a hundred and twenty pounds of woman crushingly on top of her man's battered body.

She jerked away, only to find that he held her in place with his strong arms.

"I'm hurting you," she protested.

"I'm not complaining."

Well, Carl wouldn't complain, would he? He was too busy being a man.

Which was how she thought about him, she realized. A man. Not a canine. Not a *Were*. Not her herd at all. Not any more. Now he was a man. Her man.

Damn. Joe Smealy had been right about this, at least. If you let yourself get entangled with an impaired, things could get complicated.

And she was thoroughly entangled with Carl now.

But that was something she would think about later. Right now, she needed to get off of Carl before she punctured one of his broken ribs through his heart.

She reached back, stripped his hand off her naked bottom, and turned herself around.

She hadn't consciously intended for it to happen, but she ended up facing him, her hips straddled over his.

His swollen excitement pressed against her moistened and waiting lips.

If that wasn't a sign, Danielle didn't know anything about fate.

She captured him in her hands, adjusted the aim, and lowered herself onto his engorged member.

Carl stroked a hand across her face. "Oh, yeah."

They weren't the most romantic words in the universe, but they filled Danielle with a sense of accomplishment.

She raised herself, then lowered again, pressing her hips to his, feeling her body adjust to take all of his length deep within herself.

She stared at his eyes looking for any sign of the shift. She wasn't sure what she would do if she saw it. Maybe run screaming from the house. Instead, the human Carl looked back at her, his eyes filled with the same confusion and pain that she felt after the events of the past twenty-four hours.

For now, that was enough.

She leaned forward, putting her hands on either side of his shoulders, kissed him on the mouth, and then let her hips find the rhythm that brought the two of them together.

She hadn't thought she could climax again, so soon after Carl's tongue had brought her over the edge. But as the friction built, she realized that she'd been mistaken. About this, and so many other things.

Carl groaned; his face tightened as he fought for control. Fought, and won. Then his hips joined hers in the dance of life, extending their mutual pleasure, allowing her body and his to discover new ways of pleasuring one another.

As she neared the edge, each nerve in her body became hypersensitive. Carl's faint beard, noticeable after a day without shaving, felt harsh against her skin. His hand, clasped to her shoulder to press her to him, burned with heat. Beads of perspiration collected under her breasts, each drop leaving a distinct sensation of moist warmth and evaporating coolness.

The sensual overload should have been unpleasant, or even painful. Instead, pain and pleasure mingled into a simple rush of awareness. The rush swept over her entire body, and then suddenly collected in her womb.

Her previous lovemaking with Carl should have prepared her for this to happen, but somehow it didn't. Despite everything she'd experienced before, the power of her orgasm surprised her. Caught her up in a torrent of sensual delight.

For an intoxicating moment, she felt that she and Carl were united in more than simply the physical bond that connected them. She imagined she could hear the echoes of Carl's thoughts and senses within her own mind. That heady feeling of joy, accomplishment, and pleasure washing away the memory of injury, those feelings of affection, the regret for what they'd done to one another and the destruction they had caused.

That emotional and mental bonding felt strange, uncomfortable, but wonderful at the same time. Danielle slid forward, bringing her breasts to his muscled chest, and pressed her lips against his neck in an attempt to preserve that closeness and sharing.

For the first time since she'd discovered her mother's broken body, Danielle felt whole, and safe, and wanted.

Damn, she was in trouble.

* * *

Carl disentangled himself from Danielle's sleeping body. A part of him wanted to simply stay there indefinitely. But Carl was a scientist and a scientist deals with facts rather than fantasy.

And the facts were ugly. He was a marked man. Whether the warders had ordered his termination before the games and riot, word would be out now. They would have analyzed video records from the guard tower. They would recognize the wolf and identify it as Carl in his *Were* form.

It was time for some hard decisions.

He covered Danielle's sleeping form, wrapped a sheet around his body and headed out of the bedroom. He needed to find some data, develop some hypotheses, and test the reality that had fallen over the world.

In many ways, he was different from Danielle. But in one key respect, they were similar. Both were fighters. And Carl intended to keep on fighting as long as he was alive.

Mike the Vampire lay nestled in a pallet in a tumbledown room just outside the bedroom where Danielle and Carl had slept. He'd stacked abandoned furniture around his makeshift bed to give it just the hint of coffin.

Carl wasn't an expert on vampirism. Hell, like most normals, he'd simply taken for granted the official line. Now, he wondered if the coffin thing was instinctual vampire behavior, or Mike's idea of a funny statement.

Mike's chest remained perfectly still. He wasn't breathing, but he wasn't dead either. Or rather, he wasn't any more dead than the average vampire. He also wasn't, Carl felt certain, inhabited by a demon. Like so much of the supposed knowledge about the magical, that was simply a convenient myth. A lie. A justification for cold-blooded killing.

The terrible reality was that no one else had done serious scientific work on the magical. The magical virus had infected a tenth of mankind, but no credible research had been done on the results of the infection.

Fear and panic, rather than science and reason, had formed the basis for virtually every decision made about relationships between the normal and the magical.

Snori peeked his huge head around the doorway. "Thought I heard someone moving in here." He held up a radio scanner. "I think we'd better get a move on soon."

The troll jerked Carl's mind back to the here and now. "What have you heard?"

"Warder bands are all encrypted, of course. But there is a lot of chatter. More than I've ever heard before. And there's nothing but white noise on the short wave. Like there was a major sunspot outbreak. Only there wasn't."

"Sounds like the warders are jamming. I wonder what that means?"

Snori ran a hand over his bald head. "Well, it could mean that they're going to attack and they don't want any hams to blow the secrecy. I've heard about zones that suddenly just weren't there any more."

Snori wasn't being paranoid; it was a real possibility.

"They have to do something," Carl admitted. "They'll want to come after me. But I'm not sure they'd want to take out the entire zone. In the first place, killing and disposing of a million or so magics wouldn't be cheap or easy. In the second place, I have to think that even some of the warders would balk. It's not like just encouraging an occasional riot."

Snori shrugged. They didn't have enough information to do more than speculate. And here Carl had thought he was the one who could offer scientific method.

"All right," Carl decided. "We've got to get away from the zone border and go deep underground."

"What about Danielle?"

There was no way to avoid that question. What about Danielle? He didn't want to leave her. But could he trust her after she'd betrayed him to the warders?

"What do you think?" Not that he could evade ultimate responsibility for choosing. Still, Snori had shown amazing insight already. Carl knew he couldn't be unbiased when it came to Danielle.

Snori grinned. "I think she's a keeper, boss. Just get this warder nonsense out of her head. It isn't as if she's a real normal."

"Huh?" Maybe he'd been wrong about Snori's insights.

"Come on, boss. Wake up and smell the coffee." Snori put his hands together and cracked his knuckles. The sound sent echoes through the room. "You fought her, didn't you? You saw how quick she moved. Can any normal fight like that?"

"It's the warder training," Carl explained. "We saw another warder that had the same trick."

Snori slammed a massive fist into his palm. "Warder training." His voice practically dripped with contempt. "That's such a bull line I need boots just to listen to it. Here I thought you were the scientific type. You know, look at the facts rather than people's made-up explanations."

Carl didn't feel comfortable with where this conversation was heading, but he had no choice but to follow it.

"Martial arts training can bring out exceptional talents," he reminded the troll.

"Right. That's why you can go into that blur mode, right?" Snori looked around for a place to spit, then thought better of it and swallowed. He leaned forward and lowered his voice to a modest roar. "They're using our own kind against us. The warders are like old-time Janissaries."

Carl had revised his estimation of Snori once already. Now he did so again. "Janissaries like in the medieval Ottoman army?"

"Like the Turks gathered up children from their captive people, raised them, and then used them to keep their own cultures under control. Yeah, just like that."

He looked more closely at the troll. "Who were you before you became a troll, anyway?"

Snori laughed. "I was nobody before I became a troll. Since then, I've been reading. Nobody ever said that a troll can't read, you know. No laws in the zone."

Carl rubbed his eyes. He didn't know if Snori was right, but he couldn't say the troll was wrong either. And if Danielle was magical, that would solve no end of problems. Assuming she didn't kill him when he told her.

One thing was certain, he wouldn't abandon her. If she was magical, the warder leadership would see her as a disposable tool. And, thanks to Carl, the warders might just decide that it was time for them to dispose of her. Of course, if she was magical, that solved another problem. He'd wondered how a magical could have a relationship with a normal. And he wanted a relationship with Danielle. Needed it down to the bone. And last night he'd decided Arenesol was right. Even if he found the cure, he wouldn't take it. His magic enhanced, it didn't impair.

He made his decision. "Wake up Mike and I'll get Danielle. We've got to get out of here."

Snori smiled. "You going to tell her what I said?"

Carl shrugged. Danielle held her secrets tight. She'd never told him why she'd become a warder, but he didn't believe it was out of greed or a lust for power. If he just told her that she was one of the group she hated, she wouldn't believe him and might get violent.

Besides, if Snori was right about the warders, that meant that there might be plenty more magical living amongst the normal. "Not right away. I've got to think about this."

"Don't wait too long, boss. She's not the kind of woman who like it if you know secrets about her and don't tell."

Carl didn't think that kind of woman existed. "Let me worry about that. You worry about getting Mike out of his coffin."

He turned and headed back into the bedroom where he and Danielle had slept.

She was still lying in the bed, her eyes closed, her breath soft and deep.

Her short blonde hair stood out from her head like crabgrass grown wild. One long leg lay across the bed, scraped and bruised from her battles. The thin blanket covered but didn't conceal her. To Carl, she looked perfect.

He bent and kissed her.

* * *

Even asleep, a part of Danielle's mind was aware of what happened around her. Warders live too close to the edge of danger to let sleep control them completely. When Carl returned to the room, that part of her knew that she was no longer alone.

Still, her subconscious mind brushed away the warning. This presence wasn't dangerous, it assured her. She could continue to sleep in safety. After what she'd been though, she needed to recuperate, to replace her depleted energy.

Her subconscious's assurance made the surprise more complete. She awakened, panicked, to find something clamped over her mouth.

Danielle's reaction was immediate and forceful. She smashed both fists toward whatever blocked her breath.

A solid thump told her she'd connected. Whatever had covered her mouth vanished.

She inhaled deeply and opened her eyes just in time to see dark hair disappear over the edge of her bed.

"Carl?"

A faint moan was her only answer.

She pushed herself up. She couldn't have slept for more than a couple of hours, but she felt incredibly refreshed. Making love with Carl had filled her with energy and with a sort of bubbling happiness that she didn't even recognize.

That happiness faded when she peered over the bed and saw Carl slumped on the floor.

Carl had been trying to strangle her. Her mind reeled at the realization. Had sex just been his way of softening her up?

Only belatedly did the tingle from her lips reach her conscious mind. A tingle and the faintest touch of moisture. As if she had been--kissed.

"You idiot, Carl," she growled. "Didn't anyone ever tell you to be careful when you wake up a warder?" She wrapped the scratchy blanket around herself and got down on her knees beside him. "Carl? Carl, wake up." He was at least breathing, deeply and evenly. She patted his cheek.

"Everything all right in there?" Snori opened the door to Danielle's bedroom without waiting for an answer.

"Uh--"

"He told you, did he? Well, I think maybe you over-reacted just a--"

"Told me what?"

Snori stopped. "Oh. Uh, never mind. So, why did you deck him?"

Danielle opened her mouth to answer, then snapped it shut. Her imagination supplied an assortment of implausible conversation starters that could lead her to slug Carl, but she couldn't think of any she would want to review with the troll. "Let me take care of him and you can get ready somewhere else."

"Carl is my friend. I wouldn't want him to get hurt."

"I'm not going to hurt him." Danielle knew her exasperation showed through but she couldn't help it.

"Really?"

Really. Joe Smealy had ordered her to terminate Carl and she wasn't going to do it. For the first time in since the start of her warder training, she intended to disobey a direct order.

"Just get out of here."

Snori nodded and headed out, closing the door behind her. Carl chose that moment to groan and open his eyes. "What--"

"Quiet." She examined Carl's pupils and was relieved to see that neither was dilated.

"Our trainers used to come into the barracks at night," she explained. "If we didn't awaken and defend ourselves, we washed out. I didn't wash out."

Carl managed a rueful smile. "So I'm lucky I wasn't badly hurt?"

She nodded. "Snori said you had something to tell me. Well, I'm listening."

His eyes evaded hers. A bad sign. Could he have a wife on the side? But that was impossible. His file hadn't mentioned even recent romantic involvement. Unless he'd found someone since they'd been in the zone.

"It's just speculation," he finally said. "I don't feel right talking about it until I discover the facts."

That sounded more hopeful. He wouldn't need to find the facts about a secret wife.

Danielle shook her head. She might not be a warder any more, but she certainly didn't believe in old-fashioned pre-return-of-magic fairytales. Her fantasies about running away with Carl were just that. Fantasies.

"Whatever. In the meantime, do we have a plan, or are we just going to wing it?"

Carl pulled himself back to his feet, stretched gingerly as if expecting to find new broken bones, and then started tossing clothes to Danielle. "Snori has picked up hints that there is a major warder follow-up to last night's riots. They'll need to do something after the stupid stunt that Arenesol and I pulled off. Capturing me would be a start. So, at the minimum we can expect incursions. But Snori thinks that there may be more. Possibly even liquidating the entire zone."

"We wouldn't do that." The *we* slipped out even though she'd just told herself that she wasn't a warder anymore.

"There've been reports of zones that just vanished."

"There are always crazy rumors," Danielle argued. "But that doesn't make them true." Some of the rumors had been horrible, though. Could she have closed her ears to them simply because she didn't want to hear the truth?

"It doesn't make them lies, either," Carl reminded her. "We're going to head for the core until we figure out what to do next."

"All right. I guess we'll have to wait and see." They had been too tired and too badly injured the previous evening to get far from the zone border. Finding the relative safety of the center of the zone could be a first step.

Goose bumps stood on her arms when she realized what she was thinking. She'd never thought of the zone's center as safe before. It was home to the worst of the impaired. Home to the most completely magical, she corrected herself. She had cast herself outside the pale of normal civilization. So much of what she knew, her thoughts, and her basic vocabulary, would be destructive rather than helpful in the new world she was entering.

But her training could be helpful, too. She knew how the warders would operate, what they'd be looking for. "We'll break up and head back toward Zang Boulevard. There's a market near the old Zang curve where we can rendezvous. Mike and Snori can leave first. You and I will follow taking an indirect route."

Carl looked amused. "Are you the boss now?"

"Somebody's got to be. I've had a lot more training in this than you have."

"Sounds like a plan to me," Mike put in.

Danielle's skin still crawled when she saw the vampire. But she knew this was a conditioned reflex. Mike hadn't done anything to her personally--or was it vampirely? She forced herself to smile at him.

"You doing all right, Mike?" Carl asked.

"Except I owe my life to a troll. The other vampires are never going to let me live this one down."

"Yeah?" Snori demanded. "What about the other trolls? When I tell them I'm blood brothers with a vampire, I'll be a pariah."

"Sounds like you two are back to normal," Carl said. "Unless anyone has a better plan, let's follow Danielle's. You two head out directly. We'll join you in what, three hours?"

He directed that last question to Danielle, deferring to her tactical expertise.

"Let's say four. We'll want to check out a few things."

Snori and the vampire nodded, then disappeared.

Danielle glared at the tattered remnants of her panties, then at Carl. "If you're going to do that again, make sure I have a spare pair handy."

"Are we going to do that again?" His face broke into a smile that made him look much younger.

"No promises," she told him. But she promised herself that they would. She was walking away from the life she knew, from the life she'd been raised and trained for. And there had damned well better be some advantages. More sex with Carl sounded like a pretty tremendous advantage. Lots more sex.

"And definitely not now," she told him when he closed the distance between them and kissed her neck. "Besides, I'm gross and sweaty."

"I like you sweaty."

"Figures. Men are all weird."

"Call me the weird *Were*," he answered.

It wasn't very funny, but somehow she couldn't help laughing.

They made a quick stop at a tiny market off Jefferson and bought new underwear, a pre-return-of-magic t-shirt advertising Nude Fishing, something that made no sense at all to Danielle but that offered a lot more protection than her grimy sports bra. She also bought a toothbrush and a couple of chocolate croissants. She wasn't sure whether it was the chocolate, clean teeth, or clean clothes, but Danielle felt a little more human. She couldn't say the same for Carl, though. His smile had faded almost as soon as they'd left their hideout.

Chapter 12

"Want to talk about it?" Danielle finally asked.

They'd been walking in silence for fifteen minutes, ducking out of sight when one helicopter swooped overhead, and keeping to the shadows whenever they could.

"Talk about what?"

She resisted the urge to slug him. "Let's see. One of your friends blew himself up and saved your life. Your entire plan to develop a cure for the magic virus has gone out of control, your investments in the zone were largely destroyed in the rioting and your chances of getting the money the network owes you are slim. Oh, and your girlfriend betrayed you to the warders. Other than that, I can't think of a thing."

"You did betray us?" His voice was harsh with accusation. "I was hoping Arenesol was wrong about that."

"Of course I betrayed you. What did you expect me to do? Try to help an illegal impaired breakout?"

"Is that what it was?"

"It seemed that way to me at the time." She sat down at an abandoned bus stop, the Plexiglas and plastic structure still providing some shelter from the blazing sun and from the constant spying of warder choppers.

She patted the bench next to herself, but Carl ignored her gesture and paced in front of her.

"Does it still seem that way to you? Can you still justify it? All those dead elves."

And Joe had lied to her. She'd believed him when he'd said they would simply overawe the Tiger escape.

Carl's words only rubbed salt in the wounds Joe had left. Still, Danielle wasn't the kind to back off. "What do you want me to do, Carl? Grovel? I made a decision based on the information I had. Believe me, I'm aware of the consequences. I'll have nightmares about it for years. Would I do something different knowing what I know now? Sure. But it isn't as if you took me into your confidence. You treated me like an enemy, so why are you so hurt that I acted like one?"

He spun toward her, opened his mouth, then shut it.

"Can I make a suggestion?" she asked when it became obvious that he wasn't going to say anything.

"I'd love to hear it."

Sarcasm dripped, but she decided to take him literally.

"I can't undo what I did. I wish we'd both done a lot of things differently. But we're humans. At least I'm a human and you're a *Were*. That means that neither of us comes close to perfection. But we need to be honest with each other. If we can't talk about things, can't work them out between us, we're going to end up fighting all the time." And they'd end up killing each other. She didn't want to say that.

"That makes sense." His agreement was reluctant, but he did agree.

"All right. I admit that I made a mistake telling the warders about Arenesol's breakout. I didn't plan on a slaughter. We were just supposed to turn them back."

"We?"

She barked a laugh. "See, Carl, it isn't easy to break the habits of a decade of training. And that's how long I've been working to become a warder. Ever since--" she trailed off.

"Ever since what?"

She'd said they needed to be honest. Well, this was her first test. She didn't want to tell him about finding her mother--it was a personal memory. But she owed it to him. If he looked at her and walked away in disgust, it was better now than later. Wasn't it? Actually, she wasn't so sure.

She took a deep breath. "Early in the return of magic, before people really knew what was going on, I snuck out of high school. I was going to the mall with a couple of girlfriends and I stopped by our apartment to change first.

"My mother had lost her job, but she just slept all the time so I didn't have to worry about her. Now, I know that she suffered from depression. At the time, I just thought she was lazy." *Too lazy to care about me.*

"I didn't bother checking on her when I got home. I was worrying about how much trouble I'd be in if she caught me, and didn't consider that she might be in trouble too. But I heard something in her bedroom when I was on my way out the door. So I decided to peek in."

Despite the decade that had passed, Danielle shuddered at the return of the memory.

Carl's eyes gleamed with sympathy. "Go on."

"My mother had remarried a couple of years before and my step-father was younger than she. I think I must have had a bit of a crush on him. I don't know what I was expecting when I opened the door, but it definitely wasn't what I got."

Carl nodded, waiting for her to continue.

"My stepfather was on top of my mother. I was embarrassed. I thought I'd walked in on them when they were having sex. Then I saw that his teeth stuck in her throat. There was blood—" she broke off.

"Your mother--"

"By the time the police got there my mother was dead. I must have screamed because my stepfather looked up. He--" Danielle swallowed. "He smiled at me."

She gasped a sobbing breath. The memory was vivid now. She could almost see that gory vampire face sneering, lust inflaming his eyes, his teeth dripping with her mother's life-blood.

"That was only a few days after the beginning of the return," she told him. "I got away, called 9-1-1. And I watched when the police came. They didn't have silver bullets back then, of course. Let alone wooden stakes. He killed three cops before they brought him under control. He just took their bullets and laughed.

Carl stopped pacing and sat next to her, taking her suddenly cold hand between his warm ones. "It must have been terrible."

Terrible was only the beginning. They hadn't understood the return of magic then. She'd been locked in isolation for months while doctors waited to see if she had the infection. There had been plenty of orphans. Children whose parents had gone magic and vanished, children whose parents had been killed by the magical, and children whose parents the government whisked away in one of their crackdowns.

Danielle had been lucky. Joe Smealy had been one of the first cops on the scene. He'd taken Danielle under his wing and made sure she didn't get lost in the bureaucratic shuffle—or condemned as a latent. He'd worked to send Danielle to a government school for the dispossessed. Once there, he'd made sure she was tested as a candidate for the new warder organization.

Joe had done what he could, but Danielle couldn't forget her mother. She'd sworn she would avenge her, would live to protect others from the cruelty that had taken her mother.

And now she was breaking that promise, throwing her lot in with the magical. She hoped it wasn't just her hormones controlling her life.

"So it must have terrified you when I changed to *Were* that first time we made love."

She nodded, her throat suddenly too thick to continue talking. Carl's change had brought up all of the fears she'd spent a decade suppressing. But it was more than that. Even then, a part of her had recognized her own action as a betrayal of the man and system that had adopted her, protected her when her own family had abandoned her.

Carl, wisely, said nothing. Instead, he handed her a chilled water bottle.

She drank until it was gone.

"Anyway," she handed back the empty bottle, "that's the sad story of my life."

"It is sad," Carl told her. "It must have been especially hard because of your conflicted feelings about your mother."

So much for Carl's good sense in keeping his mouth shut. "I spent months listening to a psychologist going on about Freud and Oedipus," Danielle told him. "I don't need it from you."

"In that case, what do you say we get a move on it? Mike and Snori are likely to get worried."

* * *

They met up with Snori and Mike right on time. The vampire and troll were trying too hard to look inconspicuous. Since the center of the zone was filled with people who were hiding from someone or something, they fit right in.

Snori waved them over to an outdoor table where he'd already ordered Turkish style coffee for them. Carl sipped at his politely. Danielle just looked at hers, then pushed it away. She couldn't stand the stuff.

"Any problems?" Carl asked.

Mike shook his head. "Smooth sailing."

"Except we ran into a couple of rioters who must have gotten lost on their way out of the zone," Snori added, his words barely comprehensible underneath the laughter he couldn't suppress. "We, uh, helped them along to the border."

"After taking away all their loot," Mike added.

Danielle shook her head. He could understand their action. But it was too much like Carl's attack on the guard post. Randomly striking back could be emotionally satisfying, but it didn't make a bit of difference to the reality the magical faced. Even if the looted goods were returned to their original owners, something Danielle suspected would never happen, they would simply be looted again the next time rioters descended on the zone.

They needed a fundamental change in the way they responded to the attacks. And getting that would require an alteration in the structure of the zone. As long as half the zone leaders were goons like Arenesol, and the other half were co-opted or paid by the warders, things would never get better.

Of course, first they had to survive.

"Any word on a warder attack?" Carl demanded.

Snori shook his head. "Still a lot of chatter on the encrypted warder bands. Does our pet warder have any information?"

Intellectually Danielle had known she was changing sides. But there was still an emotional charge realizing that she wasn't just being asked to ignore orders. Carl and his mob needed her to spy for them as she'd spied against them.

"I haven't checked in today." She held out a hand. "Can I borrow a cell phone? I seem to have lost mine in the confusion."

She phoned in and checked her messages, then reported back. "As soon as I finish Carl off, I'm supposed to report back to the Warder Regional office," she said. "They've identified Carl as involved in last night's attack and aren't happy that I didn't terminate you before you had the chance."

"That was quick I.D.," Carl said.

He was right. There had to be thousands of *Were* in the Dallas zone. Danielle knew they'd made progress on pattern-matching algorithms, but how would they recognize Carl when he was in wolf-form?

"Unless we had an informant."

Carl looked from Mike to Snori to Danielle.

She met his gaze coolly. She couldn't expect that making love would automatically eliminate his distrust. The Warder Academy even had a class on how to use sex to infiltrate and destroy. Fortunately it hadn't been a lab class.

"We were the only ones who knew," Snori said. "And every one of us risked their lives to save you."

Carl smashed a fist into the table. "You're right. I'm sorry. I'm paranoid after what happened, but it isn't your fault."

"And there's a general call for all warders to be out of the zone by eight tomorrow evening," Danielle added. "I haven't gotten anything personal, though."

"They're suspicious of you," Mike concluded.

Carl looked worried. "Well, you're here with us. As long as you stay in the zone, you don't have to worry about what they're thinking."

She could stay in the safety of Carl's arms, protected by the *Were* and his friends. It was tempting, but not too tempting. If the warders attacked, the zone would provide no safety.

"You want me to just sit here waiting for them to take the initiative? I don't think so. I've got to go back. I already told them that I terminated you last night after the raid. As long as you lay low they would have no reason not to believe me."

"But--"

She shook her head firmly. Her thoughts had crystallized into decision. "I know it's crazy, but I'm throwing my lot in with you and the impair--magical, Carl. Whole hog and no holding back. I saw the truth about the warders last night, and I didn't like it.

"I told you why I joined the warders. Because I thought they would protect those too weak to protect themselves. Well, I found out that they're more of the problem than the solution. If they attack now, we lose. We've got to play for time and I'm the only card you have in this game."

"We can get--"

"*We* can't, Carl. I can. We'll clean out the zone, make it a place where children can live safely. But we need time. Time to get ready for the warder attack. Time to break the links between informants and warders. The longer I can keep up the pretense of being one of them, the more warning we'll get when they come after us. I'm our secret weapon. We've got to use me."

Carl looked doubtful. "We don't know that you are a secret any more. You carried me away from the bomb blast. Someone could have seen you. I was in *Were* form and they still recognized me. And you aren't exactly low profile."

Danielle shrugged. "So?"

"You feel guilty over informing on the Tiger breakout. Well, putting herself at risk won't bring back a single elf."

He was right. She did feel guilty. But that didn't mean she didn't have to do it. "I'm not saying it isn't a risk. I'm saying that it is a risk we have to take. If they're planning a major raid, I'll be able to warn you and maybe delay it. If they aren't, I may still be able to disrupt the informant chains."

"Absolutely not," Carl announced. "You're going to stay right here in the center of the zone where it's safe. There's no way I'm going to risk you."

She was halfway across the table before he'd even began to react. Coffee exploded everywhere as she grasped him around his neck.

"Listen here, werewolf," she hissed. "I'm not some fairytale princess waiting to be rescued. If you have a valid reason for me to stay, tell me. Otherwise, back off."

* * *

The warder regional office buzzed with activity.

Danielle had been searched, disarmed down to her silver leash, and finally admitted into an underground bunker rather than the high-rise office where Joe had been stationed weeks earlier.

Armed warders tromped through the building as if expecting an attack momentarily.

She'd been waiting for over two hours before the Joe finally rushed into his office.

He rubbed his forehead, slumped in his chair, and stared at the wall for a few endless seconds before silently gesturing for her to have a seat.

She sat and waited.

He said nothing for several minutes as he paged through a computer screen. Finally he slammed his fist into the linoleum surface of the desk.

"Do you have anything to say for yourself, Warder? I thought my orders were crystal clear."

"Sorry, sir."

"Didn't I tell you to beat the *Were*?"

"Yes, sir."

"So?"

"He was better than me, sir." Even given the circumstances, it hurt her to admit that. But it was true. Carl had beat her fair and square. Once. Sure she could have handled him if she hadn't been exhausted from the earlier fights. But they'd both fought the same number of matches. Carl had preserved his strength. She'd dissipated her own.

"So freaking what?" Joe's tone made that a real question.

"Sir?"

"So he was better than you? So big deal. What are they teaching in the Warder Academy anyway? Fair play? You could have drugged him. You could have fouled him. You could have called for emergency assistance. I had sharpshooters in the crowd. They would have timed it so it looked like one of your blows landed. Warders are team players. And you didn't give your teammates a chance to help."

"Nobody told me that, sir." She shouldn't be surprised that Joe was willing to cheat. Warders were more interested in getting the job done than in protecting legalistic niceties.

"Nobody told me," he mocked. He leaned toward her and lowered his voice. "You're a graduate of the Warder Academy, not a dumb grunt. You're supposed to use your imagination, your brain. My God, Danielle, think what they did to your mother."

"Yes, sir." She was getting a royal balling out, but he hadn't accused her of treachery. Which might mean that she was safe. For now.

"What happened after the fight?" he demanded.

"I don't know, sir."

Joe slammed his fist into the computer monitor built into the desktop. Blue sparks flew across the room and a strong sizzle spoke of an electrical current meeting human flesh.

"What the hell? Put it out." Flames crawled up the arm of Joe's uniform.

The loud siren of an alarm went off. Sensitive smoke detectors were working.

Danielle yanked a fire extinguisher off the wall and blasted away at her inflamed boss. Tempting though it was, letting him burn wouldn't help anything and it would get her arrested.

Joe sputtered under the onslaught of freezing C02, caught his breath, then ordered her to stop.

"Sorry, sir."

"Yeah. Sure."

A troop of guards pounded down the hall and threw open the door to his office, assault rifles ready, chemical protection suits fully equipped.

Joe's district didn't mess around, Danielle realized.

"My computer shorted out," Joe barked. "Get out of here."

He rang for his admin, brusquely ordered a new uniform, then turned back to Danielle.

Enough of his uniform had burned to expose a hard muscular frame scarred by multiple deep wounds, some white with age and others still red with healing.

Joe had kept in shape. He was the type of active leader that Danielle had always respected. Like Carl, she realized. Except Joe was the enemy of her friends. Which made him her enemy as well. Where had Joe been the previous night? The circles under his eyes hinted that he hadn't been safely in bed.

"Can you explain what you mean?" he demanded. His voice was smooth and soft now, as if he was patiently talking to a young child.

Danielle struggled to recall where the conversation had been before he'd set himself on fire. Oh, yes. After the fight.

"I don't know what happened after the fight because I was knocked unconscious," she explained. "Someone must have moved me from the arena because when I regained consciousness, I was alone with the troll I'd fought in the match before Dr. Harriman defeated me."

"*Were* Harriman carried you out."

"Really? Well, he left me pretty quickly then."

"Go on."

"Anyway, I incapacitated the troll and went looking for Harriman. I found him, in *Were* form, near a wrecked watch tower, dragged him away from any possible witnesses, and terminated him."

"His body hasn't turned up."

Danielle nodded firmly. "It won't. Unless someone decides to dredge the algae vats he's been cultivating."

For the first time since he'd walked into the room, a smile flitted across Joe's face. It vanished so quickly she wondered if she'd seen it or just imagined it.

"You waited too long, warder. He, along with a suicide bomber, had already taken out the tower."

"Yes, sir. I saw the destruction and guessed that he might be responsible." She paused just a beat. "Did any of the impaired escape?"

Her boss slowly shook his head. "We were able to cover the area with helicopters until a replacement crew arrived."

"Excellent." Danielle paused for a moment, trying to decide what she would say if she'd really been the loyal warder she was pretending to be. "You said that you'd promote me to vampire hunting once my assignment was terminated," she reminded him. "I'd like the opportunity to do some real work, sir."

* * *

Under normal circumstances, being assigned a month of deskwork would have been a disgrace. As it was, Danielle had barely been able to disguise her satisfaction.

Joe's admin had shown her to a ratty cubicle equipped with an antique pre-return-of-magic computer, a buzzing fluorescent lamp and not much else. Coffee rings and cigarette scars formed the only decoration. The screen saver was a changing set of images of extremely female and completely nude magical creatures, each handcuffed or otherwise restrained.

"Sick," Danielle muttered as she wiped the images off the hard drive.

The admin agreed with a sniff and brought Danielle a cup of watery coffee as a sort of peace offering. Female bonding proved stronger than the admin's wish to support her boss.

"I'm Danielle Goodman," Danielle said, hoping to follow up on the implicit offer of friendship. Of all the people in the office, the admin was most likely to notice anything Danielle was doing out of the ordinary.

"Theresa Ortez," the admin identified herself. "I've been working with Joe for a couple of years now."

"Joe?" From what Danielle knew of the man, he wasn't likely to be on a first name basis with anyone on his staff.

Theresa giggled. "Mr. Smealy, then. I think of him as Joe, though. Isn't he a dreamboat?"

Danielle forced a smile. "Right now, he's mad as hell at me, which makes him a little less attractive in my eyes."

"He's upset. I understand he's never recovered from when his wife turned into an elf and ran away with another impaired," Theresa confided. "So he's single. But don't you go trolling for him. I've got him on my radar screen."

"You go, girl," Danielle encouraged. She wondered how many of the warders had stories like Joe's or her own. Personal reasons to fear and to hate the magical.

"You just let me know if there's anything you need. Office supplies or," Theresa giggled again, "a list of which warders are single and which aren't."

"And which ones put those nasty pictures on the computer," Danielle concluded.

"Yeah, a list of the ones to avoid would have saved me a lot of bother." Theresa turned to leave, then stopped at the entry to Danielle's cubicle. "A few of us girls get together for lunch. We'll meet in about an hour in the cafeteria. I know you're a real warder. And we're mostly admins and clericals. So if you don't want to join us, we'd understand. It isn't like we have a lot of stories to tell about killing--"

"I'd love to have lunch with you," Danielle told her. She didn't believe the cliché that women gossip more than men, but she suspected she could learn more from other women than from a bunch of men trying to get into her pants. Besides, the last thing she wanted now was old war stories.

Theresa giggled again, then vanished into another cubicle letting Danielle turn her attention to the computer.

If Danielle had any doubts about her decision to throw in with Carl and the magical, the next hour would have dispelled it. The task that Joe had assigned her consisted of linking incoming reports of the previous evening's riot to appropriate database entries.

The reports listed the loot collected, estimated number of impaired killed, and the amount of property damage. Intriguingly, part of her job was cross-tabulating the reports by rioters and warder agents against incoming reports from informants. Bonuses were paid only on confirmed finds, not claims. If what she could see was typical of warder offices elsewhere, the entire organization seemed to revolve around exploiting the magical. Any protection to the normals was strictly incidental.

She carefully dug deeper, afraid that the computer system would track her queries and send alarms through the building but intent on finding everything she could. This was a once-in-a-lifetime opportunity to protect her friends in the zone and she didn't intend to blow it.

No heavy hand clamped down on her shoulder, but she didn't find as much useful information as she'd hoped for either.

Within the computer system, code numbers rather than name or magical category identified informants. Danielle committed as much as possible to her memory, but the fact that informant 127z329x had reported the theft of a beer-truck wasn't actionable. Unfortunately, it was typical of what she had access to.

At noon, Theresa stopped by. "We're going down to the cafeteria, Danielle. You ready for a break?"

Danielle rubbed her eyes. She'd been ready for a break before she even sat down.

For a change, Dallas's stifling hot weather had moderated into an early fall. Mild north winds blew the Gulf of Mexico humidity south, leaving the city dry and comfortable. The girls decided to eat outside in a tree-shaded park just a block from the warder office building.

Girls, Danielle quickly decided, was something of a misnomer. For one thing, the seven women ranged in age from Theresa's twenty, up to the seventy-year-old Mary. While Danielle was the only active-duty warder in the group, Mary was a human resources manager and another woman, Karen, managed database development. These, in short, were the people who actually ran the warder office while line-level warders did their cowboy acts. That, at least, seemed to be the consensus around the picnic table.

After listening to fifteen minutes of gossip about who was sleeping with whom, which brown-nosers were moving up in the organization and which had finally gotten slammed, Danielle used a break in the conversation to ask what she really wanted to know.

"What's the story on the riots last night? I understand that the impaired took out a guard tower. Surely we're not going to let them get away with that."

Mary's look let Danielle know that her query might not have been as casual as she'd intended. "You were supposed to terminate that *Were* before he did it."

Danielle shrugged. "Unfortunately, I was unconscious. By the time I woke up, the damage had been done."

"I watched your match on the net," Theresa gushed, obviously trying to head off any conflict. "You were great. It didn't seem fair that the *Were* beat you. You were way better. Higher kicks, faster moves. You were totally awesome."

Danielle thanked her fan but turned back to Mary. "Yeah, I messed up. That's why I'm assigned to desk duty for the next few weeks even though I have no talent for it. Still, I did complete the assignment. I'm wondering if we'll be doing more, though. I don't want to be stuck on desk duty if there's a major action going down."

At the collective frowning faces, Danielle recognized she'd just slammed the work these women did.

"Not that desk work isn't important," she backtracked. "I'm just trained for fieldwork. I know I'm getting in your way here."

"I'm sure that SAIC Smealy will notify you when your skills can be better utilized elsewhere," Mary sniffed, not sounding mollified at all.

It seemed like she wasn't going to get anywhere and Danielle was looking for a way to defuse the tension and turn the conversation back in a harmless direction when Mary continued. "I understand that there will be retaliatory raids. All of our informants have been asked to forward information on who else may have been behind that tower attack."

"I'll have to talk to the SAIC about being included in some of those raids," Danielle said.

"Don't get your hopes up. We're bringing in reinforcements from other warder districts around the country. You were with the L.A. district, weren't you?" Mary made it more of a statement than a question.

"That's where I did my internship."

"I know. I have access to all the files. L.A. is sending a contingency. Did you ever meet Sergeant Mansfield? She's heading up a tactical squad. They'll get here tomorrow."

Danielle nodded slowly. If they were sending Mansfield, they were expecting to fight. And if there was going to be a fight, Danielle needed to get back into the zone. Which gave her about a day to disrupt the informant network, learn the warder plans, and warn Carl

It sounded doable.

Chapter 13

"Don't work too late, Danielle."

Theresa gathered up her handbag and shut off her computer.

"I won't," Danielle lied. "Just have a few more entries to log."

Theresa stared at Danielle for a good twenty seconds--long enough that Danielle wondered if she'd given herself away. Then the admin rubbed her toe on the ground and stared at the ceiling.

Danielle prepared herself to attack. The woman had befriended her, but Danielle couldn't afford to be betrayed now.

"A couple of girlfriends and I are hitting one of the meat markets in Deep Ellum," Theresa finally blurted. "The Golden Lying Club. Uh, the name is sort of a joke. If you wanted to join us, we'll be there around ten."

"I'll probably be too tired," Danielle confessed. "But if I have the energy, I'll try to make it."

"Either way, see you tomorrow," Theresa told her. She looked like she wished she'd kept her mouth shut.

"Thanks for your help today," Danielle said. "I swear these computer systems are a completely tangled mess."

"Hey. Us girls have got to stick together."

Theresa popped her bubble gum and headed for the door.

Half an hour later, the Warder building was largely deserted. Lights shown in a few of the cubicles and at the gym where a few overly built jocks insisted on pumping out a few more reps.

It was time to move.

Danielle had pumped Mary for information about her children, learning about her beloved grandchildren, her favorite car, and the rock-and-roll bands she had loved as a teenage girl. All the information a practiced hacker needed to break through computer security.

The door to Mary's office was locked, but it was equipped with a standard government-issue lock, designed well enough to keep out an under-motivated three-year-old. Against a trained warder equipped with a shaped paper clip, it gave way in seconds.

Mary had turned off her computer before going home for the evening. That was a bit of a disappointment, but nothing Danielle hadn't planned for.

She snapped it on, waited for it to run through its boot-up sequence, then faced the password screen.

The Academy had offered classes in breaking into computer systems. About half the time, users leave their passwords attached to the computer monitor with sticky notes. Mary wasn't that bad. Fortunately, for Danielle, Mary followed the common practice of using a family name for her password. Allison, a granddaughter, with the two 'l's' being replaced by the numeral '1,' proved to be the password.

Danielle was in.

* * *

Ten minutes later, she found the encrypted file that cross-referenced informant i.d. numbers with their identities.

The list was thousands of names long. Danielle was almost sickened as she scanned down. She knew some of these people. One was even on Carl's staff. Another was a student in her dojo.

There was no way she could remember all of those names. And naturally, Mary's computer lacked any sort of portable storage. Danielle would have to print the entire list out and then determine a way to smuggle the printout back to the zone.

Since she was planning on leaving, she had the computer overwrite the entries as it read them. Tomorrow, the warders would find that every informant was listed as being Benedict Arnold.

Double sided with a small font size, the printout still made a huge sheaf.

Being in the Human Resources Manager computer gave Danielle powers she hadn't imagined. While the laser printer ground out the pages, Danielle adjusted Warder Agent work assignments, eliminating the mandatory overtime that had been posted that morning and assigning vacation duty to as many agents as she could. With luck, that simple precaution could delay the attack for days.

Once she got back to the zone, she'd have to decide what to do with the informant names. Many magical were angry, ready to take out their frustrations. She was certain that most of the informants would be driven underground or killed if she published their names. But would that really be a good thing?

Some of them were probably just mercenary. But many might have been blackmailed into acting against their principles to protect a loved one still on the normal side of the zone border. A few might believe that they were doing the right thing, helping the lawful authorities against the armed mobs that constituted the power within the zone--just as Danielle had believed, only days ago.

Danielle realized she had no idea how many might be phantom informants: names supplied by Warders who provided the information themselves, and pocketed the informant's pay? Or even completely innocent people whose names the warders used to inflate their payrolls.

If she wasn't careful with the printout, she might create more problems than she would solve. Still, the sheer magnitude of the list made it obvious that Carl had a problem.

The printer stopped abruptly, its lights flashing to indicate that one of the pages had jammed.

Great. She yanked open the doors and started to pull out the errant page.

"What the hell--"

Joe Smealy stood blocking the door to Mary's office.

It was hopeless, but Danielle tried to talk her way out.

"Mary needed to go before she'd finished running this job. She asked that I stay and make sure it was locked up before I left. Good thing I did. This ancient printer keeps getting jammed."

Not bad for a complete improv, she told herself.

"What job?" He sounded suspicious, but not completely distrusting.

Danielle shrugged. "Like I know about human resources? She knows I'm on punishment duty and stuck me with makework."

Joe shook his head. "Wrong answer, Warder. Now how about telling the truth. For a change." He pulled a cell phone from his pocket and dialed.

She knew she only had a few seconds. When Mary picked up the phone, all the air would leak out of Danielle's story. She needed to use the one advantage she had: no one would suspect she was actually working for the enemy.

She gathered what had printed and stepped toward the SAIC. "I know Mary has been with the organization for a while, but I'm not sure you can trust her. I noticed some anomalies when I was logging the informant data this afternoon," she babbled. "At first I figured, hey, they're magical. Who can trust them anyway? But then I started to notice a pattern."

She was close now.

He spoke into the phone, "Mary? It's Joe. I might have a problem here. Just a second."

He put a hand over the transmitter. "Yeah, Goodman. What pattern?"

"This." She shoved the entire stack of paper in his face.

The fluttering paper distracted him only for a moment, but that moment was enough to follow up with a kick to his groin.

Her boss went down hard, the cell phone cracking as it hit the hard tiled floor.

Danielle leapt toward the open door.

* * *

She figured she had about one minute before Joe recovered and called security. If they used the same level security on those leaving the building as they did on those entering, she was in serious trouble.

She should have finished Joe off but she couldn't make herself do it. Even though he had lied to her, he had also saved her when she was young and damaged. And he was damaged too. Killing him when he lay there stunned was not an option.

The red exit sign pointed the way to her final turn. Beneath it, a fire alarm box sat waiting for an emergency.

Well, this was an emergency wasn't it? She yanked on the red handle.

The building filled with a wailing alarm.

She burst through the doorway into the guarded entryway.

"It's the SAIC. His office is on fire again. I tried to get him out but he's unconscious and I couldn't lift him."

Guards scrambled.

One looked at her suspiciously, but she tried a Theresa impression. "I wish I'd been stronger. A man like you would have been able to carry him off without any problem."

"I'm sure you did the best you could." The guard flexed an arm muscle and sucked in his stomach.

"The poor man." Danielle laid it on thick. "Two fires in one day. What terrible luck."

"We'll make sure he's all right."

Danielle nodded and headed out the door. She wanted her weapons, but right now, it was more important to get out.

She reached the doorway, opened the heavy glass door, and stepped into the cooler air of Dallas.

"Hey, you. Girlie. Stop."

Her distraction had run out. The time for subterfuge was over.

Danielle blurred, ducked, and took off in a zagging run.

A burst of bullets, fortunately aimed high, sent tracers flying over her head.

She ducked into a parking garage, then out the other side.

Around her, sirens blared to life.

She slowed to a walk and looked around as if suspicious.

The streets of downtown Dallas weren't anything like those of New

York or New Orleans or Boston, or even the Dallas zone. Dallas's downtown was strictly a business district. After business hours, the city folded up its sidewalks.

There were only three pedestrians in sight. All three glanced back at her, as suspicious of her as she pretended to be of them.

She needed to get off the road.

She really needed to get to the zone. Unfortunately, once Joe had a chance to look at the printout, he would know that she had turned. By the time she got anywhere near the zone border, they'd have so many guards assembled she wouldn't stand a chance of getting through.

Instead of heading toward safety, she'd have to lay low, let the initial heat die down, and plan her next move.

A city truck slowed for a red light. Its driver glanced around for oncoming traffic, saw none, and accelerated through.

Danielle grabbed onto the back, hooking her feet onto the fender while gripping the door handle and ducking her body, as much as possible, below the driver's vision.

She waited for the almost inevitable cries of alarm or the sudden braking as the driver realized he had picked up a hitchhiker. Nothing else had gone right that day. Why should this be any different?

Instead, the truck continued to accelerate.

Danielle exhaled, only then realizing she'd been holding her breath.

Stupid, Danielle, she told herself. Oxygen debt wasn't going to solve any problems.

Neither was riding this truck to whatever city garage it was heading toward. Still, she held on as long as she could, grateful that every second it was moving her away from the Warder office building, away from the alarms, and away from anyone who would recognize her. As long as the truck didn't get on a freeway or run past a warder patrol, she was in good shape.

She stayed on until the truck veered off Commerce Street, hopping down when she noticed a neighborhood drug store.

She stepped in.

Twenty minutes, three stores, and ninety dollars later, she was equipped and ready.

A padded bra maximized her assets and filled out her athletic figure. Purple spray-on hair dye would distract the casual observer's eye, playing into the psychological fact people see only what they expect to see. A slinky jade-green blouse replaced the rumpled warder tunic jacket she'd worn at the office--after an intermediate switch into a truly ugly but brilliantly ubiquitous pale green nurse's scrub. Her black pants were sufficiently generic she didn't need to change those.

It was time to blend into the Dallas nightlife.

The Golden Lying Club had a long line outside. Tough-looking bouncers in sleeveless T-shirts, their arms crossed over muscular chests, guarded the club from the *hoi polloi* and did their best to convey the message that Golden Lying was exclusively for the beautiful people of Dallas.

Danielle pushed forward. "Some of my friends were going to club here tonight," she told one of the door guards.

"Yeah? Your friend have a name?"

He sounded suspicious, but not too suspicious. Danielle noticed that many of those kept waiting outside were unattractive, and some of the attractive ones looked suspiciously like they were being paid to make the club look popular. They even had coolers and portable sound systems to entertain themselves.

The best looking were whisked inside without much of a wait at all. Which meant the bouncer's suspicion said she might not be one of the beautiful people they were trying to appeal to.

Not that she cared what some brainless, muscle-bound bouncer thought about her.

"Her name is Theresa Ortez," she said. Theresa had said the gang would arrive around ten. It was only nine now. Danielle hoped that she would be gone before anyone she recognized showed up.

"Oh. Yeah." The bouncer's voice shifted into a friendly tone. "Theresa hangs out here a lot. Wouldn't mind going home with her myself, but she seems more interested in lawyers and such. Don't know what the appeal is there."

Yeah, Danielle managed to keep herself from blurting out her sarcasm. Why would a woman be interested in a man with a decent job and a brain?

"How about I suggest to her that she doesn't have to look past the front door," Danielle said, flashing what she hoped was a flirtatious grin.

"Hey." A huge smile lit the bouncer's face making him look like an overanxious boy rather than the scary man he pretended to be. "Would you really do that? Cool. I mean, she's always like butter wouldn't melt. I mean, I'm intimidated. Afraid to talk to her, even."

Danielle suppressed a momentary feeling of guilt. If she ever ran into Therese again, she really would mention the bouncer. Who knew, maybe the two of them could make magic together. Anyone would be better than Joe Smealy.

"I'll see what I can do," she agreed.

"Cool. Uh, do you mind a word of warning?"

She gazed at the bouncer trying to put a load of trust into her eyes. "Is there a problem?"

"Seriously! The managers are trying to cover it up, but we've been having problems with drugs."

Big surprise. The whole world had problems with drugs. The return of magic had only created a new category of drugs that relied on formerly unknown chemicals like elf-blood, vampire heart, and even more disgusting things.

"I'll stay clear."

The bouncer shuffled uncomfortably. "That's the problem, lady. Because the thing is, some of our patrons are drugging the others instead of just themselves. They seem to go after women. Know what I mean?"

She knew exactly what he meant. Predators weren't limited to the magical. "I'll be careful."

"Don't touch a drink anyone offers you," he urged. "Don't let them get near enough to your drink to put something in it. And, uh, don't forget to tell Theresa about me."

She patted him on his shaved head. "No guarantees, big guy, but I'll see what I can do."

The club interior was a disappointment.

Music crashed from speakers embedded in the walls and ancient disco balls flung glitters of light through the otherwise dimly lit bar.

Nooks and semi-detached rooms veered away from the dance floor.

The dance floor itself was surrounded by tables, each home to a small gang of nattily dressed Dallas women, busy entertaining one another with cutting remarks about the dancers and the women at other tables, nursing drinks, and pretending not to notice the men.

Further out, lining the walls, single men lounged hungrily, occasionally making their moves when one of the women became separated from her group.

Danielle became one of those few separated women as she made her way to one of the many bars scattered around the club.

Unlike women, who thrived in packs, the men were solitary hunters. The women chatted continually, while men made occasional grunts as they jockeyed for position, squeezing back the less male, the less formidable, the unsuccessful. Losers retreated into womanless side rooms where the unfortunate and unhappy belted down drinks in an effort to regain their confidence before heading back to the battle.

Occasionally a desperate or criminally ignorant male made a rush at one of the tables, grabbing an empty chair if there was one, or simply crouching down near the women.

Anyone could see that this ploy would be unsuccessful, and it always was. The women would have to see their co-workers the next day. Anyone who let herself be picked up too quickly, without too much alcohol in her system, would be marked as easy, a failure.

Still, the men lined up--and were shot down.

Danielle caught the bartender's attention and ordered a tequila sunrise.

It wasn't her favorite drink. In fact, alcohol was low on Danielle's list of vices. The late-night raids at the Warder Academy weeded out those who enjoyed alcohol too much. But her purposes weren't to get drunk. She was intent on finding a lair--someplace she could escape the hunt she knew would be launched after her. The drink was protective coloration.

The bartender brought her drink, and moments later, another.

"I didn't order that."

"Gentleman sent it to you." The bartender hitched a shoulder in the direction of a blond male who looked like he might have been captain of the SMU crew team a few years earlier but who was gradually letting his physique deteriorate.

He was probably younger than Carl, Danielle realized. But he lacked the male presence that made Carl stand out in a crowd.

She gave her SMU jock a smile.

He gave a hard elbow nudge to the man standing next to him and strutted over to Danielle.

"Haven't seen you here before," he remarked. That remark had to be the soul of originality.

"My girlfriends will be getting here later."

"But why wait to party?"

She could have given him any number of reasons, starting with the fact that he wouldn't be on the top half of her party list. Instead, she nodded. "I guess."

"You from around here?"

"Los Angeles," she told him, mostly truthfully.

His eyes lit up. "From out of town, are you? Well, us Texas men have an obligation to take care of beautiful women from out of state. Make sure they have a good time."

He was after a good time all right, but Danielle didn't think he would care much whether she had one.

"That's awful generous of you."

"Any red-blooded Texas male would do the same. Uh, how about another drink?"

He leaned forward, brushing his hand across the top of her glass as if gesturing at it. He was smooth. In the dusky light of the club, the trace of powder remaining at the top of the cocktail would have been invisible to someone not expecting it, not looking for it.

"I'm all right," she told him. "Two drinks and I'll be flying high."

"No problem. Unlimited ceiling here."

She gave him points for that one--it was at least a little clever.

"Well, drink up." He took a swig at his beer.

Danielle raised the doctored drink to her lips, pretended to swallow, then put it down.

"Was that your friend over there?"

"Where?"

She gestured and, when he looked away for a moment, switched to the undoctored drink.

"He's just a guy I met," the blond told her.

Danielle didn't think so. Guys who were looking for a clean pickup didn't make buddies at the bar. These two were fishing together and she was their catch.

"I'm, uh, Leslie."

"Jeff," the blond replied.

Danielle took a deep swallow. "So, you want to dance?"

"Sure. Better drink up first, though. That bartender will probably scoop up your glass when you step away."

She took a swallow, then wobbled to her feet.

"I feel a little funny. Maybe we could just--"

"It's okay, honey. I'll take good care of you."

The man Jeff had dismissed as "just a guy" appeared and the two men draped Danielle's arms around their necks and headed for the exit. Exactly as if she was a friend who'd drunk too much.

"You were right, that was easy," the second man said.

"We're not home yet," Jeff murmured.

They headed for a fire door, avoiding the bouncers lined up outside the front.

A sign indicated that an alarm would sound if the door was opened. The sign lied.

The two men had an unmarked white van parked just outside the club in an alley. They bundled Danielle in, letting her collapse onto the carpeted back. So far so good. Now get a move on, she mentally commanded. She hoped that their base was far from downtown.

"Are you sure you want to go through with this?" the second man asked, the truck's cargo door still open in his hand. "We never had to drug one before."

"Are you kidding, Fred? Check her out. None of the chicks we picked up had half the looks of this one. You see her chest? Those have to be D cups. With her in the video, we'll make a fortune."

"Well, I guess."

The two men climbed into the cab leaving Danielle sprawled across the back.

She faked unconsciousness as the two men drove her away from danger. She might be heading into more danger, of course. They'd spoken of a video. Which could mean more men. Possibly men with weapons. Still, what choice did she have? Staying with these men was a risk. Waiting around for the Warders to catch up to her was no risk at all--it was guaranteed disaster.

The men drove north, away from the dubious safety of the zone and toward the Dallas suburbs that had been showcases of wealth at the turn of the twenty-first century when telecom had been the future and Dallas had been the Telecom Corridor. Despite the economic depression that the return of magic had created, the north still held traces of the glamour of that lost era.

The men turned their radio to a call-in show that seemed targeted directly at them. The D.J. laughed uproariously at his own jokes, which lampooned stupid magics and slutty women.

A few minutes into the show, a public service announcement described Danielle as wanted for impersonating a Warder. The description was accurate, but it didn't match her current appearance. Oddly, she felt safer being taken to an unknown destination. If it was unknown to her, it would be unknown to the Warders as well. All of their profiling technology would be worthless.

The van shifted off the freeway onto a side street.

Once, the City of Plano had been home to broad boulevards, endless green lawns, shopping malls, and miles of luxury SUVs. Now, the kidnappers' van lurched over swelling potholes and veered around vehicles that had been abandoned in the road and were too much trouble for the city to tow away.

Until she'd met Carl, Danielle had believed that the economic depression of the past decade was a side effect of the huge costs imposed on normal society by the maintenance of the zones and protection of the normals.

Her experience with Carl, first watching him transform the zone, and then watching the riots, had eliminated her certainty. Was the myth of magical responsibility for bad economic times just another of the lies that perpetuated the Warder system?

* * *

"Cuff her and carry her," Jeff commanded.

Fred jingled an old-fashioned pair of handcuffs and opened the back door to the van. They'd parked in a garage and quickly lowered the automatic garage door.

Danielle considered letting Fred cuff her so that she could enter the building without suspicion but decided against it. Regardless of how flimsy the handcuffs might be, they would slow her down, especially if he was smart enough to cuff her hands behind her back. The delay wasn't worth the risk.

As Fred opened the door, she reached for his groin. Reached, grabbed, and pulled.

Fred's high-pitched screech cut off abruptly when she brought her free hand up and put a finger to her lips. "Quiet."

"What--"

"I say, you do. Understand?" She gave Fred a bonus squeeze to make sure he was paying attention.

He nodded abruptly.

"How many men in the house?" Squeeze.

"Two more." He looked pained enough to be telling the truth.

"Fred. What's the holdup? Come on, we've got a movie to film. I'm hot to get started if you know what I mean."

"Tell him you're coming."

"Coming, Jeff," Fred parroted.

"Hey, what's going on back there?"

Danielle didn't know whether Fred had signaled or Jeff just got suspicious, and she didn't wait around to figure it out. She yanked hard on Fred's scrotum and slammed a ridge-hand into his temple. He folded, giving her the opportunity to seize the handcuffs and cuff his hands. He had the keys somewhere--she wasn't about to search his pockets for them--but she didn't think he would be able to get free in time to be much help.

She'd just finished with Fred when Jeff rounded the van. He carried a police-style truncheon and, when he saw her rising from the semi-conscious Fred, he swung it at her awkwardly, like a baseball batter.

If he'd turned and run, Jeff might have been able to warn the others. Well, Danielle hadn't picked him for intelligence.

She stepped outside his reach and gave his arm just a little extra momentum and a slight angle change--driving the club directly into his kneecap.

Jeff joined Fred on the floor. Danielle picked up the short club, judged its balance, and applied it to the back of his head. Good stick. She'd keep it.

The entire operation had barely taken fifty seconds. Just enough time for the men inside to start to worry why Fred and Jeff hadn't appeared.

Danielle tested the connecting door between the garage and the main portion of the building. Locked.

She launched a turning back kick into the door directly to the left of the latch.

The builders had obviously counted on the heavy garage door for security because they'd used a cheap hollow interior door here. The flimsy wood shattered under Danielle's kick.

She let her body spin through the kick and charged through the disintegrating portal.

The building was a three-story colonial-style brick monstrosity. It had probably been built as a Mc-mansion for one of the Dot-Com executives of turn-of-the-century Dallas. Repossessed by a bank and left empty, it had now been converted into a crude video studio.

She found the two men Fred had told her about sitting in a maze of computers, flat screen video monitors lining the walls. Images of naked and bound women writhed all too convincingly on several of the screens.

One of the men reached for a gun when she stepped into the video room.

He moved so slowly, she didn't even have to use the blur as she brushed Jeff's club against his hand and the gun, then caught the automatic pistol as it flew from his forcibly relaxed grip.

"Freeze, assholes," she ordered.

"Jeez. What the heck did those losers bring home this time? Wonder Woman?" the second man, the one with his hands high in the air, demanded.

"Warder Agent Goodman. You're under arrest," she stated. She flashed her I.D. card in their direction, then returned it to her pocket before they could get a good look.

"Hey, we heard about you on the web. You're wanted for impersonating an officer. Terrible description, though. They didn't say anything about purple hair. Or those big breasts. Gotta give Jeff credit for spotting those honkers."

It was unfortunate that they recognized her, but there wasn't anything she could do about that. She'd just improvise.

"All right, you two. Lead the way out to the garage. You're going to carry in Fred and Jeff. Then we're all going to sit down and talk about what happens next."

"Just forget about ever seeing us and we'll make it worth your while," the man who'd gone for his gun offered.

"Shut up, Harry," the other man ordered. "She may be a warder, but she's on the run. She isn't going to turn us in."

"Hey, great," Harry started. "Why don't we--"

"She might kill us, though."

"Oh." Harry thought about that. "Not so great."

The other man shook his head then turned his attention back to Danielle. "I'm guessing you're looking for a safe house, right? Someplace to lay low until the heat lets up."

Danielle glared at him. "I'd worry more about yourself than about me."

"I'm worried, all right. Because I figure the only thing keeping us alive right now is that you'd rather avoid the stink of four rotting bodies."

Harry started to laugh, took a good look at Danielle's face. He froze. "You serious?"

"Would you want the four of us hanging around with you if you were trying to hide?"

Sweat beaded on Harry's face. He turned a pale shade of green, turned, and quietly vomited in the corner.

"Don't mess on the equipment," the second man ordered.

"Shit, Simon. We're going to die and you're worried about a lousy camera."

"Everybody's going to die someday. We just need to find a way to convince the warder that she'd be better off letting us live for a while, and then convincing her to keep letting us live once she leaves."

"And you can start by doing what I tell you," Danielle ordered. "Now get out to the garage and carry in Fred and Jeff before they wake up. Because any trouble they cause is going to be big trouble for you two."

"Right, boss," Simon said.

Fred was struggling a little when they made it out to the garage but he hadn't dislodged Jeff's unconscious form.

"Simon, you carry Jeff. Harry, get Fred."

Harry whined something about his sore arm but stopped complaining when Danielle chambered a bullet in the gun she'd taken from him. Danielle didn't especially want to kill these men. On the other

163

hand, she wouldn't feel any terrible guilt about it if they pushed too hard. Even if she was the first woman they'd actually tried to drug, they'd been ready to drug, rape, and film their disgusting activities. Their business sickened her.

With her encouragement, Harry and Simon carried their semiconscious counterparts back into the house.

What had once been a living room had been converted into a bedroom-appearing movie set, a huge bed set out in the middle of the room. Three cameras surrounded the bed allowing for explicit angles in whatever perverse sexual behavior they might decide to perpetrate.

Danielle gestured toward that bed and Harry and Simon dumped Fred and Jeff.

"Sit on the floor," she ordered the two carriers.

They complied, letting Danielle find a comfortable chair for herself.

"Now let's talk about the next couple of days," she suggested. "I'm looking for a reason to keep the four of you alive. But I'm coming up empty. Anybody have a suggestion?"

Harry started off indignant. "You can't just kill us. I mean, it would be murder. It isn't as if we've done anything to you."

Danielle laughed. "You're a funny man, Harry." She paused. "The problem is, I don't have a very good sense of humor. I'm a warder. I kill for a living."

"But …" he stumbled for the word, then repeated it. "But you're only supposed to kill the impaired."

"Shut up, Harry. You're going to make her mad." Simon lounged against the bed, but he kept his eyes focused on Danielle.

"I'm already plenty mad," Danielle observed. "Your nasty business of drugging women, dragging them back here, raping them and then what, killing them? It sickens me."

"We don't kill anybody," Simon said. "And you're the first one Jeff actually drugged, if he drugged you at all."

"Snuff video pays more than rape," Harry observed. "Jeff wanted us to do them. But we, well, I mean, that is beyond gross, don't you think? Besides, you have to be careful who you sell them to."

Of the two men, Simon was the more intelligent and more dangerous. But Harry was the more annoying.

"Harry, if you want to get yourself killed, that's all right with me," Simon observed. "Try not to make her kill the rest of us, though, will you?"

"I'm still looking for a reason to keep you alive," Danielle told Simon. "So far, your friend has only given me more reasons to kill you.

Your turn."

She could almost see the wheels turning in Simon's mind. If they could somehow turn her in, they might get whatever reward the warders offered. Danielle doubted that the warders would shut down their studio. Even if they did, the four men could simply set up business elsewhere.

"You're going to need food, changes of clothing, maybe a false identity," Simon said. "We've got money and contacts. We can help."

"Go on."

Simon considered. Sweat trickled down his forehead.

Danielle guessed he'd had contact with warders before. If so, he would know that their training drove out all moral compunction about killing.

"I am a graduate of the Warder Academy," she mentioned casually.

Simon shuddered and even Harry seemed to sit up and take notice. The Academy trained the elite of the warders. Its four-year post-college program was featured on multiple entertainment webs that focused on how academy students were brutalized and transformed into killing machines.

The Academy's reputation served to make its graduates more fearsome, but the reputation also reflected the truth. No one graduated without a confirmed kill to her name.

"We can write full confessions," Simon suggested. "Detailing what we've done."

"Why would I care?"

"It makes you safe from us. If we turn you in, you'll be able to get us back. They wouldn't ignore written confessions."

"She's just trying to trick you into confessing," Harry protested. "She doesn't have anything on us."

"If you don't shut up, I'm going to kill you myself," Simon said. "She doesn't need evidence. She's a warder."

Danielle stood up, yanked a stack of paper from a printer, and tossed it to Simon. "Start writing."

Simon grabbed the paper and pen from the air. It was a smooth catch. So smooth that Danielle raised him another notch in her risk meter.

"What about after?" Harry demanded as Simon bent over his paper and started to write.

"I thought I told you to shut up!"

"Afterwards, I turn in your confessions, of course," Danielle explained.

"But--"

"That's it, Harry. Shut your goddamned mouth." Simon let anger creep into the cool tone of his voice. "Think about it. This place is finished. When she leaves, we leave. She wouldn't have to turn in our confessions if she killed us, right?"

"But what will we do?"

"We find someplace else, some other line of work. The thing is, we'll be alive."

* * *

For three days, the city of Dallas suffered from door-to-door searches, roadblocks, and heavily armed patrols. Best of all, there were no new incursions into the zone. Danielle's disappearance, or maybe the friendly rearrangements she'd made in the work assignments, seemed to have unnerved the local warders.

Eventually, Danielle knew, pursuit would stretch all the way to Plano. But the ever-widening circles meant that the search would become less intense and the searchers would grow increasingly discouraged. It gave her a chance.

Harry and Jeff spent most of their time in the room where Danielle locked them every night. Simon, on the other hand, trailed behind her with his video camera.

She drew the line at his filming her asleep, in the shower, or dressing, but otherwise allowed him to amuse himself. She didn't trust the pornographers, wouldn't trust Simon out of her sight. Still, if following her around with his video camera amused him, it was better than worrying about what he was up to.

She retreated into the routine of martial arts, trying to fuse what Carl had shown her into her own style.

After three consecutive meals of delivered pizza, Fred announced that he was sick of it and that he would cook them real food.

Danielle had gritted her teeth but she knew that if she let them have some activities and outlets, they were less likely to turn on her. She was pleasantly surprised when Fred showed an unexpected talent for cooking and brought out meals that would have made any restaurant proud.

"You know you'll have to change jobs once I leave," she told them as they sat down for one of Fred's masterpieces. "I won't let you go back to that nasty business of yours."

"But you've got a suggestion," Simon observed.

"Not for all of you," she admitted. "For Fred. He could be a chef. This is incredible." She poked at the fluffy pastry that Fred had whipped up.

"Oh yeah. Sure. Who would hire me?" Fred demanded. "They're all looking for people who went to one of those fancy schools. I just read books and experiment."

Once, that wouldn't have mattered. But after the Return, society had retreated behind increasingly rigid rules--rules that were supposed to protect, but that often kept people from finding a job or business that suited them.

Something flashed in her brain. It was one of those ah-ha moments that seem to change everything. "You're right," she admitted. "Anywhere normal, you're just another criminal."

"Just what I said."

"In the zone, though, nobody cares about those rules."

All four men jerked in their seats as if she'd electrocuted them. "The zone? That's for the impaired."

Danielle's sense of excitement swelled. This was the biggest idea she'd ever had. What if the zone wasn't only for the impaired? What if the zone could be the real world, relegating the portion of the country controlled by the so-called normals to irrelevance?

"The zone is where it's happening," she explained, her voice rising slightly as she thought things through. "The rest of the country is dead-end. I mean, look at this neighborhood. It used to be classy but now it's junk. In the zone, you get ahead by who you are. Nobody cares if you have a credential. They don't care if you're a dwarf with two heads."

Simon's gaze bore through her, but she could see the ideas percolating through his brain.

"I never thought of the zone," he admitted.

Chapter 14

In the end, the thought of the zone was too much for Harry and Jeff. Danielle, Fred, and Simon smashed the phones, left the two others tied up, and headed out with Danielle driving the white van she'd arrived in a few days earlier.

Danielle posted the confessions to the local Warder office—via snail mail--and then headed south and east. With mail service as poor as it was any more, Harry and Jeff would have plenty of time to work themselves free and find someplace to change their lives. She thought she'd cured them of any interest in drugging innocent women.

Unlike Los Angeles, which sprawled in every direction not closed off by the ocean, Dallas had grown mostly to the north and west. With the return of magic, Dallas swelled with refugees from the lost cities of Houston and San Antonio. But it had shrunk in its physical reach. A medieval urge for the protection that comes from being surrounded by others had taken seat.

The old towns and highways to the east of Dallas were largely deserted. Occasionally they passed a pickup truck or an aging sedan. Once in a while, they drove past a house with the flash of television in the window and electrical lighting reflecting off iron bars.

Mostly, though, they drove through darkness.

"Used to be we couldn't even see the stars," Fred observed. "The city lights blinded them out."

There was still a glow from the city. But it wasn't as bright as in Danielle's childhood memories from before the return. Storefront lights were mostly dimmed now. Streetlights had been shot out and not replaced.

"That's a good thing," Simon observed. "Too much light and it'd be hard to get into the zone."

Danielle shook her head. There might not be as much electricity as there had been in the old days, but there was plenty to run the searchlights for warders patrolling the zone.

"We'll abandon the van here," she told them. "Jeff and Harry will be free by now. I'm betting that Jeff will call the warders within two minutes of getting his hands free."

Simon laughed. "He's too stupid to know they'll lock him up. You know the really funny thing, though?"

"What?"

"He didn't have to drug chicks. He's so good looking he could always get someone to volunteer. It's not like many people have good options these days. But he flipped when he saw you. And he figured he couldn't have you without cheating."

"Women wanted him?"

Simon rolled his eyes. "None of the guys I know could understand it. We figured it was a woman thing."

Danielle didn't remind him that he'd been Jeff's partner. She'd let both of the men know what she expected of them once they'd reached the zone--what would happen if they even thought about playing their evil games in the future. She had a lot to be forgiven for herself and couldn't help believing in a second chance. But one second chance was all these guys had coming.

They parked behind an abandoned gas station. Danielle hesitated, then left the keys in the van. It was a calculated risk, but she decided to hope a professional thief would take it and obscure its identity before the warders turned it up and used its location as a clue to finding them.

They set off on foot, traversing the five-mile no-man's land between normals and the zone.

Without conscious choice, Danielle had approached the zone from the same angle that the Tiger elf clan had tried to make their escape.

As she and the men crept closer, she began to see evidence of that failed breakout.

The first bodies they saw were elf women. More graceful and smaller than the men, the women could move more silently, more carefully. They would also have been less likely to stand and fight.

So they'd gotten farther. In fact, many had made it past the usual warder barriers. Her warning to Joe had let the warders deepen their lines. If she'd simply kept her mouth shut, these women would be alive and free.

Instead, their rotting bodies lay where they'd been shot.

"I think I'm going to be sick." Fred's face turned so pale it almost glowed.

"Pull it together," she insisted.

Simon looked as worried as Fred, but he said nothing.

Some of the killing had been done from the infamous warder helicopters. Even after a week, the foliage was still in ruins from the high-powered machine gun fire from those gunships. The helicopters hadn't created all of the destruction, though. Several bodies had telltale powder burns surrounding small holes on their foreheads--they had been finished off by warders going through the area and making sure that no escapee remained alive.

"Are you sure this is a good idea?" Fred demanded. "I'm starting to have second thoughts about the zone."

"Nobody tries to get into the zone," Danielle reminded them. "The warders will be looking the other way."

She hoped. Unless they were still on alert, looking for her to return to the zone after her aborted visit to Warder Regional Headquarters.

Simon had been walking the point. Now he held up a hand in warning.

Someone was coming.

Fred froze.

She'd trained the two in this, at least. The human eye can detect movement where it can see nothing else. Fred wouldn't move until she told him to, or until he panicked and ran. Which would get all of them killed. It was the chance she'd taken when she'd agreed to take them into the zone.

She waited, but Simon didn't give the all clear.

That was bad. Very bad.

She clicked into blur mode and crept forward, making each move so swift that she would appear simply to be in a different position rather than moving between them.

The blur heightened all of her senses.

Simon's breath sounded like a nearby train engine. Beyond him, the roar of millions of cicadas, crickets, and mosquitoes filled the air.

But human-made sounds are distinctive and her trained senses sorted out the noise made by at least two moving humans.

They moved more carefully than any normal human. Without her enhanced senses, even Danielle wouldn't have picked them up. That Simon had was pure luck.

For an irrational second, Danielle let herself imagine that they might be survivors of the massacre--two elves creeping around, still looking for some way to escape.

And maybe it's the tooth fairy, she told herself sternly. She knew perfectly well who else could walk so softly. Warders.

* * *

Against two warders, Simon and Fred could only handicap her, distract her attention.

As she passed him, she signaled to Simon to remain in place. This was her fight.

A one-against-two battle was not especially difficult for a trained warrior. Unless the two have trained together, they are likely to get in each other's way. A skilled fighter divides and conquers.

Warders, though, were trained to fight in teams. And a trained team could defeat a single warrior, even if that fighter was more skilled.

Like her, the two hunters disdained any artificial light, relying on their enhanced senses to see through the dark.

"There's nobody here." An untrained ear wouldn't have even heard the sound of that voice. To Danielle, it cracked like thunder.

"The sensors say there is."

Danielle fought a brief sense of vertigo. She knew the second voice.

Mary had mentioned that Sergeant Mansfield would be coming to Dallas, but Danielle hadn't even considered the possibility of running into her. Mansfield, the woman responsible for training the warders in both blur and unarmed conflict, could eat Danielle for lunch.

"Probably three big dogs," the first voice argued.

"She's here," Mansfield stated with the certainty that only years of hunting can give. "Close."

From the changing angle of the voices, they were heading straight for Fred and Simon and would pass within ten feet of Danielle.

If she'd been alone, Danielle thought she could get past them. Mansfield was good, though, and it could have gone either way. With untrained men to protect, Danielle didn't have the option of simply fading into the bush. Unless she wanted to abandon Fred and Simon. But she'd abandoned too many already. She wasn't going to leave any more behind her.

Besides, the guys were important if her idea for the zone was going to work. With his cooking skills, Fred could help make the zone more of an attraction to tourists from the normal side of the line. Tourists who could see the promise of the zone and compare it to the hopelessness of the normal side of the line.

Simon, with his video talent, could help communicate the message of their new zone throughout the world-- to other zones and to normals.

Even more importantly, the two would be wonderful examples of how people with ability, even if non-magical, could prosper in the zone. They would serve as a beacon of hope to those who, stuck on the normal side of the line, had given into despair.

Of course, Danielle knew she'd work just as hard to keep no-talents like Jeff and Harry alive. Go figure.

A sense of anticipation froze her.

It was the oldest trick in the book, but the snick of a shell being chambered almost made her start.

"Stay alert. I sense her," Mansfield hardly breathed the words.

"You're crazy," the male voice replied.

Danielle could see them now. Mansfield's solid form, almost as wide across as it was tall, took the lead. Behind her walked a massive, almost troll-like, man. Mansfield carried a large-caliber shotgun: the man, an assault rifle.

"Call for a chopper," Mansfield ordered. "We've got her."

They were past her now, almost to where she'd left Simon.

Danielle let her trained reflexes take over, allowing her brain to watch rather than direct.

She bent, picked up a rock, closed the distance, and slammed the rock into the male warder's helmet before he was aware that he was under attack.

She wasn't sure she had done it quickly enough to head off his call to the helicopter, so she knew she needed to keep going, to take on Mansfield.

The instant she'd connected with the man's helmet, Danielle had rolled away, intent on avoiding the shot she was sure would follow the hollow sound of her rock striking the helmet.

The air displaced by the solid slugs was almost a punch.

"Got him, did you? That sucker won't be a loss to the warders."

Mansfield had vanished into the high grass that marked the return of prairie to this part of what had once been the second-largest city in Texas.

"I'm not interested in fighting," Danielle said. "I'm just heading back to the zone."

"And I'm just here to stop you," Mansfield said. "There'll be a hundred warders in the area within fifteen minutes. You don't seriously think you can finish me off before then, do you?"

Danielle kept quiet.

She was still holding the remains of the rock she'd broken on the warder's head. Now she threw it to an angle of where Mansfield's voice had come from.

Mansfield only laughed. "You didn't think I'd fall for the old shoot at a rock trick, did you?

The woman was good. Damned good. But was she as good as she thought she was? Danielle wasn't sure, but she knew she had to find out.

She circled around, counting off the seconds. Mansfield had been lying about the fifteen minutes. Even if Danielle had headed off the male warder's call, Mansfield would have called in her own helicopters. Danielle had five minutes at most.

She almost stumbled over something soft and yielding.

A stench reached her sensitized nerves like a shout. The distinctive smell of rotting corpse.

Recalling Arenesol's penchant for dynamite, she steeled her senses and reached for the corpse.

No dynamite. The elf had been a teenager and looked more normal than magical. She'd probably been a child when the return hit and moved to the zone with her parents. If her ears had been pointed at all, that, like so much else, had faded with a week of decomposition.

The only weapon the girl had carried was a light silver sword.

A sword was the kind of impractical statement that children like to make, but it was better than another rock.

Danielle picked it up. Things would have been easier if her nightstick hadn't dented Harry's pistol barrel. But she hadn't planned on fighting her way back to the zone. She'd hoped this part of the journey would be a walk in the park.

She didn't think she'd made a sound as she unsheathed the small sword, but she must have been wrong. A spread of shot whistled over her head where she bent over the corpse; a single silver slug ripped away a tuft of her hair.

Well, she'd never been a fashion plate anyway.

Mansfield's conceit in using an old fashioned shotgun was Danielle's only advantage now. She had already closed half the distance before she heard the weapon's action as Mansfield chambered a new shell.

Her sword met the shotgun just as Mansfield pulled the trigger, Danielle's weight deflecting the aim and the sharp blade embedding itself in the barrel.

Mansfield swore, then threw the ruined gun away, the sword still stuck to it. "Just you and me, kid. In another minute, it'll be just me."

Danielle hadn't been on blur for long, but she hadn't had much sleep for the past week and that weakened her. She felt the burr begin to ebb away.

With it, she had a small chance against the Sergeant. Without it, she knew she'd be outclassed by the woman who'd taught the Academy instructors most of what they knew.

Mansfield must have caught her look of dismay. "You had potential, kid. You're throwing it all away."

Danielle re-engaged the blur just in time to block a flurry of kicks and punches. But Mansfield pressed in too quickly to give Danielle a chance to counter.

Only one blow got through Danielle's guard, a hard fist to her floating ribs, but that punch ached and sucked energy from her system.

Desperately, she remembered what Carl had done to her when they'd fought. It had only been a week earlier, but already it seemed to be another life. Carl didn't have the blur, but he had his *Were* abilities. Very soon, Danielle would have neither. Still, she didn't think Mansfield would have faced the set of moves that Carl had put on her.

As her blur blinked out, she stepped back and tried to remember, to emulate, the way Carl had moved into the small circle kung fu/t'ai chi that had defeated her.

"Straight lines, Goodman," the sergeant instructed as if they were in a classroom. "That fancy stuff is fine for forms, but it isn't fighting."

Danielle hoped Mansfield believed that. Danielle had certainly believed it until Carl worked his moves against her. But Carl was a master. She'd had only had a week to integrate them into her own system. And a week wasn't long.

Mansfield seemed impossibly fast, shifting from stance to stance without seeming to move in between. She phased in and out of the blur, preserving her energies when she didn't need it. That was something else for Danielle to integrate into her own arts--assuming she survived this fight. Mansfield definitely hadn't taught this lesson to her fellow warders and Danielle hadn't even known it was possible. People like Mansfield were always aware that their students may some day be their rivals.

Danielle guessed she should feel complimented that Mansfield thought she was worthy of using her secret weapon. She decided she could do with one fewer compliment.

She kept her hands in motion, knowing that she wouldn't have time for conscious reaction. She had to rely on her training, her skills, and her instincts.

It wasn't a good time to remember that Carl had fought her off with these techniques, but he hadn't beaten her until her own blur had faded. She couldn't fight defensively, waiting for Mansfield to lose her blur. The area would be crawling with warders before then.

Mansfield landed a hard shot to Danielle's calf--a fraction of a second after Danielle lifted her leg. Without that instinctual move, she would have lost her knee and the fight.

"You've learned something, but not enough," Mansfield told her. "Too bad."

For the first time since she'd lost her sword, Danielle went on the attack.

Mansfield didn't even bother trying to decipher her feints and real attacks. She blocked everything, relying on the blur to speed her wherever she needed to be.

After the first few seconds, Danielle knew her attack was pointless. Still, she pressed on for a full twenty seconds sucking every reserve of energy she could find in her body. She wouldn't surrender, wouldn't let them capture her without giving everything she had to the fight.

Mansfield blocked Danielle's last kick--a spinning roundhouse that she knew was too slow before she launched it.

"I guess that's about it, then, Goodman."

If Danielle couldn't escape, at least she could let Simon and Fred try to get past the warder. "I'll keep her busy!" she shouted. "You two keep moving toward the zone."

"We can help you," Simon answered.

"Trust me, you can't."

"Come on, Simon. Let's do what she says before we get killed."

Fred and Simon weren't the hero types, fortunately. She heard the loud tramp of their footsteps as the two men circled around the two warders and headed west, toward the zone.

Mansfield's eyes widened. "You're helping impaired escape?"

"They're not impaired, they're normals. And the only thing they're trying to escape is the world you warders have created."

She knew Mansfield understood her words. It was equally obvious that the Sergeant didn't have a clue what she meant.

"You hate the impaired," Mansfield reminded her, spitting out the word with contempt. "Why would you want to expose any normal to that perversion?"

Could she hope to explain, to persuade Mansfield that she was fighting on the wrong side of the biggest battle of the century? Danielle didn't think so, but talking was better than getting killed. Every second she gained meant that the boys were a step closer to safety.

"I thought my step-father killed my mother because he was a vampire. But it wasn't the vampire, it was the man who was evil. When I lived in the zone, I learned that they were just people, some good, some bad. Same as normals. The only thing is, I decided I wanted to be one of the good ones."

"Damn. That *Were* seduced you, didn't he."

Danielle tried to suppress the smile. It hadn't been Carl who'd done the seduction. She had wanted it, insisted on it.

She obviously didn't suppress it enough for Mansfield.

"Perversion."

The Sergeant launched herself at Danielle, her arms outstretched in a completely inartistic attack.

Danielle's arms went automatically into one of Carl's circular blocks, one hand pushing Mansfield's attack off and the other, morphing from block to attack, slamming a palm thrust into the older woman's ribs.

Mansfield blinked out of the blur and glared at Danielle, surprise written over her face.

Danielle blurred and followed up, hammering elbows, fists, and chops into the Sergeant until the older woman collapsed.

"Guess you learned something after all," Mansfield said. She leaned against a tree, her fight, at least temporarily, gone. "Too late, though. Listen."

The turbine roar of warder black helicopters shook the sky.

Danielle took off running.

She angled away from the path that Simon and Fred would have taken, hoping that the warders would be confused by multiple infrared signals.

She was only a couple of miles away from the zone. Close, but way too far. Even in blur, it would take precious minutes to cover the distance. And blur would make her stand out like an infrared beacon to the warders manning the huge choppers that circled overhead.

Although her instincts told her to run, to cover whatever distance she could, she slowed to a deliberate pace, trying to send the message that she was a natural inhabitant. A deer, maybe, or a feral dog, or even one of the wild pigs that had once ranged only in east Texas but that now covered greater territory as the rains increased and as humans withdrew more tightly into their cities.

She splashed through a creek, climbed the limestone cliff on the other side, and looked down into the zone.

It was so close, she could almost touch it.

In the distance, she caught sight of two figures nearing thick strands of barbed wire. She hoped it was Simon and Fred, although it was too far to see.

Three hulking gunships, machineguns jutting from their ugly frames, floated between herself and the questionable safety of the zone.

As she watched, one of them veered from the circular pattern the others followed and headed directly for her.

Danielle scrambled back down the stream bank in a shower of limestone.

The warm water circled around her legs. It wasn't too deep. While Texas was wet relative to what it had been before the return of magic, it still lacked the huge rivers and lakes of most other states. It was enough, though. When she lay down, it was deep enough to fully submerge her.

She let herself float with the current, away from searching

helicopters. Away from the zone as well, but there wasn't a lot she could do about that. With a great deal of luck, the warm water would distort her infrared signature, make her invisible to the technologies that the warders would throw against her.

* * *

Danielle had floated for miles during the night, sometimes paddling along, occasionally holding her breath and plunging to the bottom of the stream as warder choppers circled overhead. Once in a while, the water shallowed and she'd had to walk. Only once, the stream crashed over a fall, taking her with it. She'd barely missed bashing her brains out on that one, but she'd survived with nothing worse than a few abrasions.

With daybreak, she left the stream.

She was out in the country now. Pine forest encroached on the tall-grass prairies of central Texas and provided cover.

She was desperately hungry, but she knew better than to try to raid one of the few farmhouses that formed the outposts of humanity's losing battle against the growth of chaos.

Warder training concentrated on staying alive when vampires or trolls tried to kill you. Wilderness survival wasn't even on the curriculum. So, while Danielle knew that it was safe to eat some bugs and plants, she didn't have a clue which ones.

Instead, she sucked it up, promising herself that she would get Fred to whip up something special when she made it back to the zone, and reminding herself that she needed to live long enough to get it.

She stayed off the roads, cutting across country and using trails that might have been left by neighborhood children, by game, or even by long-vanished Texas Indians, wiped out by the encroachments of the Anglo settlers.

Occasional abandoned farmhouses stood out like rotting teeth. Not all of this was the result of the return and global warming, of course. Increased farming efficiency and genetically modified crops had reduced the world's need for farmland. Still, Danielle couldn't help thinking about the elves who had tried to flee the Dallas zone. This was the kind of country they would have dreamed of finding, its pine forests providing sanctuary and its black soil rich harvests. Instead, the elves lay rotting outside the zone and the abandoned farms continued to disintegrate back into wilderness.

She left the streambed behind her, reasoning that the warders would recognize that she had used it for escape and would eventually send trackers along its length.

It took her only a couple of hours to retrace the miles that the creek had carried her during the night.

She holed up in an abandoned Washateria, the carcasses of washing machines and dryers still hanging from the walls.

The concrete floor provided a trace of cool in the hot day.

She let herself drift to a halfway state between full wakefulness and sleep, recharging her energy while she waited for the night and for her chance to return to the zone.

Two hours later, she heard the dogs.

Los Angeles warders didn't use dogs. They relied on technology, on trained warder senses, and on outsmarting their targets. But a warder can be transferred anywhere. The Academy had given Danielle a rudimentary knowledge of the use of hounds in tracking. She knew how terribly effective they could be.

The dogs eliminated the option of waiting for night. She dragged herself to her feet and started across no-man's land.

She couldn't move quickly. Helicopters patrolled in the distance, but if they spotted a running figure, they could be overhead in seconds.

The dogs and their keepers weren't constrained by any such limitations. Their baying sounded continually closer.

She took off her shirt, ripped off the sleeves, and fashioned them into a makeshift sling before putting the rags of the shirt back on. As she jogged, she kept her eyes open for smooth rocks, stuffing a small supply into her pockets.

Against assault rifles and heavy machine guns, a sling and a few rocks weren't much, but they were better than trying to fight the dogs empty-handed. And it definitely looked like she was in for a fight--almost certainly her last.

Rob Preece

Chapter 15

Carl listened to the two men. He'd been suspicious at first. Normals slum in the zone--they didn't migrate there. But these two sounded more and more convincing. Or rather, they sounded like Danielle had convinced them.

After she had been gone for a few days, he'd forced himself to consider the possibility that he'd been wrong--that Danielle had been playing him for a fool or had realized that her allegiance was with her fellow warders rather than with the magical. But if he could believe the story that Simon and Fred offered, Danielle was out there, trying to make her way back to the zone. Back to him.

"These two are criminals," Mike the Vampire reminded him. "They'd lie about their mother for a beer. The warders are using them and you're the target."

"Danielle trusted us," Simon shook his head at Mike's interruption. "If she'd left us, she could have gone on ahead and gotten through. Instead, she stayed and let us escape."

It was exactly the kind of thing Danielle would do.

But Carl wouldn't let her get away with being a sacrifice. If Danielle were out there in trouble, he'd share it with her. There was no other answer.

Carl considered taking out an armed party. He dropped the idea almost at once. The Tigers had been armed and it hadn't helped them. Their numbers had only made them easier to spot.

"I'll go," Mike offered. "It's hard to kill a vampire."

Carl shook his head. "You've got work to do here."

He had work in the zone as well. They had put the week that Danielle had bought them to good use, building up defenses, organizing the mobs to a shared purpose, but they were a long way from really pulling together.

Still, the knowledge that Danielle was close changed his priorities.

"The warder was kicking her butt," Fred told him. "It's probably too late to help her."

Carl only nodded. What Fred said made sense, but the warder helicopters were still circling, obviously looking for something. Danielle was the most likely something out there.

A part of him knew beyond mere logic that Danielle was still alive, still trying to get back.

He drove Danielle's little electrical car toward the southern zone border and abandoned it there, shifting to *Were* form before making his move.

He considered waiting until nightfall. With his heavy fur, a wolf made an indistinct infrared image. But the distant sound of hunting hounds persuaded him that he didn't have the time.

Danielle needed him now.

He hunkered low, following an abandoned storm drain out of the zone past the first line of warder defense.

He emerged into a thicket of hackberry trees and rusty barbed wire, pushed his way through, and sniffed for any sign of warder patrols.

His sensitive nose picked up only distant hints of humans, weapons, and dogs.

The wolf inside him hated dogs. Part of the instinctive makeup of every wolf sees dogs as evil cousins--beings who willfully abandoned freedom to serve human masters. But servility didn't make them safe. Both the human and wolf sides of his personality knew that dogs, especially packs of trained dogs, could be fearsome opponents.

He would deal with them when he had to. First, though, he had to find Danielle.

The roar of helicopter blades slicing the late afternoon air battled with the high-pitched baying of hounds that had caught the scent of prey and were moving in for the kill.

If he went charging about looking for Danielle, Carl would just become a target himself.

But doing nothing was no option.

He headed for the loudest of the dog packs hoping that he would run into Danielle before he ran into the dogs.

He did his best to project general dogginess to any warders who might be looking down.

Whether it was Danielle's distraction or some other reason, he didn't run into any of the warder patrols that kept a watch on the zone and prevented escapes. To his *Were* senses, the traps, mines, and sensors were obvious and avoidable.

Which was lucky, because from the sharp baying of the hounds, Danielle didn't have much time left.

He forgot about stealth, ignoring a wealth of wolf instinct, and sprinted.

Helicopters swooped nearby, but they ignored him. Like Carl, they seemed intent on the drama between the hunting dogs and the hunted woman.

Running at wolf speed, it took only minutes to cross the miles that separated him from the hunting dogs.

He arrived just as one of the baying hounds changed pitch, his bark morphing into a surprised squeal of pain.

He skidded to a stop in the shadow of an abandoned barn. Both his human and wolf sides concurred on the need to survey the scene, to plan a way to help his packmate.

Danielle ran into sight.

She looked stunning.

Sweat glued the remains of a man-styled shirt to her body like cellophane. Her black pants were torn, exposing long, tanned and muscular legs. Legs a man could lose himself in.

Carl felt himself transforming to human form at the sight and ruthlessly suppressed the shift. He needed to protect his mate, not join her in death.

* * *

Danielle climbed to the hood of a rusting pickup truck, swung her sling, and loosed.

The dogs were getting wise to her weapon. The one she'd aimed at swerved and her shot missed.

But that swerve created a momentary break in the circle of dogs surrounding her. She took advantage of the apparent opening, darting from the truck where she'd taken temporary refuge and heading toward the zone.

The dogs might not like the sling or the rocks Danielle shied at them, but they weren't cowards.

They rushed after her.

Danielle had already picked her next stand, a low ridge near an abandoned barn. She ran recklessly toward it, blurring one more time to put all of her flagging energy into speed.

The bloodhounds in the pack gave voice. For the most part, though, this was a hunting party. Rottweilers, Doberman Pinchers, and a Chow took the lead. Only occasional snicks of sound warned her how close they really were.

Danielle's blur let her move faster than any normal human. But dogs are faster than humans and she was flagging. Her efforts wouldn't be enough. The animals would hamstring her, knock her to the ground, and hold her until their human masters arrived.

Another canine broke from the barn almost directly in front of her.

Danielle forced down her despair. She would die fighting.

To her surprise, the animal caught the largest dog, a Rottweiler, in the flank, knocking the animal down and out, then turned to snarl at the others.

It wasn't a dog. It was a wolf. What was Carl doing here?

The dogs stopped abruptly, not unnerved by Carl's attack so much as cautious. They'd been caught by surprise once and didn't want more of the same.

Danielle scrambled the rest of the way to the rise and turned to face them.

Seeing no other wolves, the pack circled around, rushing in to snap at him, and retreating from Carl when he countered.

"I'll keep them distracted," he shouted. His voice came out mostly as a hoarse bark but Danielle had spent time with him and knew what he'd be saying. "Get away while you can."

As if.

A Doberman got too close to Carl and he sank his teeth into the animal's throat and shook, then dropped it when three other dogs charged.

They were hunting well as a pack, distracting him, not letting him finish them off piecemeal.

Two of them mistimed their circling and got too close together. He rushed them, making them pay for their mistake.

Again, though, the other animals charged, forcing him to back away and bare his teeth at them, and preventing him from finishing either of the animals off.

Against a pack of twenty, with more coming soon, Carl was one dead wolf.

* * *

Danielle took aim and let a rock fly.

Alone against the dogs, her sling had been only marginally effective. Dogs were smart. Once they'd figured out what a sling can do, they learned to avoid the shot. She'd been forced to feint, to waste time setting up targets. And the dogs were happy to help her waste time. Their humans were coming. They needed only to delay her.

With Carl distracting the dogs, her sling became a deadly threat. The animals couldn't dodge when a stone flew hard and straight into their flanks or faces.

She landed four consecutive hits before the animals broke away, fleeing into the brush and out of range of her shots.

"Move it, Carl. I'm hungry," she shouted.

The wolf loped over to her. Blood marred his perfect fur.

"I told you to head for the zone," he growled. "We wasted too much time."

"So stop wasting more," she answered. "Come on."

She took the lead while Carl trailed behind guarding against the dog pack.

The dogs regrouped and gave voice, but they had learned their lesson. Against Danielle or Carl alone, the dogs would attack, confident of victory. When she and Carl hunted as a team, they could force the dogs to hold their distance and wait for the arrival of their masters.

If the warders had been on foot, they would have gotten away then. Carl could move faster than any normal human, and Danielle was getting the knack of Mansfield's trick, quickly switching from blur to normal modes. This allowed her incredibly fast sprints across open land without completely depleting her sadly low energy stores.

But the warders weren't limited to running. Black helicopters circled overhead. Turbine engines propelled armored personnel carriers through the rough bush. The warders were still a ways away, but they were closing fast.

"Any ideas?" she asked.

The wolf grunted. "You were supposed to head for town."

"I wasn't going to leave you out here alone, Carl."

"Too bad you aren't *Were*," he told her. "We might blend in with the dogs."

She'd never thought of being normal as a handicap before. But being magical would solve a lot of problems. She hadn't let herself think about anything long-term with Carl, but what would they do if they somehow survived the current disaster? They hunted well together, but did a hunting team form the basis for anything permanent, anything human? Could a normal and a *Were* have a chance together?

She forced herself to consider Carl's words. He was right. They needed to find a way to blend in. Since she couldn't turn wolf, the answer had to be to blend in with the humans, to become a warder again, at least for a little while.

She turned, heading at right angles to the zone.

"Backtracking won't work," Carl argued, speaking as clearly as he could through his wolf vocal cords. "The dogs will spot us."

She nodded grimly. "Unless you have a plan of your own, why don't you play along with mine?"

"Fair enough." He ranged ahead, drove away the pair of dogs who had decided to test whether he and Danielle were tiring, and then dropped back behind her. "Lead the way."

His trust gave her a flush of pleasure.

She outlined her plan to him quickly, ignoring his expressions of disbelief. Sure it was chancy. So what? It wasn't like they had a lot of other choices.

After half a mile, she veered from her trail, then circled back.

The dogs closed around them when she and Carl finally stopped, but she'd chosen her spot with that in mind. They crouched on a gently sloped hill with the shattered remains of a windmill at the top. Between her sling and Carl's growls, the dogs didn't dare close.

Timing was critical now. The dogs' handlers would catch up soon, and the helicopters would target them shortly afterwards.

Soon, but not yet. For now, the helicopter gunships circled around overhead, apparently aimless. Her quick cutback and the large number of infrared signatures had confused them.

And Danielle's plan only needed a few moments.

A line of armored personnel carriers roared over a low rise, splashed through a small trickle of water, and followed along their original trail.

"Now," Danielle shouted.

Carl didn't argue. Instead, he rushed toward the last of the APCs.

The dogs must have thought Christmas had arrived early. Their torturers, so powerful when together, had separated and one was running. The pack charged after Carl.

He slowed, letting them almost surround him and relying on Danielle's sling to keep any from striking a fatal blow.

She followed more slowly, using what cover the ground provided and popping up to hammer a rock into whatever dogs snapped too closely at Carl.

"What the--"

The last APC ground to a halt. To them, it must have looked like the pack of dogs was running away from something. As she had planned, Carl blended into the pack.

The Warder captain commanding the APC dropped his mouth open as the dogs ran up to his vehicle, one of them actually ramming its head into the tread and dropping, unconscious.

Carl transformed his run into a leap, taking the APC captain full on the chest and shoving him off the vehicle.

He was already in human form as he dropped through the open hatchway and into the vehicle.

A few of the dogs snapped at the APC out of frustration, but too many quickly remembered their other, less protected target.

Danielle broke from cover as the APC charged toward her.

The pickup had been one of the several problems with her plan. She knew how to navigate an APC, but Carl didn't. Yet the vehicle had to come to her. She'd never make it through the circle of increasingly angry and frustrated dogs.

The APC didn't even slow as it rolled six feet from where she stood.

She blurred, then leapt, grabbing an antenna and pulling herself up onto the monstrous weapon.

"Just keep driving." Carl's voice, very human-sounding. Very deadly sounding.

Carl, his body human and beautiful, had grabbed a pistol from somewhere and was pointing it at the pilot's head. Three other warders watched in stunned disbelief.

"We've got to respond to their signals," the young pilot said, his voice cracking as he fought panic and tears. "Don't you think that we've lost APCs before? They'll target us."

"We've got a couple of minutes," Danielle said. "So let's talk about what you're going to say."

"I'll report situation normal," the pilot answered quickly. Too quickly. He was planning something.

Even in her basic training, Danielle had been taught a code for trouble, a panic button response that would sound normal to any untrained hijacker.

"What happens if you send the panic button?" Danielle asked quietly.

"How'd you know about, uh, I mean, I'm not sure what you're talking about, ma'am."

She clenched the fabric of his collar, pulling his uniform tunic tight against his Adam's apple. "I'm an academy graduate, corporal. Don't try to lie to me."

"Yes, ma'am. I mean, no, ma'am."

"If you send the panic signal, my guess is you become target number one. That about right?"

The poor pilot looked around to the other warders, but they pointedly looked away. Without the captain whom Carl had so unceremoniously dumped over the side, they weren't trained to make decisions. They certainly didn't want any share in the blame that would follow whichever way the pilot finally leaned.

"At least we would have prevented our weapon from falling into enemy hands," he finally answered, his voice a pure sulk.

"Maybe they'd award you a medal. Posthumously," Danielle sneered.

A thin line of sweat ran down his neck. "Better than being shot after we let you get away."

She had to give it to him. The soldier, hardly more than a boy, was being honest with her when it would have been easier to just buck responsibility upstairs.

"We're going to the zone. Suppose that you just stay there with us, out of their reach."

"Wait a minute," Carl broke in. "The zone is for the magical. We can't just have anybody dropping in because they don't like the way things are run outside."

"Bullshit. That's exactly what we've got to have. So what do you think, corporal? Want a chance of life with us, or to die a glorious but immediate death?"

"Uh, live."

"Good choice." She looked around at the other three warder soldiers. "What about the rest of you? You can bail now, or stick with us. If you bail, they might not shoot you. But if you stick with us, you're in it for the long haul."

"I'm out of here." One of the soldiers stood, climbed the ladder to the hatchway, and leapt.

The other two looked at Danielle, then at Carl. "We lost our APC. That'll mean stockade at best," one said. "Guess I'll stay."

Danielle wasn't sure how far she could trust them, but their personal weapons were stored in a chest that Carl guarded with a ferocity that none of the soldiers were likely to challenge.

"Let's head for the zone," she ordered.

"What should I tell Command?" the pilot whined.

"Tell them you see something and you're following up."

"They'll send reinforcements."

"Yeah. So?"

He didn't have an answer to that. Of course, she didn't either, but she didn't need tell him that.

She wasn't sure how they would get into the zone on a huge armored personnel carrier, nor whether the warders would simply follow her in and launch the invasion she had worked to prevent, but she felt a lot better protected by a few tons of armored aluminum and plastic laminate rather than just a ragged shirt.

"Ask for them," Carl broke in.

"Huh?" Both the pilot and Danielle stared at him like he'd grown horns.

"Don't resist reinforcements, demand them. If they're like any other bureaucracy, they're more likely to say no if you ask for help than if you don't."

Danielle shrugged. "Worth a try. And remember, corporal, any funny stuff and one of those gunships has your name on it."

"Trust me, I'm no hero."

He picked up the radio and began a string of jargon that Danielle's training barely let her translate.

When he finally switched off, sweat stood out from his forehead in huge beads despite the air-conditioned comfort of the APC.

"I think they bought it. But they're sending two units as backup."

She nodded. It would have been nice for things to go right for a change, but she was past expecting it. "Let's see what this baby can do, then."

"Really?"

This poor soldier definitely needed someone to mother him. Danielle had never known herself to have maternal instincts, but she patted him on the shoulder. "We're on your team now, corporal. Let's see if we can stay alive for a while."

He nodded. Apparently her words had given him the reassurance he needed.

"Which direction, ma'am?"

"North-northwest," she told him. "We'll circle away from the main group."

He punched the acceleration pedals and roared off the path taken by the other armored vehicles.

Carl shoved the gunner out of the way, taking over the weapons control system.

"You know how to handle those weapons?" she asked him.

"I can read directions."

It wasn't the answer she was looking for, but what choice did she have? The pilot and the two remaining warder soldiers had made noises about cooperating, and they certainly didn't want to die, but they wouldn't mind becoming heroes by capturing the renegade warder and dangerous *Were*, either. She certainly wouldn't count on them to fire on any enemies.

The APC bounced over bumps, slammed its way through small trees, and made surprisingly quick progress across the open countryside.

"Left those other two behind for now," the corporal grinned. "They don't have the balls to play." He glanced at her. "Meaning no respect, ma'am."

"Try to outdistance them gradually," she told him. "The boys upstairs are watching."

Sure enough, two black helicopters circled around the APC's path; occasional streaks of tracer shells snaked to the ground and indicated that they thought they'd spotted something alive and weren't taking any chances.

"Don't guess Bert is going to make it," the pilot told her after an especially long burst of fire targeting the area where Danielle and Carl had boarded the APC. "I thought jumping out was pretty dumb with all that shooting going on. By the way, I'm Gus."

"Is Bert the private who decided he'd take his chances outside?"

"That would be him." Gus laughed bitterly. "He always had the ridiculous idea that the warders were there to protect people, so we shouldn't have any enemies. Probably thought they'd send a helicopter down to rescue him."

Danielle didn't say anything. Until a week earlier, she'd shared Bert's beliefs. Like Bert, her naive faith had almost gotten her killed. Bert, though, had only hurt himself. Her own willingness to ignore the truth had gotten a lot of other people, innocent people, killed.

"How close will this thing be able to get us to the zone?" she asked, hoping for a change of subjects.

"Lady, we can drive this thing down Main Street."

"What about the guards?"

"They're looking inward, not outward. We'll go right through them."

"And once we're past them, inside?"

"Then we get shot up," Gus admitted. "Our rear armor isn't much to write home about. These pieces of junk aren't like the old Bradleys. Now those systems could stand up to a beating."

Danielle could understand the economizing. How much armor does it take to mow down a teenaged elf-girl? Still, right now, she wished she had a bit more protection.

"This baby is complicated," Carl announced from the fire control seat. "And the IFF system is designed to keep us from firing at anything remotely designated as a friendly."

Which meant that they weren't going to get any help from the APC's weapons.

"Maybe it will make it hard for them to shoot at us too," Danielle suggested. "We'll just tell them we're in hot pursuit and drive through."

As plans went, this one sucked.

Nobody suggested anything smarter.

Chapter 16

Danielle hung onto the braces as Gus smashed through a tree, drove straight through a shallow brook, and then rolled over a massive barbed wire fence.

"Here goes nothing," Gus muttered as he brought his hands to the track levers.

"Ten more minutes and I'll have this fire control system hacked," Carl promised. His fingers flashed across the keyboard as he sought some way, any way, to arm his weapons against their enemies--enemies that the computer stubbornly insisted were friends.

They didn't have ten minutes, though. Command seemed increasingly frustrated with their story about confirmed sightings. No one else had seen anything, and Command had finally realized that their supposed prey was moving too fast.

"Just got orders to return to base," Gus reported.

"Make that ten seconds," Danielle instructed Carl. "We're going in now."

"Uh--"

"Punch it," she ordered Gus, cutting off Carl.

A storm of bullets bounced off the APC's frontal armor as they approached a guard tower.

"Guess they decided we're a foe," Gus said. "Didn't take them long to reprogram their computers. How about some counterfire, Carl?"

"Working on it," he reported. Miles of engine-straining performance had overwhelmed the machine's air conditioning and sweat glistened on Carl's forehead . He punched a few keys, swore, and then punched another one.

"Almost there."

"Knock down the tower," Danielle ordered Gus.

"They're pretty sturdy," the corporal argued. "It might break something." But he jammed both levers full forward.

The APC rocked as it was struck by something a lot heavier than a machine-gun bullet.

"Just do it before they chop us into pieces," she ordered.

Gus nodded grimly, his face pale. "I'm on it, ma'am."

The guard tower erupted in a storm of machine gun fire, rocket grenades, and TOW missiles.

Gus zigged and zagged. Twice, Danielle actually saw anti-armor rockets brush past the APC.

The machine gun fire cut off abruptly and Danielle realized that they were beneath the tower's firing angle. They were going to make it.

Then a warder calmly stood, pointed a shoulder-mounted missile at them, and fired.

Gus just ducked.

The missile smashed into the APC, bringing the vehicle to an abrupt stop, knocking Danielle to the floor, and plunging them into the dim red lighting of the battery backup system.

Gus recovered his chair, restarted the engine, then revved it. The vehicle spun in place. "Lost a tread," Gus said. "We aren't going anywhere."

The weapons roar was even louder this time than the first and the APC shook under its force.

"Sorry I got you into this, guys," Danielle told Gus and the others.

Gus started to nod, then slammed a fist against the APC's armor. "Great shot, Carl!" She hadn't really noticed, but Carl's cursing had suddenly taken a different tone. As she watched, the tower crumpled on itself.

"Sorry I'm a little late coming to the party," Carl announced. "The worst thing is, we'll have to leave this baby here just when we got things going our way. They <u>really</u> didn't want anyone hacking that code. All sorts of traps in it."

"Let's go," Danielle shouted. She reached for the hatch.

"Let me give those choppers something to think about first," Carl said.

He was stroking rather than hammering the keyboard now, coaxing extra effort out of a friend rather than beating cooperation from an enemy.

The APC shuddered again as it launched a flurry of lead into the air.

"I put it on automatic," Carl announced. "Anything that flies too close gets shot at. Might give us a bit of cover."

And it might not. Either way, it was time to leave the comfort of their vehicle and make a break for the questionable safety of the zone.

She popped the hatch, blurred, and flew up the ladder.

A couple of warders were halfheartedly popping at the APC with personal weapons. They scattered when Carl pressed a button on the keyboard and blasted the neighborhood.

"Move," Danielle commanded.

Gus, the two other soldiers whose names she hadn't managed to learn, and finally Carl emerged from the battered APC.

"You'd better lead," Carl said. "If three soldiers come barging into the middle of the zone, they're likely to get shot."

Danielle wasn't so sure why her reception would be any better than that for the soldiers, or why Carl got to play hero, but this wasn't the time to argue.

"Come on," she shouted.

She blurred again, moving quickly ahead to ensure that the men weren't going to get shot at, and then letting them catch up.

Carl morphed into his wolf form and cleared the terrified remainder of the tower warders from their posts. Weapons that would have been effective against the onrushing APC were too slow and awkward against the fast-moving *Were*.

Danielle didn't see the black helicopter dropping from the sky until it was almost on top of them. It swerved to avoid the storm of computer-controlled fire coming from the now distant APC and descended.

A door opened in the chopper and a rope ladder dropped out. Danielle saw a group of camouflaged warders preparing to lower themselves down. Presumably they wanted to capture her since the gunship's huge cannons remained silent.

Carl howled and charged toward them, but he was too far away to catch them before the warders arrived. Not that he could do much when he got there. The warders would be equipped with silver bullets.

She'd picked up a handgun and fired a couple of shots into the helicopter, but the warders' body armor protected them. Her automatic locked empty, ejecting its cartridge.

Well, damn. This wasn't the ending she'd been looking for.

"Keep running," she told her adopted soldiers. "I'll hold them off as long as I can."

Which would be about half a second. Still, it was better than nothing.

"Bullcrap," Gus answered. He reached into his shirt, and withdrew what looked like a flare gun, only larger and uglier.

"I always wanted to try this." He fired directly into the open door.

The helicopter exploded into a fireball.

"Guess I really can't go back now," he grinned, tossing the single shot weapon on the ground. "Hope you weren't kidding about the zone being open to us normals."

"Let's head there and find out," Danielle said.

* * *

Carl had used the week she'd bought him through her hacking of the warder computers and the manhunt her escape had created. While Carl had been bringing her in, Mike the Vampire had focused zone defenses around the southern end.

Still, as Danielle crouched in a newly dug slit trench, she wondered if it mattered. The invading warders had too much armor, too many helicopters, too many trained soldiers for her to believe that Carl's impromptu militia could do anything but make them angry.

The first wave of armor met a pathetic love-tap of fire as magical creatures opened up with what few weapons they'd been able to hide from the frequent warder raids. One APC bogged down, but most simply shrugged off the low-caliber fire.

Behind them, warder infantry moved in a gray wall.

This was going to be ugly. And Danielle knew it was her own fault.

Danielle looked around for something to use as a weapon and felt a hand on her shoulder.

"Stay down, honey." Carl's voice sounded confident despite the limited damage his troops were having.

"This looks bad."

"It'll get better later."

"Will there be a zone left by later?"

Carl nodded seriously. "I hope so."

Danielle did too. The alternative was unthinkable. Unthinkable or not, though, she couldn't imagine anything the zone could do that would stop that incoming tide of equipment and soldiers.

The magics had cleared a kill zone of a few hundred feet inside the zone barriers, but the warders swept through it with minimal damage and plunged into the narrow alleys and ramshackle buildings of the zone.

That's when the miracle happened.

Trolls reared back and heaved brownies at the APCs, the small winged creatures flying so fast that the APC machine guns couldn't track on them. The brownies dropped grenades into open hatches, attached plastique explosives to closed hatches, and then flitted off.

Badly aimed automatic-fire shots from the warder infantry bounded off the trolls and only managed to take out the few warder officers who

194

had survived the brownie attack and then opened their hatches to see what was going on.

The elves struck next.

Using elf camouflage, they had blended into the buildings and streets. With the APC crews distracted by the brownies, they now rose and planted explosives inside the APC track mechanisms.

One after another, the fearsome APCs ground to halts, their crews bailing to the relative safety of the line of foot soldiers behind them.

Mike's motorcycle-mounted vampire legion attack had to be one of the dumbest military plans since the charge of the light brigade. But when the already demoralized warder soldiers saw those vampires coming at them, their teeth bared and ready to suck blood, they broke.

A rush of werewolves turned the retreat into a rout. The invading warders streamed back across the borders, their helicopter gunships blasting any magical who tried to follow.

"Welcome back, Danielle," Carl told her. "We missed you."

Danielle listened to her heart pound in the still darkness of the night. Making love with Carl only got better as they learned those secret spots that heighten pleasure and as they lost their inhibitions and experimented. During the few days since the warder attack had been beaten off, they'd tried to make up for the weeks of sexual tension that Danielle's now-shed prejudices had created. She'd abandoned her own room and moved into Carl's spacious suite in a recently opened hotel--his lab was still considered too dangerous to use.

She practically purred as she draped herself across his handsome body—and stopped abruptly. The pounding didn't come from her heart—or his. "I think we're about to have company," she told Carl.

He grabbed for his pants while Danielle hunted for a weapon. She'd only come up with a broken off chair leg when their door burst open and a tactical team of warders poured in.

"Well look what we have here." Joe Smealy, her ex-boss, ex-mentor, and now her enemy, strode into the supposedly secret room where she and Carl had gone after the zone-wide celebration of their victory over the warders.

"The zone is no threat to you," she told Joe. "Why don't you just go back and let us live in peace."

He shook his head slowly. "You could have been one of the best, Danielle. But you threw it away for sex with an animal. Disgusting."

"We have ten thousand armed magics within a mile," Danielle reminded him. "If you shoot, every one will be here."

"So if you'd just accompany me back to the chopper, we can

dispense with killing all those animals. At least for now."

Beside her, Carl moved slightly. She clamped a hand on his wrist. If he transformed, the warders would shoot him down no matter what the danger to themselves.

"What happens if I come with you?"

Carl stiffened. "Danielle. No."

She ignored Carl's protest. "Are you prepared to offer a bargain?"

"Aren't you the noble one, Danielle? I guess that was always your weakness. But of course I will. If you come with us, we'll leave the zone alone. Hell, we'll bring it food and medical supplies."

For an instant, she'd forgotten that Joe was a practiced liar. He'd keep whatever bargain he made exactly as long as it was comfortable for him to do so.

"We've reproduced the magic virus," Carl said. "If you don't head back, we'll release it."

The warder commandos looked to Joe for direction, obviously intimidated by Carl's threat.

Joe slowly shook his head. "I don't think you'd do it. Maybe if we tried to wipe out the entire zone. But you wouldn't risk it to protect one rogue warder. After all, if the virus does get out, we'll nuke you back to the Paleolithic."

She looked from the man she'd admired half her life to the man she'd never heard of a few months earlier—but now loved. Both were strong leaders. Both believed that they had right on their side. But Joe was tangled up in a world of lies. Hatred had turned him rotten from the inside. That same hatred had nearly destroyed her.

"Danielle. You're under arrest for violation of the inter-species breeding ordinance 100007 and for failure to obey a lawful termination order."

A part of her wanted to obey. She'd spent her life obeying, ever since she'd broken the rules, snuck out of school, and, to her teenaged mind, been responsible for getting her mother killed. The sudden psychological insight helped her resist any effort to peacefully surrender, but it didn't do anything to resolve the problem. "Stay here, Carl. I'll go along with them." She dropped the makeshift club she'd found.

"The hell!"

If she got Carl killed, she would never forgive herself. She stood from the bed and walked toward Joe. "You mean what you said about helping the zone, right?"

"Oh yeah. Sure."

How could she have believed him for all those years? The lie was in his face for any idiot to see. She must have been blind.

One of the warders reached out to her, plastic cuffs in his hand. From his overly controlled movement, she could tell that he was already in full blur.

Well, two could play at that game.

She blurred, sliced a knife hand to the warder's groin, and held on as she spun around.

"Shoot them both down," Joe ordered. He fired a blast in her direction.

She had anticipated his move, though. She swept the first warder's feet from under him and then rolled forward over him toward Joe. The burst of automatic fire went high, over her head.

Their bed transformed into an explosion of feathers, foam rubber, and metal springs as two more warders opened up at where Carl had been moments before. Except that Carl had disappeared.

Good. He was safe. For now.

"You two go after the wolf. Alex, stay here and help me take care of the female."

Danielle faced the two men who separated, circled around. "Don't make this hard on yourself," Joe urged.

His voice sounded perfectly normal to her—which had to mean that he had blurred as well.

He was good. The other warder feinted, distracting her just enough to let Joe slice in a crescent kick followed by a punch to her midsection.

Danielle reeled away fighting for breath.

She gasped in a hint of oxygen and concentrated on staying alive.

The two men teamed perfectly, attacking together, protecting one another when Danielle tried to strike back. She landed a few blows but took much worse in return.

Then, she faced Joe alone. Carl, who had somehow lost the team assigned to follow him, faced her other opponent, his slow motions belying his calm competence.

"This won't turn out well for you, Goodman," Joe snarled at her. "The impaired can't be trusted. Ever."

He might be right, but that didn't make the magical anything but human.

"Maybe your wife didn't leave you because she was magical," Danielle suggested. "Maybe she was just looking for anyone who wasn't you."

Joe's eyes narrowed and he rushed her, his hands grasping like a crab's claws. He was out of control and vulnerable.

Danielle sidestepped and hammered in a series of punches but Joe spun around as if he didn't even feel them. His rage added to the blur's endorphin overload and made him all but oblivious to pain.

"You're going down," he growled. "Now,"

Danielle nodded. "If you're good enough."

Joe rushed her again. This time, though, he stopped abruptly when he'd gotten inside her guard, sucked it up as she landed three hard punches, and then grappled.

He was strong.

He grasped her close, choking her against his body armor, which deadened the kicks and punches that that she continued to throw.

"Say goodbye, Danielle," he urged.

Carl had incapacitated the other warder and circled around looking for an opening, but Joe backed into a corner and continued to squeeze out Danielle's life.

"If you let her go now, I'll let you walk out of here," Carl promised. "If you hurt her, you're a dead man."

Joe just laughed.

Oxygen debt sent a wave of dizziness through Danielle and she shifted from blur mode to let herself survive a little longer.

She gave up striking at Joe's armored body, quickly saw that he had protected his face and eyes, and went to work on a finger.

Joe's gloved hands resisted her grasp. Only the smallest metallic click let her believe that she was having any effect at all. Either he was impossibly strong or—

"You think I'd come here without the best equipment?" Joe bragged. "You're finished, Danielle."

She sagged against him, letting him carry all of her weight, then kicked off against the wall.

Joe stumbled and loosened his grasp, although only for a fraction of a moment.

That moment was enough, though. She grabbed a breath and twisted, not trying to escape, but telling herself to be like water, letting Joe flow over her without getting a grasp, sweeping his feet from under him.

Joe couldn't completely counter her move, but she didn't catch him by surprise either. When he fell, he twisted so that his heavy armored body fell on her.

She felt her ribs giving way and then Joe's hands were back on her neck squeezing hard. The dull thud-thud-thud of her heart in her ears sounded like chopper blades.

She had almost lost consciousness when she felt the wolf's body slam into Joe knocking him away from her.

Her technique, stupid if she'd been alone, had given Carl the opportunity to get into the fight.

Joe rolled away, took one look at the enraged wolf, and blurred for the window.

Danielle rolled to her feet and followed, but too slowly. Before she could reach him, Joe broke through the window. Perfectly timed, a nylon ladder dropped from a chopper--it hadn't been Danielle's heart after all. Joe grasped the ladder

She watched as the helicopter zoomed away.

Carl, in human form again, joined her at the window.

"I have a feeling he'll be back."

She couldn't disagree. Watching Joe climb that weblike ladder reminded her of a spider.

The helicopter spun back around and raked the hotel with machine gun fire.

"Get down," Carl commanded.

She started to obey, then stopped. Something was off.

Joe was shouting commands to the helicopter, ordering it back into the attack.

The black gunship ponderously turned, it's cannons pointing straight toward the window where Danielle stood waiting.

"Get down." Carl was screaming but Danielle couldn't move. Not that it made any difference.

The chopper's turn seemed slow, but Joe was hanging at the end of a long rope. The leverage turned a gentle movement into the crack of a whip.

Joe used the mechanical strength of his gloves to hold on. But, as he reached for a new handhold, his grip slipped.

For the first time since she'd known him, Danielle saw panic flit across Joe's face. He grasped for the line with his free hand--too late.

The helicopter pilot picked that minute to adjust its sights. It was only a slight jerk, but it was too much for Joe.

He seemed to fall in slow motion, his eyes filled with an insane gleam. Then he accelerated and smashed into the ground a hundred feet below the gunship.

"Goodbye, Joe," Danielle murmured.

"What happened?"

"When we were grappling, I felt something snap in his glove. I must have frozen one of the reinforced joints. When he relied on it, it wasn't there."

"You're quite a fighter," Carl said.

Those weren't the most romantic words in the world, but Danielle felt lucky to be alive. "What happened to the other warders?"

"They ran into Mike and Snori. We'll let them go in the morning. With the message that another attempt like this is going to cause the second magical plague."

"In that case, maybe we should get back to bed."

Carl gestured at the bullet-infested remains of what had once been their love nest. "Here?"

"How about the floor. Except I get to be on top."

* * *

For most of the zone, Joe Smealy's death was a cause for celebration. Danielle couldn't quite bring herself to join. He had been a liar, but she still believed he'd been doing what he thought was right.

"Gus and the guys are one thing, but we can't let just anybody in," Carl explained, his voice almost artificially patient. "For one thing, they'd smuggle more warders in to sabotage us. And for another, we don't want to live with them any more than they want to live with us."

She and Carl faced off in the middle of Carl's compound, now converted into a makeshift headquarters. A sort of combination government office and military command center. Around them, Mike the Vampire, Snori, the dwarfs, and a cluster of elves tried to be inconspicuous.

Danielle didn't bother trying to sound patient. She knew she was right and wasn't going to back down. "You're thinking exactly the same way that the warders think. Letting fear control your actions."

"Fancy talk," he growled. He stepped into her personal space trying to intimidate her with his size and maybe the sexual magnetism that had worked so well. But sex was sex and life was life. Carl was wrong and Danielle didn't plan on backing down no matter what he might say.

"Of all people, you should be able to understand this," she said. "You were a normal until a few months ago. You've lived both worlds. You can see how the two need each other if we're going to break out of this downward spiral."

"We've been treated like dirt for years. We need time to create our own civilization. If the normals overrun us now, we'll just be forced into a new zone." His hands twitched at his side as if he wanted to attack—or maybe to caress her. Danielle couldn't tell.

"Look at me," he continued. "They had me convinced that the answer was a cure to the magic. To force the magical to give up their talents. I had to get away from them to see that magical talents are a gift, not a curse."

"You don't get it, do you? I thought you would be the first to want to open the door to the future rather than keep looking backward." She spun on her heels and started away from him.

"Come on, Danielle," he urged. "Let me show you what we're building here. Maybe once you have a chance to really feel the promise, you'll see that it's a magical thing. The normals wouldn't understand."

She spun around. "I am a normal, remember."

"You're not normal," he told her. "You're as magical as any of us. Where else do you think your blur comes from? You're as much a victim of their lies as any of us. Because you are one of us, Danielle. Not one of them."

Danielle froze.

She'd wondered how Carl could reconcile his newfound magical chauvinism with the apparent feelings that they shared. She'd imagined, hoped, that this showed that Carl was more open and perceptive than he appeared.

Those hopes burned into ashes. Carl hadn't accepted her for who she was, he'd projected what he wanted into her. He'd decided that she was a magical because he needed her to be one.

Unfortunately for Carl, his theory was dead wrong. She wasn't magical. The blur wasn't a magical talent. It was the result of years of hard work with biofeedback and countless hours of training.

Unfortunately for Danielle, Carl's reaction meant that her hopes, her plans, and her dreams were impossible. She couldn't live her life with Carl, and she couldn't persuade anyone to create the powerful hybrid of magical and non-magical that every instinct told her was humanity's only way to move forward.

* * *

Carl watched Danielle walk away, her hands clenched in fists that he knew could break concrete—could break his heart.

He wanted to call her back, to run after her, to do anything but let her leave. But what could he add to what he'd already told her?

"You blew that one, boss," Mike the Vampire told him.

"Yeah?" Carl turned on his friend and jammed his hands into his pockets so he wouldn't do anything rash. "So what was I supposed to do? Sell out the entire zone just so I could get a little nookie?"

"Is that what Danielle is to you, boss? Nookie?"

Carl yanked his hands back out of his pocket and slammed a fist into the apartment's brick wall. Two bricks crumbled with a crunch that would have been satisfying if he hadn't felt something shatter in his hand as well.

"Damn it, Mike." He manipulated his hand, trying to see if he could still make his fingers move. He could, but barely. "It doesn't matter what she means to me," he continued. "I'm working for all of us."

Mike didn't look particularly grateful. "Like I said before, you blew it. The worst thing is, you're too stubborn to do anything about it."

The vampire didn't look as angry as Danielle had when she'd walked away, but he walked away too. Leaving Carl standing alone, his fist throbbing and the rest of him feeling like he'd been sucker-punched.

He considered smacking the wall again, but managed to restrain himself. He could work around one broken hand. Two would get in the way.

* * *

Fred and Simon had holed up in one of the many abandoned buildings close to the zone border. Fred's restaurant had only been opened for a couple of days, but it was packed when Danielle arrived.

"You look like hell," Simon told her. He was working as maitre-d, dressed in a tux, but greeted her with a hug and smile that took a bit of the sting out of his words.

"It's good to see you too."

"We owe you and Carl a lot," Simon said. "He lent us the money to set this place up and sent a bunch of his friends and workers to eat here."

"Yeah. He's a goddamn saint," she said. Still, she was surprised to learn what Carl had done. How could he be so reasonable about some things and irrational about others?

"Uh-oh. Love problems?" Simon asked.

Danielle resisted the urge to strangle the man. This had nothing to do with love. It had everything to do with Carl's stubborn refusal to accept that the future could be better.

"Can a person get anything to eat around here?" she demanded.

Simon led her back to a table near the kitchen where Fred quickly joined her.

She knew she was right and Carl wrong and seeing Simon and Fred becoming successful proved it. But the empty feeling inside of her said that being right didn't matter. At her emotional core, she didn't want to be right--she wanted to be right with Carl, and for Carl to want to build a new world with her

After dinner, she went into the kitchen and helped with the dishes.

The blur, she learned, didn't really help with the washing. Unfortunately, learning that cost Fred and Simon half a dozen plates.

Fred finally took the drying rag from her hands and set her down in the corner. "We can't afford your help, honey. So why don't you let us help you?"

She couldn't help bristling. "I don't need any help."

"We all need help," Simon said. He had wrapped an apron over his tux and was sweeping up the shattered remains of the last plate she'd destroyed.

Simon pretended to be talking to Fred. "Boy, that Carl sure looked worried when we came in without Danielle, didn't he?"

"Almost like a man in love," Fred answered.

"So what?" It took an effort not to shout, but Danielle managed. Barely. That 'L' word got to her in a way she would have thought was impossible.

* * *

The next morning Fred fed Danielle a stack of pancakes liberally smeared with butter and whipped cream, together with coffee so thick she was surprised that her spoon didn't stand up in it.

Simon sat down next to her and aimed a fork at her plate.

"Hey." She blurred and pushed it away. "Get your own pancakes."

"You think Fred would feed me like this?"

"If you asked him nicely."

"I'd rather mooch off of you. You sure you want to eat all of those?"

She looked down at the heaping plate of pancakes and then at Simon's hungry eyes.

"I'm real sure."

He sighed. "It was worth a try, anyway. And speaking of trying, have you thought any more about what we talked about last night?"

Danielle nodded. "I've thought about it, but I don't see it doing any good."

"Don't give up on him, Danielle. Carl's a good man, and he loves you."

He might love a Danielle, she realized. Unfortunately, his was a magical Danielle who existed only in his mind.

"It isn't about that," she explained. "Carl's caught up in old pain-- pain that I spent my life battling and only now am starting to get away from. Do you think I can afford to go back to that, Simon?"

Simon considered, then shrugged. "I'm on your side, Danny. But I hope you'll give him a chance."

She reached over and kissed him gently on the cheek. "I'm glad I didn't kill you that first day, Simon."

He grinned. "Me too."

Danielle had to blow her nose and dry her eyes when she left Fred's restaurant, but she sucked it up and went looking for Carl. This wasn't about them, it was about making the zone right and she couldn't run from that fight.

Chapter 17

Danielle returned to her combination house and dojo and threw her few things into a workout bag. When she met with him again, she wanted to be on her own, independent.

Everything she owned filled half of a small workout bag. Once she dumped her warder uniforms, she'd be down to the dress she'd bought for her first date with Carl, some underwear, and a spare karate gi. She needed to get out more often.

"Going somewhere?" The deep male voice, indisputably Carl, caught her completely by surprise.

"Hi, Carl. Yeah, I figured I'd move out. It isn't like you need a herder any more."

She tried not to look at him, but failed miserably. He looked younger than he had when she had first met him, more fit and darkened by the sun. But his commanding presence was as strong as ever. One of his hands was wrapped in a bandage and she started to reach out to caress his wound, then snatched back her hand before she touched him. She should know better than to play with fire.

"You were always more than a herder, you know. I wanted you from the minute I first saw you."

"Yeah. Well, you got me. So I guess that means you can move on with your life."

He shook his head slowly. "I'm having trouble with that."

"Am I supposed to feel guilty or something?" She knew she was being snippy but didn't know how to stop it without throwing herself into his arms.

"No thanks," he said. "But we have a lot of things to talk about and running away isn't going to make that any easier."

"I'm not running," she lied. "I'm fighting."

"If you say so."

Well, she couldn't just leave that like the elephant in the corner. "What sort of things were you wanting to talk about?"

He ticked off on the fingers of his good hand. "What we do about the zone; what we do about the informants you uncovered when you were at warder headquarters; and what we do about us."

"There is no us," she protested.

Carl looked unhappy. "Maybe not now, but I'm hoping that there can be."

He looked so sincere that she wanted to kiss him. Or maybe kick him. Her feelings were genuinely conflicted and Carl's strange idea of a conversation was only making it worse.

"Carl, we disagree about everything. Want me to list a few? First, I want to let normals into the zone. You want to keep them out. Second, I've decided not to turn over the names of informants I found. You want to go after them. Third, you need a magical mate, but I'm normal. And fourth, you think sex with the local ex-warder is kinky. I'm looking for something a little more, well, settled."

"Really?"

She narrowed her eyes. "Really what?"

"Are those really the things that are keeping us apart?"

"Do you really want a longer list?"

He shook his head. "Let's see if we can deal with that list first."

"Deal how?"

"If you think the zone would be secure with the informants running around, I'm willing to give them a warning and a chance. It isn't as if they were breaking any laws."

Danielle looked at him. She wanted to be angry. Anger would give her the strength to continue to fight him. But she couldn't work up a good anger when he was being so agreeable. "Someone will have to make sure that the warders are controlled in the future. That they don't send their agents into town to riot, loot, and cause problems," she said.

Carl nodded. "We need a real police force. One designed to protect people rather than attack anyone. "Snori the Troll has agreed to head up that effort, building from what he's done with the defense militia. It turns out that he was a police lieutenant in Houston in the old days before the return."

A surge of disappointment surprised Danielle. She was twenty-five and barely out of warder school. Of course no one was going to consider her for that type of position.

"I thought about you," Carl said, as if reading her mind.

She must have jumped.

"I didn't have to read your mind, you were an obvious candidate. But you don't have the experience in the zone that Snori has, nor the experience with old-fashioned policing. Besides--"

"Besides, I'm a normal," she finished Carl's sentence for him.

"Besides, I thought you'd want something more active than a desk job," he said.

206

Right. He still thought she was magical—and wouldn't get a clue.

"Then there's the matter of letting normals into the zone," he continued.

"I'm not going to give up on this," she told him. "After you left yesterday, I thought about this a lot," he explained. "And I talked to some of the guys. I understand your position, but you have to understand that this is the first time the magical have tried to do anything together as a team. If we were overrun by normals, we might end up being pushed into a corner of the small corner we're already in. Maybe it's just fear, but it's real and it isn't just me."

Danielle tried, but she couldn't hold back her laughter. "Overrun? You're kidding. Think about what you said. How many normals do you think will flock to the zone?"

"Maybe only a few at first, but once we get things going, there could be thousands, or more."

"Once you get things going, you will have a process in place to make sure that nobody is allowed to segregate the city, to impose special rules on one group."

Carl nodded slowly, digesting her words, incorporating her thoughts into his world-view. "You know, you're right. So, we can let them in. Maybe with limits at first."

She couldn't believe it. Carl was going along, giving up his prejudices and fears.

She stuffed the last of her underwear into her workout bag and slung it over her shoulder. "Great, Carl. It sounds like you are taking some sensible steps. You've got my vote in the next election. Now, would you get out of my way?"

She tried to step around him, but his muscular body blocked the doorway to her room. She considered trying to duck between his legs but didn't want to give him that satisfaction.

"Are you going to let me move?"

Carl shook his head. "We have one more topic on our list."

"Don't be stupid. Humans react to danger in certain, predictable ways. Given what we've been through over the past couple of months, it's no wonder that we fell into bed together. But don't try to make it into something that it isn't."

He shook his head slowly. "You've still got your betrayal issues, don't you?"

"I don't know what you're talking about." Just because her stepfather and then her mentor had turned on her didn't make her crazy.

"I think you do. Right now, I'm not sure if you're afraid of men, or afraid of the magical, or both. I hear your fear talking. But you're bigger than your fear, Danielle. You don't have to let it cripple you."

She wouldn't admit, even to herself, that his shot had hit home. "All right, I'm listening."

He brushed his good hand against her shoulder, tracing it down her arm. "I hope you are, Danielle, because I'm not very good at this stuff. When it comes to science or business, I've always felt confident, in control. But ever since I met you, I've been out of control."

"You want me to tie you up or something?"

He laughed. "Sounds like fun, but later. But what I'm saying is that I like it. You've opened up possibilities for me that I never had before. You--" his voice trailed off for a moment. "Ah, hell."

He pulled her to him, his lips descending toward hers.

In her mind, Danielle turned into his motion, blocking his grab and then flipped him over her hip. She'd done it a thousand times in the dojo. But this time, her muscles didn't cooperate. In fact, when his lips touched hers, every muscle in her body liquefied. She would have collapsed to the floor if Carl's strong body hadn't kept both of them erect.

Her universe centered around the kiss, the sensation of Carl's body against her own, his chest hard against her own softer curves, his male hardness pressing against her abdomen, and his lips, tongue, battling for control of her soul.

Time passed. Danielle had no idea how long. Until Carl finally pulled back.

"I didn't mean to do that," he admitted.

"It was a little powerful."

"What I mean is, I don't want to use sex to persuade you. I want you to want to be with me, to share my life and to let me share yours. I know that being with me has torn apart everything you've lived for, but I can't think it's all bad. We exposed the lies that held you, together. I know that it hurt. I hope part of it is wonderful, too."

Danielle needed to get away from him. With his strong arms around her, she could feel protected and safe, but she couldn't think rationally. Any movement, though, seemed completely impossible.

"Carl, listen because this is important. The blur is something we learn, not something I got from a magical infection. I'm not a magical. And I'm not interested in becoming magical."

Carl shrugged. "So?"

"So, I'm a normal. One of the people you were just saying everyone is nervous about. If you hang around with me, you'll never be elected Mayor or President or Pack Leader. I'm poison for you. You've got to let

208

go of me."

His deep laughter warmed her heart. "First, you're a hero. Everyone knows that your work gave us the week we needed to prepare for the invasion and nobody cares whether you are normal or magical. Second, I love you for being Danielle, not for your talents or lack of talent. And third, who wants to be elected?"

Danielle was still stuck on number two. "Can you say that again?"

"That I don't want to be elected?"

"No. Before that."

He stopped, thought, then smiled. "I told you I wasn't much good at the emotional stuff. Of course I love you, Danielle. Being with you makes me complete."

"Oh." Her voice came out small and weak. Not at all the powerful statement she wanted to make. "So what do you think we should do about it?"

"I was hoping we might get away for a couple of weeks of rest and recuperation and, well, sex."

Her heart sank to her shoes. "A couple of weeks?"

"We would have to come back to the real world eventually. We've got a city to build. That'll take longer. Like forever."

"Forever sounds good."

"What do you say we start those couple of weeks right now?"

Carl swung Danielle up in his arms, almost hiding a wince when his wounded hand brushed against her back, and headed downstairs. Toward his bedroom.

"Are you going to tell me what happened to your hand?"

He shook his head. "I've been doing too much talking. For the next couple of hours, I'm going to be no talk, all action."

His lips pressed to hers making sure that she wouldn't say anything either. Not that she had anything that needed saying more than she needed to love, and make love, to this wonderful man.

Epilogue

Blood splattered over the narrow alley behind the shiny new high-rise that redefined the zone's skyline.

Danielle knelt briefly, judging the vampire's speed and direction by the shape of the splatter.

"He's heading north. And he can't be more than a minute ahead."

The wolf's howl was her only answer, but she'd been with Carl long enough now to recognize the meaning. He was on the hunt.

"I'll go ahead. You herd him to me," she ordered.

If a wolf could mutter, Carl would have, but she didn't give him the chance to morph back into human form. Instead, she blurred and left him.

Using the tricks she'd learned from Sergeant Mansfield, Danielle controlled the blur, using it when she moved, switching it off momentarily when she needed to stop.

She should have let Carl take the point. In wolf form, his alpha-male instincts demanded it. And his hearing, far better than a mere human's, would offer more advantages than Danielle's sharp sight. Still, she'd been confined too much lately. She'd desperately needed to get out. When the alarm had come in, she had used her seniority in the zone police force to demand it.

Carl's howl sent eerie shivers down her spine. She hesitated to think what they would do to the vampire they were hunting.

Even her unenhanced hearing could pick up the abrupt stumble as the vampire ground to a halt, then plunged forward--straight for her.

"Dallas Zone Police." She stepped out in front of the runner. "You're under arrest."

The vampire practically ran into her, back-peddled, then collided with three more vampires.

So much for modern surveillance equipment. The camera had only seen one of these punks.

"Rush her," one of the vampires suggested.

"You idiot, it's Supervisor Goodman."

Carl's howl sounded close now.

She had to hand it to the young vampires. That howl would have frozen her. Instead, it galvanized them into motion.

The four spread around her looking for an opening.

Danielle let her hands begin to make the slow circles that she and Carl had worked into their martial arts repertoire. She couldn't help the smile plastered to her lips. She hadn't had this much fun in, well a long time. Not that she wasn't happy to be a new mother, but she'd practically bitten off Snori's head when he'd ordered her to take a month's desk duty when she'd come back from the hospital.

"Now," the oldest of the vampires shouted. He feinted toward Danielle's face but the strike was so obvious that Danielle didn't even bother parrying. Instead, she caught one of the others with a punch to the stomach and then the one behind her with a back kick to the head.

The sharp snick of a switchblade told her that the remaining two vampires wouldn't give up easily.

The leader moved toward her, intent on her movement, looking for a chance to slice, to draw blood, to claim a victory out of defeat.

Carl's jaws clamped on his knife hand just as the vampire launched himself forward.

Two hundred pounds of wolf bore the vampire to the ground and sent the blade spinning into the darkness.

Danielle turned and looked at the fourth vampire. "I'll hold one hand behind my back," she offered.

He fell to his knees. "Don't tell my parents. They'll kill me."

Once, Danielle might have sympathized. As a new parent herself, she thought that this punk's parents should have known a lot more about what their son was up to.

"Hand over the blood," she ordered.

Reluctantly, the vampires reached into their knapsacks and handed over the bags of blood they'd stolen from the blood bank.

"Idiots," Danielle told them as she scooped up the plastic bags and radioed for a biological pickup. "The bloodbank isn't a candy store for punks."

"We, uh, were just testing its security," the leader suggested.

"Guess you failed the test then," Carl told them. He'd reverted to human form.

"Oh, hell, Mayor Harriman. I guess so."

"You four are going to do some serious community service," he said.

"Yes, Mr. Mayor," the leader said. "We're sorry."

Danielle laughed. "By the time you finish cleaning the Trinity River filtration system, you'll be very sorry."

The disgusted noises from the four vampires told Danielle that she'd suggested the right punishment. Vampires' noses, even more than *Were's*, were extremely sensitive to biological scents, and undead bodies reacted poorly to water. The four vampires would spend some miserable hours helping the zone and, with luck, learn a valuable lesson.

Once the biologic team showed up to reclaim the blood, and the four vampires were carted off in a paddy wagon, Carl turned to Danielle.

"That was a charming way to start our first date since little Tyler came onto the scene. Do you have any suggestions on what to do next?"

"It's a bit early to be working on a little sister."

"I'm in no rush. We've got plenty of time for that. But we need to keep in practice, right?"

"I thought you'd never ask."

Danielle took Carl's arm and walked with him slowly through the streets of the zone, so different now than when she'd first encountered it three years ago. Most of the buildings were renovated and inhabited now. The streets were bursting with new businesses--bridal shops, jewelry stores, furniture rental shops, taco stands. New schools had sprung up on vacant lots. There were parks with fountains and tennis courts.

Sure, there were problems. Some lingering resentments. But normals and magics mixed freely now, in the zone. Their experiment in Dallas had proved that cooperation and tolerance could overcome fear and hatred. There was even talk about some cities tearing down guard towers, taking advantage of magical creativity for the city at large.

Danielle had no qualms about bringing children into the world she and Carl had helped to create. She'd only been teasing about the little sister, but she hoped there would be more children--lots more. A whole herd of them.

A new generation growing up free from the old hatreds, to build on what she and Carl, and Mike and Snori and even Arenesol had started.

The End